THE BEST SHORT STORIES

THE BEST
SHORT STORIES

◆

Guy de Maupassant

Introduction by
CEDRIC WATTS

WORDSWORTH CLASSICS

For my husband
ANTHONY JOHN RANSON
with love from your wife, the publisher.
Eternally grateful for your unconditional love.

Readers who are interested in other titles from
Wordsworth Editions are invited to visit our website at
www.wordsworth-editions.com

First published in 1997 by Wordsworth Editions Limited
8B East Street, Ware, Hertfordshire SG12 9HJ
Introduction added in 2011

ISBN 978 1 85326 189 3

Wordsworth Editions
is the company founded in 1987 by
MICHAEL TRAYLER

Typeset in Great Britain by Antony Gray
Printed and bound by Clays Ltd, Elcograf S.p.A.

CONTENTS

INTRODUCTION

'Talent is lengthy patience. It is a question of looking at
anything you want to express long enough and closely
enough to discover in it something that nobody else has
seen before. [...] The most insignificant thing contains
something of the unknown. Let us find it.'

(Maupassant: Preface to *Pierre et Jean*.)

'What is wanting to his universal success is the mediocrity of
an obvious and appealing tenderness. He neglects to qualify
his truth with the drop of facile sweetness; he forgets to strew
paper roses over the tombs.'

(Joseph Conrad, assessing Maupassant.) [1]

1

Guy de Maupassant was born on 5 August 1850, the first of two sons of
well-to-do parents who for a while resided in a château near Le Havre
in northern France. In 1863 his mother, Laure, legally separated from
the father, Gustave, who enjoyed a Sybaritic life-style. While Gustave
worked at a bank in Paris, Laure and the two sons moved to a house at
Étretat, on the Channel coast. She nurtured Guy's literary interests, for
she was cultured and well-read, and was a great friend of Gustave
Flaubert, whom she enlisted as the lad's mentor. (Flaubert had declared
his love for her brother, Alfred.[2]) The writer Louis Bouilhet also
provided guidance.

Guy was educated in Yvetot, at a Roman Catholic seminary from
which eventually, his mother said, she had to withdraw him because
'they refused to grant him a dispensation from fasting ordered by his
doctors';[3] and later he entered the Lycée Pierre Corneille at Rouen,
where he gained his baccalaureate in 1869. During the Franco-Prussian
War of 1870-1, in which the French would be ignominiously defeated,
Guy was conscripted into the army, serving as a clerk at Rouen until
the enemy approached. Although it has been claimed that he 'fought
bravely', what he told his mother was this: 'I fled with our army in

retreat; I was almost captured. [...] I ran very well.'4 With the aid of money from his father, Maupassant procured a substitute, so that he could escape from military service. Subsequently, helped by Gustave's influence, he gained employment as a civil servant in Paris at the Ministère de la Marine (the Naval Ministry, 1872–8), and later (1878–2) at the Ministère de l'Instruction Publique (the Ministry of Education). His salary was augmented by an allowance from Gustave. Guy enjoyed boating and female company during visits to Argenteuil on the Seine. Temperamentally, however, he was inclined not only to hedonism but also to scepticism: while corresponding with Flaubert, he lamented 'the futility of everything, the unconscious wickedness of Creation, the void that is my future'.5

During Maupassant's time as a civil servant, he contributed to a range of journals, notably *Le Figaro*, *Gil Blas* and *L'Echo de Paris*. Here he honed his literary skills. In 1880 he published not only a controversially frank volume of poetry, *Des Vers*, but also, to great acclaim, the tale 'Boule de Suif', which was included in Émile Zola's collection of 'naturalist' writings, *Les Soirées de Médan*.6 Literary 'naturalists', influenced by Darwinian evolutionary theories, emphasised the importance of heredity and environment on characterisation, and often manifested a secular, sceptical outlook. Writers associated with this movement included Ibsen, Strindberg and Chekhov. Nevertheless, although Maupassant has evident connections with the literary naturalists, his preface to the novel *Pierre et Jean* refers loosely to 'a realist or naturalist' school, says that realists are 'Illusionists', and emphasises that the artist should be 'free to understand, observe, and create as he sees fit'.7 Maupassant published prolifically, gaining prosperity as a novelist and short-story writer. In addition to six novels, three travel books, several plays and the poetry, he wrote hundreds of short stories. Perhaps he over-produced: he has been accused of repetition or recycling of topics and situations.8

His tales dealt predominantly with the provincial bourgeoisie, urban employees and civil servants; but prostitutes, soldiers, peasants and members of the nobility were also scrutinised. The Normandy that he knew so well was amply commemorated. Sales of Maupassant's work were certainly helped by the frankness with which he treated sexual matters, at a time when, in England and America, censorship in various forms inhibited many fiction-writers. Instead of voicing dismay or anger, his narrators generally accept, as a matter of social fact (and sometimes of satiric comedy), adultery, promiscuity, domestic violence, and the functions of a brothel in a given locality. It has been objected that 'his brothel-keeper and prostitutes are rather too respectable to be true'.[9] The nature of Maupassant's eventual death makes its own sombre comment.

Guy de Maupassant earned international renown with such collections of stories as *La Maison Tellier* (1881), *Clair de Lune* (1884) and *Miss Harriet* (1884), and with such novels as *Une Vie* (1883) and *Bel-Ami* (1885). In addition to Flaubert and Zola, his famous literary associates included Ivan Turgenev, J.-K. Huysmans, Alphonse Daudet, Edmond de Goncourt and Alexandre Dumas (Junior); and he would influence writers as diverse as Joseph Conrad (who claimed to be 'saturated with Maupassant'[10]), R. B. Cunninghame Graham, Ambrose Bierce and Ernest Hemingway. For instance: Conrad's *The Secret Agent* and 'A Smile of Fortune' are indebted respectively to 'Ce Cochon de Morin' (in this collection entitled 'That Pig of a Morin') and 'Les Sœurs Rondoli'. Cunninghame Graham's 'Christie Christison' has marked resemblances to 'Le Port'. Bierce's 'The Damned Thing' recalls 'Le Horla', a story of the horrifically supernatural, which in turn may recall macabre fiction by Edgar Allan Poe. Hemingway himself drew attention to similarities between 'La Maison Tellier' (alias 'Madame Tellier's Establishment') and 'The Light of the World': Alice in his tale is clearly related to Maupassant's proficient brothel-keeper. Other writers influenced by the French story-teller include William Somerset Maugham, termed 'The English Maupassant' by Desmond MacCarthy, and O. Henry, famed for his deft dénouements.

Furthermore, Maupassant's tales have been widely fostered by other media. Notably: 'Boule de Suif' was freely adapted in John Ford's classic Western film, *Stagecoach* (1939), and in Stephen Hartke's opera *The Greater Good, or The Passion of Boule de Suif* (2006). [11] Another distinguished movie was *Une Partie de Campagne* (1936), directed by Jean Renoir. 'Le Rosier de Madame Husson' ('Madame Husson's "Rosier" ') was transformed into the comic opera *Albert Herring* (1947), with a libretto by Eric Crozier and music by Benjamin Britten. This tale suited Britten's recurrent interest in the type of the transgressive pariah. Television found the stories congenially adaptable, as was demonstrated by the 'France 2' channel's series entitled 'Chez Maupassant' (2007–8), for which the directors included the eminent Claude Chabrol. The title 'La Maison Tellier' became the name of a French rock group, founded in 2004.

Although Guy de Maupassant enjoyed immense fame and prosperity, his life-span was harshly curtailed by the syphilis that he had probably contracted as a lusty young man; it had blighted his eyesight and his mental stability. His younger brother, Hervé, had died, insane, in 1889: a precursor of Guy's fate. In 1892, after attempting suicide, Guy entered an asylum at Passy, and died there on July 6th, 1893, aged forty-two. His influential writings have nevertheless ensured his cultural longevity.

2

The tales in this volume illustrate well Maupassant's distinctive combination of qualities as a story-writer. These include: a lucid, proficient style, deft and generally unobtrusive; strongly ironic plotting; swiftly incisive characterisation; sharply detailed descriptions; sympathy for the kind-hearted, particularly for genial prostitutes or brothel-bosses; varying degrees of scepticism towards religion and some of its representatives; contempt for the middle class's hypocrisy (depicted sometimes as widespread, sometimes as localised); and disgust at the wastefulness and cruelty of war.

All these are represented in 'Boule de Suif', the most successful of his tales, deemed by Flaubert a masterpiece. (The title, referring to a buxom prostitute and her bulging bosom, means 'Ball of Tallow', and has been pleasantly rendered by various translators as 'Dumpling', 'Roly-Poly' and 'Butterball'.) At once we encounter a paradox. Numerous commentators have claimed that Maupassant displays 'indifference', offers 'no social comment' and 'never makes a moral judgement', so that 'the story appears to tell itself': indeed, these views constitute a critical cliché.[12] The cliché, however, is false. On the contrary: in 'Boule de Suif', an intense moral indignation is evident. The eponymous heroine, a prostitute, initially displays hospitable generosity in sharing her food with the various well-to-do or pious passengers in the packed coach; but, at the end of the story, when she herself is hungry, those whom she has helped ignore her disdainfully. She is more patriotic and courageous than any of her fellow-travellers, and initially spurns the Prussian officer who seeks to sleep with her. When the travellers find that their journey can continue only if she will bestow her favours on him, all of them (even the nuns) gradually resemble pimps, urging her to grant the Prussian his wish. And when, reluctantly, she does so in order to help the others, they reward her with only their scorn and contempt. Their hypocrisy, selfishness and cruelty (which make mockery of the heroic unity hailed in 'The Marseillaise', whistled by Cornudet, a smug democrat) is systematically exposed and implicitly condemned. Sometimes Maupassant's ironies intensify so as to verge on satire: he employs selectivity and some exaggeration to make critical points about human fallibility, as when describing the predatory greed of the coach-borne travellers.

Contradicting the familiar critical notion that Maupassant displays 'indifference', 'Boule de Suif' contains ample moralising and some provocative generalisations. For instance, the narrator remarks:

> The earthquake [...], the flood [....,] or the army, covered with glory, murdering those who defend themselves, making prisoners of the rest, pillaging in the name of the Sword, and giving thanks to God to the thunder of cannon – all these are appalling scourges, which destroy belief in eternal justice, all that confidence we have been taught to feel in the protection of heaven and the reason of man.

Here Maupassant writes in the tradition of French philosophical scepticism, the tradition firmly established by the *Dictionnaire Philosophique* and the writings of Voltaire. Still more provocative (and refutable) is the narrator's comment on female deference to authority; and here even Boule de Suif, as 'an ardent Bonapartist' who scorns Cornudet the democrat, incurs criticism:

> But the countess and the manufacturer's wife, imbued with the unreasoning hatred of the upper classes for the Republic, and instinct, moreover, with the affection felt by all women for the pomp and circumstance of despotic government, were drawn, in spite of themselves, towards this loyal young woman, whose opinions coincided so closely with their own.

If the allegation of the affection of 'all women' for despotism seems bizarrely misogynistic, the misogyny is offset in the tale by the depiction of Boule de Suif herself as courageous and altruistic, in contrast to the men she encounters, who are depicted as variously cruel, greedy, vain, cowardly and hypocritical. The narrator's detailed observations often seem at times to subvert his generalisations. Many men, certainly, are condemned by the moralist's commentary. 'Long-bearded democrats of [Cornudet's] type have a monopoly of patriotism, just as priests have a monopoly of religion [...].' French army officers, we are told, are frequently 'afraid of their own men – scoundrels often brave beyond measure, but pillagers and debauchees'. In fact, such provocatively explicit moral comments make one ask why Maupassant was so often regarded as a writer who refrained from moralising, as when the critic Geoffrey Brereton spoke of 'the moral comment which he refrains from making'.[13] One reason is that, compared with the elaborate judgemental rhetoric of, say, Charles Dickens or George Eliot, Maupassant seems relatively restrained: lust and infidelity don't shock him. Another is that the final paragraphs of his tales are often (though not always) morally reticent, leaving the reader to supply concluding moral generalisations. Again, the *implicit* judgements sometimes notably exceed the *explicit* judgements. What makes the stories so generally persuasive is the deftly precise summoning of detail in the observations of character, location and incident. In 'Boule de Suif', for instance, the food, which figures so importantly, is rendered with cunning specificity, as when we are told that 'A solid wedge of Gruyère cheese, which had been wrapped in newspaper, bore the imprint "Items of News" on its rich, oily surface.' Here the absurd realistic juxtaposition (news, cheese) and the sensuously-apt adjective 'oily' vindicate Maupassant's declared interest in the transformation of the mundane by close scrutiny.[14]

Maupassant's descriptions may also evoke, fleetingly and without explicit elaboration, a symbolic range. Thus, when Boule de Suif feeds the hungry passengers from her remarkably cornucopian provisions, we may be briefly reminded (with ironic differences) of the feeding of the multitude by Jesus, or of the Holy Mass. As in the Mass, the wine is served from one cup. One great irony of the tale is, of course, that Christian tales of martyrdom are explicitly evoked by the passengers (particularly the nuns) to coerce Boule de Suif into overcoming her repugnance at the thought of granting her body to an enemy officer. Although these evocations, having ulterior motives, are hypocritical, and result in scorn for Boule de Suif, their allusions emphasise that, in Christian terms, she is more worthy than are the supposedly pious and virtuous people around her.

Indeed, one of the marked complications in the appraisal of Maupassant's scepticism arises when we observe how frequently our moral bearings in his fictional world are provided by Christian morality,[15] particularly the more liberal New Testament teachings of Jesus. Jesus was merciful to the woman 'taken in adultery' and famously accepted Mary Magdalen, traditionally regarded as a 'fallen woman', among his disciples. He thus provided warrant for Maupassant's tendency to depict prostitutes as having hearts of gold or, at least, of sound metal.

That preoccupation is represented, in this collection of tales, not only by 'Boule de Suif' but also by 'Madame Tellier's Establishment', in which the prostitutes, attending a girl's first communion, weep readily, affecting the whole congregation, so that the priest (unwittingly crowning the irony) feels that a miracle of piety has taken place. In 'Mademoiselle Fifi', there is no doubt of the narrator's sympathy with the Jewish prostitute who, bullied by an arrogant Prussian officer, stabs him to death and escapes. Here heavy emphasis falls on the destructive brutality of the conquerors of France. This time, the priest is a patriotic collaborator with the killer. 'Two Friends', a companion-piece, stresses the arbitrary cruelty (and unproclaimed heroism) that accompanies warfare: the angling comrades now become food for fish, while the fish they have caught make a meal for the ruthless Prussian. We may be reminded that a fish was an early Christian symbol.[16]

A gentler Maupassant is evident in 'Clair de Lune' ('Moonlight'), in which a misogynistic priest is challenged by the beauty of a moonlit night which seems to bless the lovers he observes, so that now he is obliged to recall that the Bible tells not only of woman as temptress but also, in 'The Song of Solomon', of the ecstasies of heterosexual love. The power of love to transform but also, sometimes, to destroy: that is the theme of numerous tales in this collection. In 'Miss Harriet', the eponymous English lady, grey-haired, her youth gone, is tardily awakened to love for an artist, and feels that in their appreciation of nature they have a basis for a fuller mutuality; but, on finding that he is philandering with a younger woman, she is disillusioned, and commits suicide. A homophilous variant is found in 'Two Little Soldiers', in which Jean is so distraught when his dear friend Luc falls in love with a young woman that he drowns himself. As further testimony to emotional isolation, his suicidal anguish goes unrecognised by the friend.

In 'Mademoiselle Pearl', the narrating character rather ruthlessly obliges the eponymous lady and Monsieur Chantal to realise that they should have been united long ago; their love has long gone unfulfilled. As if making an ironic comment, the slight, short tale 'Love' is virtually a parable of fatal fidelity (and of casual cruelty inflicted by men on nature). In contrast, 'Happiness' claims that even if a young woman from a rich family sacrifices wealth and social propriety to live with a peasant, love may be ample reward. This tale obviously challenges Henry James's insistence that Maupassant is cynical.[17] Indeed, James's charge is not even sustained by 'A Sale', in which one drunken peasant tries to sell his wife by weight to another, employing Archimedean physics; for the narrator's attitude is rather one of amused contempt and scorn for the emotional and moral degradation shown. If a cynic is 'a man who knows the price of everything and the value of nothing', as Lord Darlington claimed,[18] then Maupassant, on the contrary, is sensitive to the values which thick-skinned human beings neglect; and such sensitivity is a radical source of his ironies. Though Joseph Conrad felt that Maupassant lacked 'tenderness', the very lack of tenderness in human relationships is what the tales often deplore.

A life may be ruined by a brief incident and the interpretation or misinterpretation of it. This sombre recognition becomes the theme of 'The Piece of String', 'The Necklace' and 'That Pig of a Morin'. The last of those three tales wins some sympathy for Morin, the sexual assailant, but is, arguably, an effectively feminist piece in its depiction of the strongly attractive and astute young woman. Perhaps the most feminist of the stories is 'Useless Beauty', in which Gabrielle successfully revolts against her aggressively possessive husband, declaring: 'I am a woman of the civilised world – we all are – and we are no longer, and we refuse to be, mere females to restock the earth.'[19] Indeed, one feminist critic has said that here:

> Woman, free from phallocracy, rises to new heights of power [...], and she does it without sacrificing either her femininity or her maternity.[20]

Feminists may, however, be irritated by the narrator's eventual surge of rather vapid lyricism in which he extols certain women as 'living statues who waken, as though in some voluptuous dream, desires vague and mysterious and unnameable'. Gabrielle seems rather more intelligent and markedly more lucid than her rhapsodist. Here we may recall that Henry James once remarked of Maupassant: 'The philosopher in his composition is perceptibly inferior to the story-teller.' But then we may be reminded, in turn, that T. S. Eliot praised James for having 'a mind so fine that no idea could violate it'.[21]

A very sombre aspect of Maupassant is represented by 'The Olive Orchard'. Once again, a priest is shocked into a reappraisal of his life. In this case, the priest is horrified to learn that he has engendered a brutal son: the violence with which he himself had threatened the mother is now punished by the emergence of this monstrous offspring from the past. In a final bitter irony, the son may die for a crime of which he was innocent.

If the ironic pattern there is dark and almost tragic, the ironies elsewhere are closer to comedy. In 'Madame Husson's "Rosier" ', a young man is rewarded in cash for being a model of virginal innocence; but he promptly celebrates his good fortune by going to Paris for a spell of dissipation. Even here, the aftermath of comedy is sombre enough: eventually the 'Rosier' ('Rose-king, paragon of purity') dies of delirium tremens, an alcoholic's fate. Jean-Paul Sartre, the eminent bourgeois philosopher, once denigrated Maupassant as an upholder of bourgeois orderliness;[22] but the tales show, often enough, how order may be mocked, subverted or disrupted.

3

Near the end of 'Miss Harriet', the artist Léon Chenal, reflecting on that solitary woman's life-story, condemns 'implacable Nature':

'How many unhappy beings there are! I felt that there was laid upon that unhappy creature the eternal injustice of implacable Nature! It was all over with her, without her ever having experienced, perhaps, that which sustains the greatest outcasts – the hope of being loved once!'

Nevertheless, 'implacable Nature' can offer consolation, too. Chenal says this of Miss Harriet:

'She would now disintegrate and become, in turn, a plant. She would blossom in the sun, the cattle would browse on her leaves, the birds would bear away the seeds, and through these changes she would become again human flesh.'

It is a tenuous consolation, a slow materialistic resurrection. Wordsworth had said of an earlier woman,

> No motion has she now, no force;
> She neither hears, nor sees;
> Rolled round in earth's diurnal course,
> With rocks, and stones, and trees.[23]

Wordsworth's austere consolation lies in the association of the dead person with the durably and invulnerably nonhuman: rocks, stones and trees cannot feel pain. Maupassant's consolation is more creative: Miss Harriet, absorbed in the natural world, will eventually contribute to living beings; she is part of a cycle whereby old life pervasively nourishes new life.[24]

Thus, as we survey the many tales in this volume, we may realise that one of their most positive features is the attention given to the natural environment. If the tragi-comic turmoil of human existence fills the foreground, the background offers a consolatory commentary. Earthquakes and floods are exceptional. What is far more common, as Chenal in 'Miss Harriet' suggests, is the daily beauty of sky, sea and countryside, and the innocent sensual gratification there available:

'You sit down by the side of a spring which gushes out at the foot of an oak, amid a growth of tall, slender weeds, glistening with life. You go down on your knees, bend forward and drink that cold, clear water which wets your face; you drink it with a physical pleasure, as though you kissed the spring, lip to lip.'

The artist is pagan enough; but a kindred delight in nature is found by the priest in 'Clair de Lune', who is able to reconcile it with the Song of Solomon. Though Maupassant has long held the reputation of being a sceptical sensualist, such a reputation needs qualification. During his appreciation of the delights of the natural environment, he sometimes hints at the inadequacies of a solely sensual response. Some of the descriptions deserve to be termed 'epiphanies': they convey those moments when, according to Stephen Dedalus, the mundane is redeemed by the radiantly significant.[25] The reader of the following stories will find, among much that is entertaining and thought-provoking, such brief burgeonings of radiance.

CEDRIC WATTS

NOTES TO THE INTRODUCTION

I am grateful to Professor Laurence Davies for his constructive comments. In the Introduction and these notes, all editorial emendations and insertions are enclosed in square brackets. The abbreviation 'n.d.' means 'no date specified'.

1 The first epigraph is from Maupassant's Preface ('Le Roman') to his novel *Pierre et Jean*, translated by Julie Mead (Oxford: Oxford University Press, 2001), p. 12. Here he is paraphrasing and endorsing Flaubert's advice. The second is from Joseph Conrad's essay 'Guy de Maupassant' in *Notes on Life and Letters* (London: Dent, 1949), p. 29.

2 'I can believe I have never loved any one (man or woman) like him.' See Ernest Boyd's *Guy de Maupassant: A Biographical Study* (London: Knopf, 1926), p. 7.

3 Boyd, p. 9.

4 'fought bravely': Wikipedia website entitled 'Guy de Maupassant',
   10 April 2011. Letter to his mother: quoted in Boyd, p. 17. See also
   Michael G. Lerner's *Maupassant* (London: Allen & Unwin, 1975),
   p. 49.

5 Letter of July 1878: Lerner, p. 62.

6 The contributors were Zola, Maupassant, Henry Céard, J.-K. Huysmans, Léon Hennique and Paul Alexis.

7 *Pierre et Jean*, tr. Julie Mead, pp. 5, 8 and 5 respectively. Privately,
   Maupassant wrote: 'I believe no more in Naturalism than in Realism
   or Romanticism. [...] Why limit oneself?' See Boyd, p. 89.

8 'Maupassant [...] made his living by his pen, and was consequently
   far too productive. Declining health too made him rely on
   mechanical formulas, and so turned him into the model for slick
   short-story writers [...].' So said J. M. Cohen in *A History of Western
   Literature* (Harmondsworth: Penguin, 1956), p. 272.

9 Lerner, p. 153.

10 See Owen Knowles and Gene M. Moore: *Oxford Reader's Companion
   to Conrad* (Oxford: Oxford University Press, 2000), pp. 226–7;
   quotation, p. 227. Conrad's 1897 'Author's Note' to *The Nigger of
   the 'Narcissus'* would echo some of Maupassant's ideas.

11 Ford himself acknowledged the debt to Maupassant's tale. Hartke's
   The Greater Good, or The Passion of Boule de Suif (with libretto by
   Phillip Littell) was first performed by Glimmerglass Opera in 2006
   and was issued as a CD in 2007.

12 The first quotation is from Arthur Symons' *Studies in Prose and Verse*
   (London: Dent, n.d.), p. 98; the second is from J. M. Cohen, p. 272;
   the third is from an anonymous 'Introduction' to Maupassant: *The
   Best Short Stories* (Ware: Wordsworth, 1997), p. vi; and the fourth is
   from Percy Lubbock's *The Craft of Fiction* (New York: Scribner's,
   1921), p. 113. Maupassant's tales 'take no account of the moral
   nature of man', asserted Henry James.

13 Geoffrey Brereton: *A Short History of French Literature* (Harmondsworth: Penguin, 1954), p. 227.

14 The English translation conforms well to the original: 'Un beau
   carré de gruyère, apporté dans un journal, gardait imprimé: "faits
   divers" sur sa pâte onctueuse.'

15 Christian theology, too, is invoked. For instance, in the following
   passage of 'Madame Husson's "Rosier" ', irony (though possible and

perhaps desirable) eludes textual confirmation, so that some readers will reasonably regard the viewpoint as non-ironically Christian:

> Who will ever know or who can tell what a terrible conflict took place in the soul of the 'Rosier' between good and evil, the tumultuous attack of Satan, his artifices, the temptations which he offered to this timid virgin heart?

16 Such Christian symbolism is discussed by A. J. Greimas in a book devoted to a semiotic analysis of this tale: *Maupassant: La Sémiotique du texte: exercices pratiques* (Paris: Seuil, 1976). See particularly pp. 259–61.

17 Henry James: 'Guy de Maupassant' [1888] in *Henry James: Selected Literary Criticism* (Harmondsworth: Peregrine, 1968), pp. 118–44. He refers to 'Maupassant's cynicism, unrelieved as it is,' on p. 125, and discusses it on several pages. Subsequently, the charge has often been repeated: for instance, by H. N. P. Sloman in the Introduction to *A Woman's Life* (Harmondsworth: Penguin, 1965), p. 5: '[he is] sometimes cynical and even coarse'; and by Trevor Harris in *Maupassant in the Hall of Mirrors* (Basingstoke: Macmillan, 1990), p. xi: 'he possessed in abundance [...] cynicism'.

18 He makes this claim in Oscar Wilde's *Lady Windermere's Fan*, Act III. See *The Works of Oscar Wilde* (London: Spring Books, 1963), p. 30.

19 This ending may bring to mind the different modes of defiance shown by Nora in Ibsen's *A Doll's House* and Mrs Hervey in Conrad's 'The Return'.

20 Mary Donaldson-Evans: *A Woman's Revenge* (Lexington, Kentucky: French Forum, 1986), p. 100. Elsewhere, Maupassant can certainly seem misogynistic. He once remarked: 'Now, a woman has two functions in this life: love and maternity.' (Boyd, p. 118.) See also: Trevor Harris: *Maupassant*, pp. 141–59.

21 James: 'Guy de Maupassant', p. 119. Eliot: 'In Memory': *Little Review*, 5: 4 (August 1918), pp. 44–7; quotation, p. 46.

22 Sartre asserted: 'L'ordre triomphe, l'ordre est partout': *Situations, II* (Paris: Gallimard, 1948; reprinted 1962), p. 181.

23 'A slumber did my spirit seal' (often deemed one of the 'Lucy' poems): *The Poetical Works of Wordsworth*, ed. Thomas Hutchinson (Oxford: Oxford University Press, 1950), p. 149.

24 In 2010, the film-actor Morgan Freeman remarked: 'I want life

everlasting. That means going into the ground, going back to Mother Earth, and she will spit you out again.' ('Showcase' website, 11 June 2010.) 'Pushing up daisies' is how Wilfred Owen had rendered the matter in his poem 'À Terre'.

25 'The soul of the commonest object [...] seems to us radiant', explains Stephen Dedalus in Joyce's *Stephen Hero* (London: Cape, 1969), p. 218. Of course, paradox-loving Joyce then offers a deflationary coda. Stephen's friend Cranly stares towards the mouth of the River Liffey as if in an appropriately aesthetic trance, but then remarks: 'I wonder did that bloody boat, the *Sea-Queen* ever start?' In Maupassant's tale 'Happiness', the arising of Corsica from the distant horizon, 'as if itself to answer the question', serves well as an epiphanic instance.

FURTHER READING

(The order is chronological. The abbreviation 'n.d.' means that no date is specified in the volume.)

Henry James: 'Guy de Maupassant' [1888] in *Henry James: Selected Literary Criticism*. Harmondsworth: Peregrine, 1968.

Arthur Symons: 'Guy de Maupassant' [1899, 1903], reprinted in *Studies in Prose and Verse*. London: Dent, n.d..

Joseph Conrad: 'Guy de Maupassant' [1914], reprinted in *Notes on Life and Letters*. London: Dent, 1949.

Ernest Boyd: *Guy de Maupassant: A Biographical Study*. London: Knopf, 1926.

Jean-Paul Sartre on Maupassant in 'Qu'est-ce que la littérature' [1947], reprinted in *Situations*, *II*, pp. 180–2. Paris: Gallimard, 1948; reprinted 1962.

Francis Steegmuller: *Maupassant: A Lion in the Path*. New York: Random House, 1949.

Edward D. Sullivan: *Maupassant: The Short Stories*. London: Arnold, 1962.

Albert-Marie Schmidt: *Maupassant par lui-même*. Paris: Seuil, 1962.

Paul Ignotus: *The Paradox of Maupassant*. London: University of London Press, 1966.

John Raymond Dugan: *Illusion and Reality: A Study of Descriptive Techniques in the Works of Guy de Maupassant*. The Hague: Mouton, 1973.

Michael G. Lerner: *Maupassant*. London: Allen & Unwin, 1975.

A. H. Wallace: *Guy de Maupassant*. Boston: Hall, 1973.

Maupassant Criticism: A Centennial Bibliography 1880–1979, ed. R. W. Artinian and A. Artinian. Jefferson: McFarland, 1982.

Mary Donaldson-Evans: *A Woman's Revenge: The Chronology of Dispossession in Maupassant's Fiction*. Lexington, Kentucky: French Forum, 1986.

Trevor Harris: *Maupassant in the Hall of Mirrors*. Basingstoke: Macmillan, 1990.

Rachel M. Hartig: *Struggling under the Destructive Glance: Androgyny in* the Novels of Guy de Maupassant. New York: Peter Lang, 1991.

David Bryant: The Rhetoric of Pessimism and Strategies of Containment in the Short Stories of Guy de Maupassant. Lewiston, N. Y.: Mellen, 1993.

Charles J. Stivale: The Art of Rupture: Desire and Narrative Duplicity in the Tales of Guy de Maupassant. Ann Arbor, Michigan: University of Michigan Press, 1994.

Richard Fusco: Maupassant and the American Short Story: The Influence of Form at the Turn of the Century. University Park, Pennsylvania: Pennsylvania State University Press, 1994.

Sharon P. Johnson: Boundaries of Acceptability: Flaubert, Maupassant, Cézanne and Cassatt. New York: Peter Lang, 2000.

Peter Cogman: Narration in Nineteenth-Century French Short Fiction: Prosper Mérimée to Marcel Schwob. Durham: University of Durham, 2002.

Germaine Greer: 'Foreword' to Maupassant: Butterball, tr. Andrew Brown. London: Hesperus, 2003.

Laurence A. Gregorio: Maupassant's Fiction and the Darwinian View of Life. New York: Peter Lang, 2005.

WEBSITES:

Wikipedia provides a wide range of information on Maupassant and his works.

This spareness in the narrative often gives the artistry in a good short story higher visibility than the artistry in the more capacious and loosely structured novel.

M. H. ABRAMS (1985)

THE BEST SHORT STORIES

Boule de Suif

For several days in succession fragments of a defeated army had passed through the town. They were mere disorganised bands, not disciplined forces. The men had long, dirty beards and tattered uniforms; and they advanced in listless fashion, without a flag, without a leader. All seemed exhausted, worn out, incapable of thought or resolve, marching onward merely by force of habit, and dropping to the ground with fatigue the moment they halted. One saw, in particular, many enlisted men, peaceful citizens, men who lived quietly on their income, bending beneath the weight of their rifles; and little active volunteers, easily frightened but full of enthusiasm, as eager to attack as they were ready to take to flight; and amid these, a sprinkling of red-breeched soldiers, the pitiful remnant of a division cut down in a great battle; sombre artillerymen, side by side with nondescript foot-soldiers; and, here and there, the gleaming helmet of a heavy-footed dragoon who had difficulty in keeping up with the quicker pace of the soldiers of the line.

Legions of irregulars with high-sounding names – 'Avengers of Defeat', 'Citizens of the Tomb', 'Brethren in Death' – passed in their turn, looking like *banditti*.

Their leaders, former drapers or grain merchants, or tallow or soap chandlers – warriors by force of circumstances, officers by reason of their moustaches or their money – covered with weapons, flannel and gold lace, spoke in an impressive manner, discussed plans of campaign, and behaved as though they alone bore the fortunes of broken France on their braggart shoulders; though, in truth, they frequently were afraid of their own men – scoundrels often brave beyond measure, but pillagers and debauchees.

Rumour had it that the Prussians were about to enter Rouen.

The members of the National Guard, who for the past two months had been reconnoitring with the utmost caution in the neighbouring woods, occasionally shooting their own sentinels, and making ready for fight whenever a rabbit rustled in the undergrowth, had now returned to their homes. Their arms, their uniforms, all the death-dealing paraphernalia with which they had terrified every milestone along the high road for eight miles round, had suddenly and marvellously disappeared.

The last of the French soldiers had just crossed the Seine on their way to Pont-Audemer, through Saint-Sever and Bourg-Achard, and in their rear the vanquished general, powerless to do aught with the forlorn remnants of his army, himself dismayed at the overthrow of a nation accustomed to victory and disastrously beaten despite its legendary bravery, walked between two orderlies.

Then a profound calm, a shuddering, silent dread, settled on the city. Many a round-paunched citizen, emasculated by years devoted to business, anxiously awaited the conquerors, trembling lest his roasting-jacks or kitchen knives should be looked upon as weapons.

Life seemed to have stopped short; the shops were shut, the streets deserted. Now and then an inhabitant, awed by the silence, glided swiftly by in the shadow of the walls. The anguish of suspense made men even desire the arrival of the enemy.

In the afternoon of the day following the departure of the French troops, a number of Uhlans, coming no one knew whence, passed rapidly through the town. A little later, a black mass descended St Catherine's Hill, while two other invading bodies appeared respectively on the Darnetal and the Bois-Guillaume roads. The advance guards of the three corps arrived at precisely the same moment at the Square of the Hôtel de Ville, and the German army poured through all the adjacent streets, its battalions making the pavement ring with their firm, measured tread.

Orders shouted in an unknown, guttural tongue rose to the windows of the seemingly dead, deserted houses; while behind the fast-closed shutters eager eyes peered forth at the victors – masters now of the city, its fortunes, and its lives, by 'right of war'. The inhabitants, in their darkened rooms, were possessed by that terror which follows in the wake of cataclysms, of deadly upheavals of the earth, against which all human skill and strength are vain. For the same thing happens whenever the established order of things is upset, when security no longer exists, when all those rights usually protected by the law of man or of Nature are at the mercy of unreasoning, savage force. The earthquake crushing a whole nation under falling roofs; the flood let loose, and engulfing in its swirling depths the corpses of drowned peasants, along with dead oxen and beams torn from shattered houses; or the army, covered with glory, murdering those who defend themselves, making prisoners of the rest, pillaging in the name of the Sword, and giving thanks to God to the thunder of cannon – all these are appalling scourges, which destroy belief in eternal justice, all that confidence we have been taught to feel in the protection of heaven and the reason of man.

Small detachments of soldiers knocked at each door, and then disappeared within the houses; for the vanquished saw they would have to be civil to their conquerors.

At the end of a short time, once the first terror had subsided, calm was again restored. In many houses the Prussian officer ate at the same table with the family. He was often well-bred, and, out of politeness, expressed sympathy with France and repugnance at being compelled to take part in the war. This sentiment was received with gratitude; besides, his protection might be needful some day or other. By the exercise of tact the number of men quartered in one's house might be reduced; and why should one provoke the hostility of a person on whom one's whole welfare depended? Such conduct would savour less of bravery than of foolhardiness. And foolhardiness is no longer a failing of the citizens of Rouen as it was in the days when their city earned renown by its heroic defences. Last of all – final argument based on the national politeness – the folk of Rouen said to one another that it was only right to be civil in one's own house, provided there was no public exhibition of familiarity with the foreigner. Out of doors, therefore, citizen and soldier did not know each other; but in the house both chatted freely, and each evening the German remained a little longer warming himself at the hospitable hearth.

Even the town itself resumed by degrees its ordinary aspect. The French seldom walked abroad, but the streets swarmed with Prussian soldiers. Moreover, the officers of the Blue Hussars, who arrogantly dragged their instruments of death along the pavements, seemed to hold the simple townsmen in but little more contempt than did the French cavalry officers who had drunk at the same cafés the year before.

But there was something in the air, a something strange and subtle, an intolerable foreign atmosphere like a penetrating odour – the odour of invasion. It permeated dwellings and places of public resort, changed the taste of food, made one imagine oneself in far-distant lands, amid dangerous, barbaric tribes.

The conquerors exacted money, much money. The inhabitants paid what was asked; they were rich. But, the wealthier a Norman tradesman becomes, the more he suffers at having to part with anything that belongs to him, at having to see any portion of his substance pass into the hands of another.

Nevertheless, within six or seven miles of the town, along the course of the river as it flows onward to Croisset, Dieppedalle and Biessart, boatmen and fishermen often hauled to the surface of the water the body of a German, bloated in his uniform, killed by a blow from knife or club, his head crushed by a stone, or perchance pushed from some bridge into the stream below. The mud of the river bed swallowed up these obscure acts of vengeance – savage, yet legitimate; these unrecorded deeds of bravery; these silent attacks fraught with greater danger than battles fought in broad day, and surrounded, moreover, with no halo of romance. For hatred of the foreigner ever arms a few intrepid souls, ready to die for an ideal.

At last, as the invaders, though subjecting the town to the strictest discipline, had not committed any of the deeds of horror with which they had been credited while on their triumphal march, the people grew bolder, and the necessities of business again animated the breasts of the local merchants. Some of these had important commercial interests at Le Havre – occupied at present by the French army – and wished to attempt to reach that port by overland route to Dieppe, taking the boat from there.

Through the influence of the German officers whose acquaintance they had made, they obtained a permit to leave town from the general in command.

A large four-horse coach having, therefore, been engaged for the journey, and ten passengers having given in their names to the proprietor, they decided to start on a certain Tuesday morning before daybreak, to avoid attracting a crowd.

The ground had been frozen hard for some time past, and commencing about three o'clock on Monday afternoon large black clouds from the north shed their burden of snow uninterruptedly all through that evening and night.

At half-past four in the morning the travellers met in the courtyard of the Hôtel de Normandie, where they were to take their seats in the coach.

They were still half asleep, and shivered with cold under their wraps. They could see one another but indistinctly in the darkness, and the mountain of heavy winter wraps in which each was swathed made them look like a gathering of obese priests in their long cassocks. But two men recognised each other, a third accosted them, and the three began to talk. 'I am bringing my wife,' said one. 'So am I.' 'And I, too.' The first speaker added: 'We shall not return to Rouen, and if the Prussians approach Havre we will cross to England.' All three, it turned out, had made the same plans, being of similar disposition and temperament.

Still the horses were not harnessed. A small lantern carried by a stable-man emerged now and then from one dark doorway to disappear immediately in another. The stamping of horses' hoofs, deadened by the dung and straw of the stable, was heard from time to time, and from inside the building came a man's voice, talking to the animals and swearing at them. A faint tinkle of bells showed that the harness was being got ready; this tinkle soon developed into a continuous jingling, louder or softer according to the movements of the horse, sometimes stopping altogether, then breaking out in a sudden peal accompanied by a pawing of the ground by an iron-shod hoof.

The door suddenly closed. All noise ceased. The frozen townsmen were silent; they remained motionless, stiff with cold.

A thick curtain of glistening white flakes fell ceaselessly to the ground; it obliterated all outlines, enveloped all objects in an icy mantle of foam; nothing was to be heard throughout the length and breadth of the silent, winter-bound city except the vague, indescribable rustle of falling snow – a sensation rather than a sound – the gentle mingling of light atoms which seemed to fill all space, to cover the whole world.

The man reappeared with his lantern, leading by a rope a melancholy-looking horse, evidently being led out against his inclination. The hostler placed him beside the pole, fastened the traces, and spent some time in walking round him to make sure that the harness was all right; for he could use only one hand, the other being engaged in holding the lantern. As he was about to fetch the second horse he noticed the motionless group of travellers, already white with snow, and said to them: 'Why don't you get inside the coach? You'd be under shelter, at least.'

This did not seem to have occurred to them, and they at once took his advice. The three men seated their wives at the far end of the coach, then got in themselves; lastly the other vague, snow-shrouded forms clambered to the remaining places without a word.

The floor was covered with straw, into which the feet sank. The ladies at the far end, having brought with them little copper foot-warmers heated by means of a kind of chemical fuel, proceeded to light these, and spent some time in expatiating in low tones on their advantages, saying over and over again things which they had all known for a long time.

At last, six horses instead of four having been harnessed to the diligence, on account of the heavy roads, a voice outside asked: 'Is everyone there?' To which a voice from the interior replied: 'Yes'; and they set out.

The vehicle moved slowly, slowly, at a snail's pace: the wheels sank into the snow; the entire body of the coach creaked and groaned; the horses slipped, puffed, steamed, and the coachman's long whip cracked incessantly, flying hither and thither, coiling up, then flinging out its length like a slender serpent as it lashed some rounded flank, which instantly grew tense as it strained in further effort.

But the day grew apace. Those light flakes which one traveller, a native of Rouen, had compared to a rain of cotton-down fell no longer. A murky light filtered through dark, heavy clouds, which made the country more dazzlingly white by contrast, a whiteness broken sometimes by a row of tall trees spangled with hoarfrost, or by a cottage roof hooded in snow.

Within the coach the passengers eyed one another curiously in the dim light of dawn.

Right at the back, in the best seats of all, Monsieur and Madame Loiseau, wholesale wine merchants of the Rue Grand-Pont, slumbered opposite each other. Formerly clerk to a merchant who had failed in business, Loiseau had bought his master's interest, and made a fortune for himself. He sold very bad wine at a very low price to the retail dealers in the country, and had the reputation, among his friends and acquaintances, of being a shrewd rascal, a true Norman, full of quips and wiles. So well established was his character as a cheat that, in the mouths of the citizens of Rouen, the very name of Loiseau became a byword for sharp practice.

Above and beyond this, Loiseau was noted for his practical jokes of every description – his tricks, good or ill-natured; and no one could mention his name without adding at once: 'He's an extraordinary man – Loiseau.' He was undersized and pot-bellied, and had a florid face with greyish whiskers.

His wife – tall, strong, determined, with a loud voice and decided manner – represented the spirit of order and arithmetic in the business house which Loiseau enlivened by his jovial activity.

Beside them, dignified in bearing, belonging to a superior caste, sat Monsieur Carré-Lamadon, a man of considerable importance, a king in the cotton trade, proprietor of three spinning-mills, officer of the Legion of Honour, and member of the General Council. During the whole time the Empire was in the ascendancy he remained the chief of the well-disposed Opposition, merely in order to command a higher value for his devotion when he should rally to the cause which he meanwhile opposed with 'courteous weapons', to use his own expression.

Madame Carré-Lamadon, much younger than her husband, was the consolation of all the officers of good family quartered at Rouen. Pretty, slender, graceful, she sat opposite her husband, curled up in her furs, and gazing mournfully at the sorry interior of the coach.

Her neighbours, the Comte and Comtesse Hubert de Bréville, bore one of the noblest and most ancient names in Normandy. The count, a nobleman advanced in years and of aristocratic bearing, strove to enhance, by every artifice of the toilet, his natural resemblance to King Henry IV, who, according to a legend of which the family were inordinately proud, had been the favoured lover of a De Bréville lady, and father of her child – the frail one's husband having, in recognition of this fact, been made a count and governor of a province.

A colleague of Monsieur Carré-Lamadon in the General Council, Count Hubert represented the Orleanist party in his department. The story of his marriage with the daughter of a small shipowner at Nantes had always remained more or less of a mystery. But as the countess had an air of unmistakable breeding, entertained faultlessly, and was even supposed to have been loved by a son of Louis Philippe, the nobility vied with one another in doing her honour, and her drawing-room remained the most exclusive in the whole countryside – the only one which retained the old spirit of gallantry, and to which access was not easy.

The income of the Brévilles amounted, it was said, to five hundred thousand francs a year.

These six people occupied the farther end of the coach, and represented Society – with means – the strong, established society of good people with religion and principle.

It happened by chance that all the women were seated on the same side; and the countess had, moreover, as neighbours two more women, nuns, who spent the time in fingering their long rosaries and murmuring paternosters and aves. One of them was old, and so deeply pitted with smallpox that she looked for all the world as if she had received a charge of shot full in the face. The other, of sickly appearance, had a pretty but wasted countenance, and a narrow, consumptive chest, sapped by that devouring faith which is the making of martyrs and visionaries.

A man and woman, sitting opposite the two nuns, attracted all eyes.

The man – a well-known character – was Cornudet, the democrat, the terror of all conservative people. For the past twenty years his big red beard had been on terms of intimate acquaintance with the tankards of all the republican cafés. With the help of his comrades and brethren he had dissipated a respectable fortune left him by his father, an old-established confectioner, and he now impatiently awaited the Republic, that he might at last be rewarded with the post he had earned by his revolutionary orgies. On the fourth of September – possibly as the result of a practical joke – he was led to believe that he had been appointed prefect; but when he attempted to take up the duties of the position the clerks in charge of the office refused to recognise his authority, and he was compelled in consequence to retire. A good sort of fellow in other respects, inoffensive and obliging, he had thrown himself zealously into the work of making an organised defence of the town. He had had pits dug in the level country, young forest trees felled, and traps set on all the roads; then at the approach of the enemy, thoroughly satisfied with his preparations, he had hastily returned to the town. He thought he might now do more good at Le Havre, where new entrenchments would soon be necessary.

The woman, who belonged to the courtesan class, was distinguished for an embonpoint unusual for her age, which had earned for her the sobriquet of 'Boule de Suif'. Short and round, fat as a pig, with puffy fingers constricted at the joints, looking like rows of short sausages, and with a shiny, tightly-stretched skin and an enormous bust filling out the bodice of her dress, she was yet attractive and much sought after, owing to her fresh and pleasing appearance. Her face was like a crimson apple, a peony-bud just bursting into bloom; she had magnificent dark eyes, fringed with thick, heavy lashes, which cast a shadow into their depths; her mouth was small, ripe, kissable, and was furnished with the tiniest of white teeth.

As soon as she was recognised, the respectable matrons of the party began to whisper among themselves, and derogatory expressions such as 'public scandal', were uttered so loudly that Boule de Suif raised her head. She forthwith cast such a challenging, bold look at her neighbours that a sudden silence fell on the company, and all lowered their eyes, with the exception of Loiseau, who watched her with evident interest.

But conversation was soon resumed among the three ladies, whom the presence of this girl had suddenly drawn together in the bonds of friendship – one might almost say in those of intimacy. They decided that they ought to combine, as it were, in their dignity as wives in face of this shameless hussy; for legitimised love always despises its easy-going brother.

The three men, also, brought together by a certain conservative instinct awakened by the presence of Cornudet, spoke of money matters in a tone expressive of contempt for the poor. Count Hubert related the losses he had sustained at the hands of the Prussians, spoke of the cattle that had been stolen from him, the crops that had been ruined, with the easy manner of a nobleman who was also a tenfold millionaire, and whom such reverses would scarcely inconvenience for a single year. Monsieur Carré-Lamadon, a man of wide experience in the cotton industry, had taken care to send six hundred thousand francs to England as provision against the rainy day he was always anticipating. As for

Loiseau, he had managed to sell to the French commissariat department all the wines he had in stock, so that the state now owed him a considerable sum, which he hoped to receive at Le Havre.

And all three eyed one another in friendly, well-disposed fashion. Although of varying social status, they were united in the brotherhood of money – in that vast freemasonry made up of those who possess, who can jingle gold whenever they choose to put their hands into their pockets.

The coach went along so slowly that at ten o'clock in the morning it had not covered twelve miles. Three times the men of the party got out and climbed the hills on foot. The passengers were becoming uneasy, for they had counted on lunching at Tôtes and it seemed now as if they would hardly arrive there before nightfall. Everyone was eagerly looking out for an inn by the roadside, when, suddenly, the coach foundered in a snowdrift, and it took two hours to extricate it.

As appetites increased, their spirits fell; no inn, no wine shop could be discovered, the approach of the Prussians and the transit of the starving French troops having frightened away all business.

The men sought food in the farmhouses beside the road, but could not find so much as a crust of bread; for the suspicious peasant invariably hid his stores for fear of being pillaged by the soldiers, who, being entirely without food, would take violent possession of everything they found.

About one o'clock Loiseau announced that he positively had a big hollow in his stomach. They had all been suffering in the same way for some time, and the increasing gnawings of hunger had put an end to all conversation.

Now and then someone yawned, another followed his example, and each in turn, according to his character, breeding and social position, yawned either quietly or noisily, placing his hand before the gaping void whence issued breath condensed into vapour.

Several times Boule de Suif stooped, as if searching for something under her petticoats. She would hesitate a moment, look at her neighbours, and then quietly sit upright again. All faces were pale and drawn. Loiseau declared he would give a thousand francs for a knuckle of ham. His wife made an involuntary and quickly checked gesture of protest. It always hurt her to hear of money being squandered, and she could not even understand jokes on such a subject.

'As a matter of fact, I don't feel well,' said the count. 'Why did I not think of bringing provisions?' Each one reproached himself in similar fashion.

Cornudet, however, had a bottle of rum, which he offered to his neighbours. They all coldly refused except Loiseau, who took a sip, and returned the bottle with thanks, saying: 'That's good stuff; it warms one up, and cheats the appetite.' The alcohol put him in good humour, and he proposed they should do as the sailors did in the song: eat the fattest of the passengers. This indirect allusion to Boule de Suif shocked the respectable members of the party. No one replied; only Cornudet smiled. The two good sisters had ceased to mumble their rosary, and, with hands enfolded in their wide sleeves, sat motionless, their eyes steadfastly cast down, doubtless offering up as a sacrifice to heaven the suffering it had sent them.

At last, at three o'clock, as they were in the midst of an apparently limitless plain, with not a single village in sight, Boule de Suif stooped quickly, and drew from underneath the seat a large basket covered with a white napkin.

From this she extracted first of all a small earthenware plate and a silver drinking cup, then an enormous dish containing two whole chickens cut into joints and embedded in jelly. The basket was seen to contain other good things: pies, fruit, dainties of all sorts – provisions, in fine, for a three-day journey, rendering their owner independent of wayside inns. The necks of four bottles protruded from among the food. She took a chicken wing, and began to eat it daintily, together with one of those rolls called in Normandy 'régence'.

All looks were directed towards her. An odour of food filled the air, causing nostrils to dilate, mouths to water, and jaws to contract painfully. The scorn of the ladies for this disreputable female grew positively ferocious; they would have liked to kill her, or throw her and her drinking cup, her basket, and her provisions, out of the coach into the snow of the road below.

But Loiseau's gaze was fixed greedily on the dish of chicken. He said: 'Well, well, this lady had more forethought than the rest of us. Some people think of everything.'

She looked up at him.

'Would you like some, sir? It is hard to go on fasting all day.'

He bowed.

'Upon my soul, I can't refuse; I cannot hold out another minute. All is fair in wartime, is it not, madame?' And, casting a glance on those around, he added: 'At times like this it is very pleasant to meet with obliging people.'

He spread a newspaper over his knees to avoid soiling his trousers, and, with a pocketknife he always carried, helped himself to a chicken leg coated with jelly, which he thereupon proceeded to devour.

Then Boule de Suif, in low, humble tones, invited the nuns to partake of her repast. They both accepted the offer unhesitatingly, and after a few stammered words of thanks began to eat quickly, without raising their eyes. Neither did Cornudet refuse his neighbour's offer, and, in combination with the nuns, a sort of table was formed by opening out the newspaper over the four pairs of knees.

Mouths kept opening and shutting, ferociously masticating and devouring the food. Loiseau, in his corner, was hard at work, and in low tones urged his wife to follow his example. She held out for a long time, but over-strained Nature gave way at last. Her husband, assuming his politest manner, asked their 'charming companion' if he might be allowed to offer Madame Loiseau a small helping.

'Why, certainly, sir,' she replied, with an amiable smile, holding out the dish.

When the first bottle of claret was opened some embarrassment was caused by the fact that there was only one drinking cup, but this was passed from one to another, after being wiped. Cornudet alone, doubtless in a spirit of gallantry, raised to his own lips that part of the rim which was still moist from those of his fair neighbour.

Then, surrounded by people who were eating, and well-nigh suffocated by the odour of food, the Comte and Comtesse de Bréville and Monsieur and Madame Carré-Lamadon endured that hateful form of torture which has perpetuated the name of Tantalus. All at once the manufacturer's young wife heaved a sigh which made everyone turn and look at her; she was white as the snow without; her eyes closed, her head fell forward; she had fainted. Her husband, beside himself, implored the help of his neighbours. No one seemed to know what to do until the elder of the two nuns, raising the patient's head, placed Boule de Suif's drinking cup to her lips, and made her swallow a few drops of wine. The pretty invalid moved, opened her eyes, smiled, and declared in a feeble voice that she was all right again. But, to prevent a recurrence of the catastrophe, the nun made her drink a cupful of claret, adding: 'It's just hunger – that's what is wrong with you.'

Then Boule de Suif, blushing and embarrassed, stammered, looking at the four passengers who were still fasting: 'If I might offer these ladies and gentlemen – '

She stopped short, fearing a snub. But Loiseau continued: 'Hang it all, in such a case as this we are all brothers and sisters and ought to help each other. Come, come, ladies, don't stand on ceremony, for goodness' sake! Do we even know whether we shall find a house in which to pass the night? At our present rate of going we shan't be at Tôtes till midday tomorrow.'

They hesitated, no one daring to be the first to accept. But the count settled the question. He turned towards the abashed girl, and in his most distinguished manner said: 'We accept gratefully, madame.'

The Rubicon once crossed, they set to work with a will. The basket was emptied. It still contained pâté de foie gras, a lark pie, a piece of smoked tongue, Crassane pears, Pont-l'Evêque gingerbread, fancy cakes, and a cup full of pickled gherkins and onions – Boule de Suif, like all women, being very fond of indigestible things.

They could not eat this girl's provisions without speaking to her. So they began to talk, stiffly at first; then, as she seemed by no means forward, with greater freedom. Mesdames de Bréville and Carré-Lamadon, who were accomplished women of the world, were gracious and tactful. The countess especially displayed that amiable condescension characteristic of great ladies whom no contact with baser mortals can sully, and was absolutely charming. But the sturdy Madame Loiseau, who had the soul of a gendarme, continued morose, speaking little and eating much.

Conversation naturally turned on the war. Terrible stories were told about the Prussians, deeds of bravery were recounted of the French; and all these people who were fleeing themselves were ready to pay homage to the courage of their compatriots. Personal experiences soon followed, and Boule de Suif related with genuine emotion, and with that warmth of language not uncommon in women of her class and temperament, how it came about that she had left Rouen.

'I thought at first that I should be able to stay,' she said. 'My house was well stocked with provisions, and it seemed better to put up with feeding a few soldiers than to banish myself goodness knows where. But when I saw these Prussians it was too much for me! My blood boiled with rage; I wept the whole day for very shame. Oh, if only I had been a man! I looked at them from my window – the fat hogs, with their pointed helmets! – and my maid held my hands to keep me from throwing my furniture down on them. Then some of them were quartered on me; I flew at the throat of the first one who entered. They are just as easy to strangle as other men! And I'd have been the death of that one if I hadn't been dragged away from him by my hair. I had to hide after that. And as soon as I could get an opportunity I left the place, and here I am.'

She was warmly congratulated. She rose in the estimation of her companions, who had not been so brave; and Cornudet listened to her with the approving and benevolent smile of an apostle, the smile a priest might wear in listening to a devotee praising God; for long-bearded democrats of his type have a monopoly of patriotism, just as priests have a monopoly of religion. He held forth in turn, with dogmatic self-assurance, in the style of the proclamations daily pasted on the walls of the town, winding up with a specimen of stump oratory in which he reviled 'that besotted fool Louis-Napoleon'.

But Boule de Suif was indignant, for she was an ardent Bonapartist. She turned as red as a cherry, and stammered in her wrath: 'I'd just like to have seen you in his place – you and your sort! There would have been a nice muddle. Oh, yes! It was you who betrayed that man. It would be impossible to live in France if we were governed by such rascals as you!'

Cornudet, unmoved by this tirade, still smiled a superior, contemptuous smile; and one felt that high words were impending, when the count interposed, and, not without difficulty, succeeded in calming the exasperated woman, saying that all sincere opinions ought to be respected. But the countess and the manufacturer's wife, imbued with the unreasoning hatred of the upper classes for the Republic, and instinct, moreover, with the affection felt by all women for the pomp and circumstance of despotic government, were drawn, in spite of themselves, towards this loyal young woman, whose opinions coincided so closely with their own.

The basket was empty. The ten people had finished its contents without difficulty amid general regret that it did not hold more. Conversation went on a little longer, though it flagged somewhat after the passengers had finished eating.

Night fell, the darkness grew deeper and deeper, and the cold made Boule de Suif shiver, in spite of her plumpness. So Madame de Bréville offered her her foot-warmer, the fuel of which had been several times renewed since the morning, and she accepted the offer at once, for her feet were icy cold. Mesdames Carré-Lamadon and Loiseau gave theirs to the nuns.

The driver lighted his lanterns. They cast a bright gleam on a cloud of vapour which hovered over the sweating flanks of the horses, and on the roadside snow, which seemed to unroll as they went along in the changing light of the lamps.

All was now indistinguishable in the coach; but suddenly a movement occurred in the corner occupied by Boule de Suif and Cornudet; and Loiseau, peering into the gloom, fancied he saw the big, bearded democrat move hastily to one side, as if he had received a well-directed, though noiseless, blow in the dark.

Tiny lights glimmered ahead. It was Tôtes. The coach had been on the road eleven hours, which, with the three hours allotted the horses in four periods for feeding and breathing, made fourteen. It entered the town, and stopped before the Hôtel du Commerce.

The coach door opened; a well-known noise made all the travellers start; it was the clanging of a scabbard on the pavement; then a voice called out something in German.

Although the coach had come to a standstill, no one got out; it looked as if they were afraid of being murdered the moment they left their seats. Thereupon the driver appeared, holding in his hand one of his lanterns which cast a sudden glow on the interior of the coach, lighting up the double row of startled faces, mouths agape and eyes wide open in surprise and terror.

Beside the driver stood in the full light a German officer, a tall young man, fair and slender, tightly encased in his uniform like a woman in her corset, his flat shiny cap, tilted to one side of his head, making him look like an English hotel runner. His exaggerated moustache, long and straight and tapering to a point at either end in a single blond hair that could hardly be seen, seemed to weigh down the corners of his mouth and give a droop to his lips.

In Alsatian French he requested the travellers to alight, saying stiffly: 'Will you get out, ladies and gentlemen?'

The two nuns were the first to obey, manifesting the docility of holy women accustomed to submission on every occasion. Next appeared the count and countess, followed by the manufacturer and his wife, after whom came Loiseau, pushing his larger and better half before him.

'Good day, sir,' he said to the officer as he put his foot to the ground, acting on an impulse born of prudence rather than of politeness. The other, insolent like all in authority, merely stared without replying.

Boule de Suif and Cornudet, though near the door, were the last to alight, grave and dignified before the enemy. The stout girl tried to control herself and appear calm; the democrat stroked his long russet beard with a somewhat trembling hand. Both strove to maintain their dignity, knowing well that at such a time each individual is always looked upon as more or less typical of his nation; and, also, resenting the complaisant attitude of their companions, Boule de Suif tried to wear a bolder front than her neighbours, the virtuous women, while Cornudet, feeling that it was incumbent on him to set a good example, kept up the attitude of resistance which he had first assumed when he undertook to mine the high roads round Rouen.

They entered the spacious kitchen of the inn, and the German, having demanded the passports signed by the general in command, in which were mentioned the name, description and profession of each traveller, inspected them all minutely, comparing their appearance with the written particulars.

Then he said brusquely: 'All right,' and turned on his heel.

They breathed freely. Everyone was still hungry, so supper was ordered. Half an hour was required for its preparation, and, while two servants were apparently engaged in getting it ready, the travellers went to look at their rooms. These all opened off a long corridor, at the end of which was a glazed door with a number on it.

They were just about to take their seats at table when the innkeeper appeared in person. He was a former horse dealer – a large, asthmatic person, always wheezing, coughing, and clearing his throat. Follenvie was his patronymic.

He called: 'Mademoiselle Elisabeth Rousset?'

Boule de Suif started, and turned round.

'That is my name.'

'Mademoiselle, the Prussian officer wishes to speak to you immediately.'

'To me?'

'Yes; if you are Mademoiselle Elisabeth Rousset.'

She hesitated, reflected a moment, and then declared roundly: 'That may be; but I'm not going.'

They moved restlessly around her; everyone wondered and speculated as to the cause of this order.

The count approached: 'You are wrong, madame, for your refusal may bring trouble not only on yourself, but also on all your companions. It never pays to resist those in authority. Your compliance with this request cannot possibly be fraught with any danger; it has probably been made because some formality or other was forgotten.'

All added their voices to that of the count; Boule de Suif was begged, urged, lectured, and at last convinced; everyone was afraid of the complications which might result from headstrong action on her part. She said finally: 'I am doing it for your sakes, remember that!'

The countess took her hand.

'And we are grateful to you.'

She left the room. All waited for her return before beginning the meal. Each was distressed that he or she had not been sent for rather than this impulsive, quick-tempered girl, and each mentally rehearsed platitudes in case of being summoned also.

At the end of ten minutes she reappeared, breathing hard, crimson with indignation.

'Oh! the scoundrel! the scoundrel!' she stammered.

All were anxious to know what had happened; but she declined to enlighten them, and when the count pressed the point, she silenced him with much dignity saying: 'No; the matter has nothing to do with you, and I cannot speak of it.'

Then they took their places round a high soup tureen, from which issued an odour of cabbage. In spite of this incident, the supper was cheerful. The cider was good; the Loiseaus and the nuns drank it from motives of economy. The others ordered wine; Cornudet demanded beer. He had his own fashion of uncorking the bottle and making the beer foam, gazing at it as he inclined his glass and then raised it to a position between the lamp and his eye that he might judge of its colour. When he drank, his great beard, which matched the colour of his favourite beverage, seemed to tremble with affection; his eyes positively squinted in the endeavour not to lose sight of the beloved glass, and he looked for all the world as if he were fulfilling the only function for which he was born. He seemed to have established in his mind an affinity between the two great passions of his life – pale ale and revolution – and assuredly he could not taste the one without dreaming of the other.

Monsieur and Madame Follenvie dined at the end of the table. The man, wheezing like a broken-down locomotive, was too short-winded to talk when he was eating. But the wife was not silent a moment; she told how the Prussians had impressed her on their arrival, what they did, what they said; execrating them in the first place because they cost her money, and in the second because she had two sons in the army. She addressed herself principally to the countess, flattered at the opportunity of talking to a lady of quality.

Then she lowered her voice, and began to broach delicate subjects. Her husband interrupted her from time to time, saying: 'You would do well to hold your tongue, Madame Follenvie.'

But she took no notice of him, and went on: 'Yes, madame, these Germans do nothing but eat potatoes and pork, and then pork and potatoes. And don't imagine for a moment that they are clean! No, indeed! And if only you saw them drilling for hours, indeed for days, together; they all collect in a field, then they do nothing but march backwards and forwards, and wheel this way and that. If only they would cultivate the land, or remain at home and work on their high roads! Really, madame, these soldiers are of no earthly use! Poor people have to feed and keep them, only in order that they may learn how to kill! True, I am only an old woman with no education, but when I see them wearing themselves out marching about from morning till night, I say to myself: When there are people who make discoveries that are of use to people, why should others take so much trouble to do harm? Really, now, isn't it a terrible thing to kill people, whether they are Prussians, or English, or Poles, or French? If we revenge ourselves on anyone who injures us we do wrong, and are punished for it; but when our sons are shot down like partridges, that is all right, and decorations are given to the man who kills the most. No, indeed, I shall never be able to understand it.'

Cornudet raised his voice: 'War is a barbarous proceeding when we attack a peaceful neighbour, but it is a sacred duty when undertaken in defence of one's country.'

The old woman looked down: 'Yes; it's another matter when one acts in self-defence; but would it not be better to kill all the kings, seeing that they make war just to amuse themselves?'

Cornudet's eyes kindled.

'Bravo, citizen!' he said.

Monsieur Carré-Lamadon was reflecting profoundly. Although he was an ardent admirer of great generals, the peasant woman's sturdy common sense made him reflect on the wealth which might accrue to a country by the employment of so many idle hands now maintained at a great expense, of so much unproductive force, if they were employed in those great industrial enterprises which it will take centuries to complete.

But Loiseau, leaving his seat, went over to the innkeeper and began chatting in a low voice. The big man chuckled, coughed, sputtered; his enormous carcass shook with merriment at the pleasantries of the other; and he ended by buying six casks of claret from Loiseau to be delivered in the spring, after the departure of the Prussians.

The moment supper was over everyone went to bed, worn out with fatigue.

But Loiseau, who had been making his observations on the sly, sent his wife to bed, and amused himself by placing first his ear, and then his eye, to the bedroom keyhole, in order to discover what he called 'the mysteries of the corridor'.

At the end of about an hour he heard a rustling, peeped out quickly, and caught sight of Boule de Suif, looking more rotund than ever in a dressing-gown of blue cashmere trimmed with white lace. She held a candle in her hand, and directed her steps to the numbered door at the end of the corridor. But one of the side doors was partly opened, and when, at the end of a few minutes, she returned, Cornudet, in his shirt-sleeves, followed her. They spoke in low tones, then stopped short. Boule de Suif seemed to be stoutly denying him admission to her room.

Unfortunately, Loiseau could not at first hear what they said; but towards the end of the conversation they raised their voices, and he caught a few words. Cornudet was loudly insistent.

'How silly you are! What does it matter to you?' he said.

She seemed indignant, and replied: 'No, my good man, there are times when one does not do that sort of thing; besides, in this place it would be shameful.'

Apparently he did not understand, and asked the reason. Then she lost her temper and her caution, and, raising her voice still higher, said: 'Why? Can't you understand why? When there are Prussians in the house! Perhaps even in the very next room!'

He was silent. The patriotic reserve of this woman, who would not suffer herself to be caressed in the neighbourhood of the enemy, must have roused his dormant dignity, for after bestowing on her a simple kiss he crept softly back to his room. Loiseau, much edified, capered round the bedroom before taking his place beside his slumbering spouse.

Then silence reigned throughout the house. But soon there arose from some remote part – it might easily have been either cellar or attic – a stertorous, monotonous, regular snoring, a dull, prolonged rumbling, varied by tremors like those of a boiler under pressure of steam. Monsieur Follenvie had gone to sleep.

As they had decided on starting at eight o'clock the next morning, everyone was in the kitchen at that hour; but the coach, its roof covered with snow, stood by itself in the middle of the yard, without either horses or driver. They sought the latter in the stables, coach-houses and barns – but in vain. So the men of the party resolved to scour the village for him, and sallied forth. They found themselves in the square, with the church at the farther side, and to right and left low-roofed houses where there were some Prussian soldiers. The first soldier they saw was peeling potatoes. The second, farther on, was washing out a barber's shop. Another, bearded to the eyes, was fondling a crying infant, and dandling it on his knees to quiet it; and the stout peasant women, whose menfolk were for the most part at the war, were, by means of signs, telling their obedient conquerors what work they were to do: chop wood, prepare soup, grind coffee; one of them even was doing the washing for his hostess, an infirm old grandmother.

The count, astonished at what he saw, questioned the beadle who was coming out of the presbytery.

The old man answered: 'Oh, those men are not at all a bad lot; they are not Prussians, I am told; they come from somewhere farther off, I don't exactly know where. And they have all left wives and children behind them; they are not fond of war either, you may be sure! I expect they are mourning for the men where they come from, just as we do here; and the war causes them just as much unhappiness as it does us. As a matter of fact, things are not so very bad here just now, because the soldiers do no harm, and work just as if they were in their own homes. You see, sir, poor folk always help one another; it is the great ones of this world who make war.'

Cornudet, indignant at the friendly understanding established between conquerors and conquered, withdrew, preferring to shut himself up in the inn.

'They are re-peopling the country', jested Loiseau.

'They are undoing the harm they have done', said Monsieur Carré-Lamadon gravely.

But they could not find the coach driver. At last he was discovered in the village café, fraternising cordially with the officer's orderly.

'Were you not told to harness the horses at eight o'clock?' demanded the count.

'Oh, yes; but I've had different orders since.'

'What orders?'

'Not to harness at all.'

'Who gave you such orders?'

'Why, the Prussian officer.'

'But why?'

'I don't know. You must ask him. I am forbidden to harness the horses, so I don't harness them – that's all.'

'Did he tell you so himself?'

'No, sir; the innkeeper gave me the order from him.'

'When?'

'Last evening, just as I was going to bed.'

The three men returned in a very uneasy frame of mind.

They asked for Monsieur Follenvie, but the servant replied that on account of his asthma he never got up before ten o'clock. They were strictly forbidden to rouse him earlier, except in case of fire.

They wished to see the officer, but that also was impossible, although he lodged in the inn. Monsieur Follenvie alone was authorised to interview him on civil matters. So they waited. The women returned to their rooms and occupied themselves with trivial matters.

Cornudet settled down beside the tall kitchen fireplace, before a blazing fire. He had a small table and a jug of beer placed beside him, and he smoked his pipe – a pipe which enjoyed among democrats a consideration almost equal to his own, as though it had served its country in serving Cornudet. It was a fine meerschaum, admirably coloured to a black the shade of its owner's teeth, but sweet-smelling, gracefully curved, at home in its master's hand, and completing his physiognomy. And Cornudet sat motionless, his eyes fixed now on the dancing flames, now on the froth which crowned his beer; and after each draught he passed his long, thin fingers with an air of satisfaction through his long, greasy hair, as he sucked the foam from his moustache.

Loiseau, under pretence of stretching his legs, went out to see if he could sell wine to the country dealers. The count and the manufacturer began to talk politics. They forecast the future of France. One believed in the Orleans dynasty, the other in an unknown saviour – a hero who should rise up in the last extremity: a Du Guesclin, perhaps a Joan of Arc? or another Napoleon Bonaparte? Ah! if only the Prince Imperial were not so young! Cornudet, listening to them, smiled like a man who holds the keys of destiny in his hands. His pipe perfumed the whole kitchen.

As the clock struck ten, Monsieur Follenvie appeared. He was immediately surrounded and questioned, but could only repeat, three or four times in succession, and without variation, the words: 'The officer said to me, just like this: "Monsieur Follenvie, you will forbid them to harness up the coach for those travellers tomorrow. They are not to start without an order from me. You hear? That is sufficient." '

Then they asked to see the officer. The count sent him his card, on which Monsieur Carré-Lamadon also inscribed his name and titles. The Prussian sent word that the two men would be admitted to see him after his luncheon – that is to say, about one o'clock.

The ladies reappeared, and they all ate a little, in spite of their anxiety. Boule de Suif appeared ill and very much worried.

They were finishing their coffee when the orderly came to fetch the gentlemen.

Loiseau joined the other two; but when they tried to get Cornudet to accompany them, by way of adding greater solemnity to the occasion, he declared proudly that he would never have anything to do with the Germans, and, resuming his seat in the chimney corner, he called for another jug of beer.

The three men went upstairs, and were ushered into the best room in the inn, where the officer received them lolling at his ease in an armchair, his feet on the mantelpiece, smoking a long porcelain pipe, and enveloped in a gorgeous dressing-gown, doubtless stolen from the deserted dwelling of some citizen destitute of taste in dress. He neither rose, greeted them, nor even glanced in their direction. He afforded a fine example of that insolence of bearing which seems natural to the victorious soldier.

After the lapse of a few moments he said in his halting French: 'What do you want?'

'We wish to start on our journey,' said the count.

'You can't.'

'May I ask the reason why?'

'Because I don't choose.'

'I would respectfully call your attention, monsieur, to the fact that your general in command gave us a permit to proceed to Dieppe; and I do not think we have done anything to deserve this harshness at your hands.'

'I don't choose – that's all. You may go.'

They bowed, and retired.

The afternoon was wretched. They could not understand the caprice of this German, and the strangest ideas came into their heads. They all congregated in the kitchen, and talked the subject to death, imagining all kinds of unlikely things. Perhaps they were to be kept as hostages – but for what reason? or to be extradited as prisoners of war? or possibly they were to be held for ransom? They were panic-stricken at this last supposition. The richest among them were the most alarmed, seeing themselves forced to empty bags of gold into the insolent soldier's hands in order to buy back their liberty. They racked their brains for plausible lies whereby they might conceal the fact that they were rich, and pass themselves off as poor – very poor. Loiseau took off his watch-chain, and put it in his pocket. The approach of night increased their apprehension. The lamp was lighted, and as it wanted yet two hours to dinner Madame Loiseau proposed a game of trente et un. It would distract their thoughts. The rest agreed, and Cornudet himself joined the party, first putting out his pipe for politeness' sake.

The count shuffled the cards – dealt – and Boule de Suif had thirty-one to start with; soon the interest of the game assuaged the anxiety of the players. But Cornudet noticed that Loiseau and his wife were in league to cheat.

They were about to sit down to dinner when Monsieur Follenvie appeared, and in his grating voice announced: 'The Prussian officer sends to ask Mademoiselle Elisabeth Rousset if she has changed her mind yet.'

Boule de Suif stood still, pale as death. Then, suddenly turning crimson with anger, she gasped out: 'Kindly tell that scoundrel, that cur, that carrion of a Prussian, that I will never consent – you understand? – never, never, never!'

The fat innkeeper left the room. Then Boule de Suif was surrounded, questioned, entreated on all sides to reveal the mystery of her visit to the officer. She refused at first; but her wrath soon got the better of her.

'What does he want? He wants me to give myself to him!' she cried.

No one was shocked, so great was the general indignation. Cornudet broke his jug as he banged it down on the table. A loud outcry arose against this base soldier. All were furious. They drew together in common resistance against the foe, as if some part of the sacrifice exacted of Boule de Suif had been demanded of each. The count declared, with supreme disgust, that those people behaved like ancient barbarians. The women, above all, manifested a lively and tender sympathy for Boule de Suif. The nuns, who appeared only at meals, cast down their eyes, and said nothing.

They dined, however, as soon as the first indignant outburst had subsided; but they spoke little, and thought much.

The ladies went to bed early; and the men, having lighted their pipes, proposed a game of écarté, in which Monsieur Follenvie was invited to join, the travellers hoping to question him skilfully as to the best means of vanquishing the officer's obduracy. But he thought of nothing but his cards, would listen to nothing, reply to nothing, and repeated, time after time: 'Attend to the game, gentlemen! attend to the game!' So absorbed was his attention that he even forgot to expectorate. The consequence was that his chest gave forth rumbling sounds like those of an organ. His wheezing lungs struck every note of the asthmatic scale, from deep, hollow tones to a shrill, hoarse piping resembling that of a young cock trying to crow.

He refused to go to bed when his wife, overcome with sleep, came to fetch him. So she went off alone, for she was always up with the sun; while he was addicted to late hours, ever ready to spend the night with friends. He merely said: 'Put my egg-noggin by the fire,' and went on with the game. When the other men saw that nothing was to be got out of him they declared it was time to retire, and each sought his bed.

They rose fairly early the next morning, with a vague hope of being allowed to start, a greater desire than ever to do so, and a terror at having to spend another day in this wretched little inn.

Alas! the horses remained in the stable; the driver was invisible. They spent their time, for want of something better to do, in wandering round the coach.

Luncheon was a gloomy affair, and there was a general coolness towards Boule de Suif, for night, which brings counsel, had somewhat modified the judgement of her companions. In the cold light of the morning they almost bore a grudge against the girl for not having secretly sought out the Prussian, that the rest of the party might receive a joyful surprise when they awoke. What more simple? Besides, who would have been the wiser? She might have saved appearances by telling the officer that she had taken pity on their distress. Such a step would be of so little consequence to her.

But no one as yet confessed to such thoughts.

In the afternoon, seeing that they were all bored to death, the count proposed a walk in the neighbourhood of the village. Each one wrapped himself up well, and the little party set out, leaving behind only Cornudet, who preferred to sit over the fire, and the two nuns, who were in the habit of spending their day in the church or at the presbytery.

The cold, which grew more intense each day, almost froze the noses and ears of the pedestrians; their feet began to pain them so that each step was a penance, and when they reached the open country it looked so mournful and depressing in its limitless mantle of white that they all hastily retraced their steps, with bodies benumbed and hearts heavy.

The four women walked in front, and the three men followed a little behind.

Loiseau, who saw perfectly well how matters stood, asked suddenly 'if that trollop were going to keep them waiting much longer in this God-forsaken spot'. The count, always courteous, replied that they could not exact so painful a sacrifice from any woman, and that the first move must come from herself. Monsieur Carré-Lamadon remarked that if the French, as they talked of doing, made a counter attack by way of Dieppe, their fight with the enemy must inevitably take place at Tôtes. This reflection made the other two anxious.

'Supposing we escape on foot?' said Loiseau.

The count shrugged his shoulders.

'How can you think of such a thing, in this snow? And with our wives? Besides, we should be pursued at once, overtaken in ten minutes, and brought back as prisoners at the mercy of the soldiery.'

This was true enough; they were silent.

The ladies talked of dress, but a certain constraint seemed to prevail among them.

Suddenly, at the end of the street, the officer appeared. His tall, wasp-like uniformed figure was outlined against the snow which bounded the horizon, and he walked, knees apart, with that motion peculiar to soldiers who are always anxious not to soil their carefully polished boots.

He bowed as he passed the ladies, and then glanced scornfully at the men, who had sufficient dignity not to raise their hats, though Loiseau made a movement to do so.

Boule de Suif flushed crimson to the ears, and the three married women felt unutterably humiliated at being met thus by the soldier in company with the courtesan whom he had treated with such scant ceremony.

Then they began to talk about him, his figure and his face. Madame Carré-Lamadon, who had known many officers and judged them as a connoisseur, thought him not at all bad-looking; she even regretted that he was not a Frenchman, because in that case he would have made a very handsome hussar, with whom all the women would assuredly have fallen in love.

When they were once more within doors they did not know what to do with themselves. Sharp words even were exchanged apropos of the merest trifles. The silent dinner was quickly over, and each one went to bed early in the hope of sleeping, and thus killing time.

They came down next morning with tired faces and irritable tempers; the women scarcely spoke to Boule de Suif.

A church bell summoned the faithful to a baptism. Boule de Suif had a child who had been brought up by peasants at Yvetot. She did not see him once a year, and never thought of him; but the idea of the child who was about to be baptised induced a sudden wave of tenderness for her own, and she decided to be present at the ceremony.

As soon as she had gone out, the rest of the company looked at one another and then drew their chairs together, for they realised that they must decide on some course of action. Loiseau had an inspiration: he proposed that they should ask the officer to detain Boule de Suif only, and to let the rest depart on their way.

Monsieur Follenvie was entrusted with this commission, but he returned to them almost immediately. The German, who knew human nature, had shown him the door. He intended to keep all the travellers until his condition had been complied with.

Whereupon Madame Loiseau's vulgar temperament broke bounds. 'We're not going to die of old age here!' she cried. 'Since it's that woman's trade to behave so with men, I don't see that she has any right to refuse one more than another. I may as well tell you she took any lovers she could get at Rouen – even coachmen! Yes, indeed, madame – the coachman at the prefecture! I know it for a fact, for he buys his wine off us. And now that it is a question of getting us out of a difficulty she puts on virtuous airs, the drab! For my part, I think this officer has behaved very well. Why, there were three others of us, any one of whom he would undoubtedly have preferred. But no, he contents himself with the girl who is common property. He respects married women. Just think. He is master here. He had only to say: "I wish it!" and he might have taken us by force, with the help of his soldiers.'

The two other women shuddered; the eyes of pretty Madame Carré-Lamadon glistened, and she grew pale, as if the officer were indeed in the act of laying violent hands on her.

The men, who had been discussing the subject among themselves, drew near. Loiseau, in a state of furious resentment, was for delivering up 'that miserable woman', bound hand and foot, into the enemy's power. But the count, descended from three generations of ambassadors, and endowed, moreover, with the lineaments of a diplomat, was in favour of more tactful measures.

'We must persuade her,' he said.

Then they laid their plans.

The women drew together; they lowered their voices, and the discussion became general, each giving his or her opinion. But the conversation was not in the least coarse. The ladies, in particular, were adepts at delicate phrases and charming subtleties of expression to describe the most improper things. A stranger would have understood none of their allusions, so guarded was the language they employed. But, seeing that the thin veneer of modesty with which every woman of the world is furnished goes but a very little way below the surface, they began rather to enjoy this unedifying episode, and at bottom were hugely delighted – feeling themselves in their element, furthering the schemes of lawless desire with the gusto of a gourmand cook who prepares supper for another.

Their gaiety returned of itself, so amusing at last did the whole business seem to them. The count uttered several rather risqué witticisms, but so tactfully were they said that his audience could not help smiling. Loiseau in turn made some considerably broader jokes, but no one took offence; and the thought expressed with such brutal directness by his wife was uppermost in the minds of all: 'Since it's the girl's trade, why should she refuse this man more than another?' Dainty Madame Carré-Lamadon seemed to think even that in Boule de Suif's place she would be less inclined to refuse him than another.

The blockade was as carefully arranged as if they were investing a fortress. Each agreed on the role which he or she was to play, the arguments to be used, the manoeuvres to be executed. They decided on the plan of campaign, the stratagems they were to employ, and the surprise attacks which were to reduce this human citadel and force it to receive the enemy within its walls.

But Cornudet remained apart from the rest, taking no share in the plot.

So absorbed was the attention of all that Boule de Suif's entrance was almost unnoticed. But the count whispered a gentle 'Hush!' which made the others look up. She was there. They suddenly stopped talking, and a vague embarrassment prevented them for a few moments from addressing her. But the countess, more practised than the others in the wiles of the drawing-room, asked her: 'Was the baptism interesting?'

The girl, still under the stress of emotion, told what she had seen and heard, described the faces, the attitudes of those present, and even the appearance of the church. She concluded with the words: 'It does one good to pray sometimes.'

Until lunchtime the ladies contented themselves with being pleasant to her, so as to increase her confidence and make her amenable to their advice.

As soon as they took their seats at table the attack began. First they opened a vague conversation on the subject of self-sacrifice. Ancient examples were quoted: Judith and Holofernes; then, irrationally enough, Lucrece and Sextus; Cleopatra and the hostile generals whom she reduced to abject slavery by a surrender of her charms. Next was recounted an extraordinary story, born of the imagination, which told how the matrons of Rome seduced Hannibal, his lieutenants, and all his mercenaries at Capua. They held up to admiration all those women who from time to time have arrested the victorious progress of conquerors, made of their bodies a means of ruling, a weapon; who have vanquished by their heroic caresses hideous or detested beings, and sacrificed their chastity to vengeance and devotion.

All was said with due restraint and regard for propriety, the effect heightened now and then by an outburst of forced enthusiasm calculated to excite emulation.

A listener would have thought at last that the one role of woman on earth was a sacrifice of her virtue, a continual abandonment of herself to the caprices of a hostile soldiery.

The two nuns seemed to hear nothing, and to be lost in thought. Boule de Suif also was silent.

During the whole afternoon she was left to her reflections. But instead of calling her 'madame', as they had done hitherto, her companions addressed her simply as 'mademoiselle', without exactly knowing why, but as if desirous of making her descend a step in the esteem she had won, and forcing her to realise her degraded position.

Just as soup was served, Monsieur Follenvie reappeared, repeating his phrase of the evening before: 'The Prussian officer sends to ask if Mademoiselle Elisabeth Rousset has changed her mind.'

Boule de Suif answered briefly: 'No, monsieur.'

But at dinner the coalition weakened. Loiseau made three unfortunate remarks. Each was cudgelling his brains for further examples of self-sacrifice, and could find none, when the countess, possibly without ulterior motive, and moved simply by a vague desire to do homage to religion, began to question the elder of the two nuns on the most striking facts in the lives of the saints. Now, it fell out that many of these had committed acts which would be crimes in our eyes, but the Church readily pardons such deeds when they are accomplished for the glory of God or the good of mankind. This was a powerful argument, and the countess made the most of it. Then, whether by reason of a tacit understanding, a thinly veiled act of complaisance such as those who wear the ecclesiastical habit excel in, or whether merely as the result of sheer stupidity – a stupidity admirably adapted to further their designs – the old nun rendered formidable aid to the conspirators. They had thought her timid; she proved herself bold, talkative, bigoted. She was not troubled by the ins and outs of casuistry; her doctrines were as iron bars; her faith knew no doubt; her conscience no scruples. She looked on Abraham's sacrifice as natural enough, for she herself would not have hesitated to kill both father and mother if she had received a divine order to that effect; and nothing, in her opinion, could displease our Lord, provided the motive were praiseworthy. The countess, putting to good use the consecrated authority of her unexpected ally, led her on to make a lengthy and edifying paraphrase of that axiom enunciated by a certain school of moralists: 'The end justifies the means.'

'Then, sister,' she asked, 'you think God accepts all methods, and pardons the act when the motive is pure?'

'Undoubtedly, madame. An action reprehensible in itself often derives merit from the thought which inspires it.'

And in this wise they talked on, fathoming the wishes of God, predicting His judgements, describing Him as interested in matters which assuredly concern Him but little.

All was said with the utmost care and discretion, but every word uttered by the holy woman in her nun's garb weakened the indignant resistance of the courtesan. Then the conversation drifted somewhat, and the nun began to talk of the convents of her order, of her Superior, of herself and of her fragile little neighbour, Sister St Nicéphore. They had been sent for from Le Havre to nurse the hundreds of soldiers who were in hospitals, stricken with smallpox. She described these wretched invalids and their malady. And, while they themselves were detained on their way by the caprices of the Prussian officer, scores of Frenchmen might be dying, whom they would otherwise have saved! For the nursing of soldiers was the old nun's speciality; she had been in the Crimea, in Italy, in Austria; and as she told the story of her campaigns she revealed herself as one of those holy sisters of the fife and drum who seem designed by nature to follow camps, to snatch the wounded from amid the strife of battle, and to quell with a word, more effectually than any general, the rough and insubordinate troopers – a masterful woman, her seamed and pitted face itself an image of the devastations of war.

No one spoke when she had finished for fear of spoiling the excellent effect of her words.

As soon as the meal was over the travellers retired to their rooms, whence they emerged the following day at a late hour of the morning.

Luncheon passed off quietly. The seed sown the preceding evening was being given time to germinate and bring forth fruit.

In the afternoon the countess proposed a walk; then the count, as had been arranged beforehand, took Boule de Suif's arm, and walked with her at some distance behind the rest.

He began talking to her in that familiar, paternal, slightly contemptuous tone which men of his class adopt in speaking to women like her, calling her 'my dear child', and talking down to her from the height of his exalted social position and stainless reputation. He came straight to the point.

'So you prefer to leave us here, exposed like yourself to all the violence which would follow on a repulse of the Prussian troops, rather than consent to surrender yourself, as you have done so many times in your life?'

The girl did not reply.

He tried kindness, argument, sentiment. He still bore himself as count, even while adopting, when desirable, an attitude of gallantry, and making pretty – nay, even tender – speeches. He exalted the service she would render them, spoke of their gratitude; then, suddenly, using the familiar 'thou': 'And you know, my dear, he could boast of having made a conquest of a pretty girl such as he won't often find in his own country.'

Boule de Suif did not answer, and joined the rest of the party.

As soon as they returned she went to her room, and was seen no more. The general anxiety was at its height. What would she do? If she still resisted, how awkward for them all!

The dinner hour struck; they waited for her in vain. At last Monsieur Follenvie entered, announcing that Mademoiselle Rousset was not well, and that they might sit down to table. They all pricked up their ears. The count drew near the innkeeper, and whispered: 'Is it all right?'

'Yes.'

Out of regard for propriety he said nothing to his companions, but merely nodded slightly towards them. A great sigh of relief went up from all breasts; every face was lighted up with joy.

'By Gad!' shouted Loiseau, 'I'll stand champagne all round if there's any to be found in this place.' And great was Madame Loiseau's dismay when the proprietor came back with four bottles in his hands. They had all suddenly become talkative and merry; a lively joy filled their hearts. The count seemed to perceive for the first time that Madame Carré-Lamadon was charming; the manufacturer paid compliments to the countess. The conversation was animated, sprightly, witty, and although many of the jokes were in the worst possible taste, all the company were amused by them, and none offended – indignation being dependent, like other emotions, on surroundings. And the mental atmosphere had gradually become filled with gross imaginings and unclean thoughts.

At dessert even the women indulged in discreetly worded allusions. Their glances were full of meaning; they had drunk much. The count, who even in his moments of relaxation preserved a dignified demeanour, hit on a much-appreciated comparison of the condition of things with the termination of a winter spent in the icy solitude of the North Pole and the joy of shipwrecked mariners who at last perceive a southward track opening out before their eyes.

Loiseau, fairly in his element, rose to his feet, holding aloft a glass of champagne.

'I drink to our deliverance!' he shouted.

All stood up, and greeted the toast with acclamation. Even the two good sisters yielded to the solicitations of the ladies, and consented to moisten their lips with the sparkling wine, which they had never before tasted. They declared it was like effervescent lemonade, but with a pleasanter flavour.

'It is a pity,' said Loiseau, 'that we have no piano; we might have had a quadrille.'

Cornudet had not spoken a word or made a movement; he seemed plunged in serious thought, and now and then tugged furiously at his great beard, as if trying to add still further to its length. At last, towards midnight, when they were about to separate, Loiseau, whose gait was far from steady, suddenly slapped him on the back, saying thickly: 'You're not jolly tonight; why are you so silent?'

Cornudet threw back his head, cast one swift and scornful glance over the assemblage, and answered: 'I tell you all, you have done an infamous thing!'

He rose, reached the door, and repeating: 'Infamous!' disappeared.

A chill fell on all. Loiseau himself looked foolish and disconcerted for a moment, but soon recovered his aplomb, and, writhing with laughter, exclaimed: 'Really, he is too innocent for anything!'

Pressed for an explanation, he related the 'mysteries of the corridor', whereat his listeners were hugely amused. The ladies could hardly contain their delight. The count and Monsieur Carré-Lamadon laughed till they cried. They could scarcely believe their ears.

'What! you are sure? He wanted –'

'I tell you I saw it with my own eyes.'

'And she refused?'

'Because the Prussian was in the next room!'

'Surely you are mistaken?'

'I swear I'm telling you the truth.'

The count was choking with laughter. The manufacturer held his sides. Loiseau continued: 'So you may well imagine he doesn't think this evening's business at all amusing.'

And all three began to laugh again, choking, coughing, almost ill with merriment.

Then they separated. But Madame Loiseau, who was nothing if not spiteful, remarked to her husband as they were on the way to bed that 'that stuck-up little minx of a Carré-Lamadon had laughed on the wrong side of her mouth all the evening'.

'You know,' she said, 'when women run after uniforms it's all the same to them whether the men who wear them are French or Prussian. It's perfectly disgusting!'

The next morning the snow showed dazzling white under a clear winter sun. The coach, ready at last, waited before the door; while a flock of white pigeons, with pink eyes spotted in the centres with black, puffed out their white feathers and walked sedately between the legs of the six horses.

The driver, wrapped in his sheepskin coat, was smoking a pipe on the box, and all the passengers, radiant with delight at their approaching departure, were putting up provisions for the remainder of the journey.

They were waiting only for Boule de Suif. At last she appeared.

She seemed rather shamefaced and embarrassed, and advanced with timid step towards her companions, who with one accord turned aside as if they had not seen her. The count, with much dignity, took his wife by the arm, and removed her from the unclean contact.

The girl stood still, stupefied with astonishment; then, plucking up courage, accosted the manufacturer's wife with a humble, 'Good morning, madame,' to which the other replied merely with a slight and insolent nod, accompanied by a look of outraged virtue. Everyone suddenly appeared extremely busy, and kept as far from Boule de Suif as if her skirts had been infected with some deadly disease. Then they hurried to the coach, followed by the despised courtesan, who, arriving last of all, silently took the place she had occupied during the first part of the journey.

The rest seemed neither to see nor to know her – all except Madame Loiseau, who, glancing contemptuously in her direction, remarked, in a loud whisper, to her husband: 'What a mercy I am not sitting beside that creature!'

The lumbering vehicle started on its way, and the journey began afresh.

At first no one spoke. Boule de Suif dared not even raise her eyes. She felt at once indignant with her neighbours, and humiliated at having yielded to the Prussian into whose arms they had so hypocritically cast her.

But the countess, turning towards Madame Carré-Lamadon, soon broke the painful silence: 'I think you know Madame d'Etrelles?'

'Yes; she is a friend of mine.'

'Such a charming woman!'

'Delightful! Exceptionally talented, and an artist to the fingertips. She sings marvellously and draws to perfection.'

The manufacturer was chatting with the count, and amid the clatter of the window-panes a word of their conversation was now and then distinguishable: 'Shares – maturity – premium – time-limit.'

Loiseau, who had abstracted from the inn the time-worn pack of cards, thick with the grease of five years' contact with half-wiped tables, started a game of bezique with his wife.

The good sisters, taking up simultaneously the long rosaries hanging from their waists, made the sign of the cross, and began to mutter in unison interminable prayers, their lips moving ever more and more swiftly, as if they sought which should outdistance the other in the race of orisons; from time to time they kissed a medal, crossed themselves anew, and then resumed their rapid and unintelligible murmur.

Cornudet sat still, lost in thought.

At the end of three hours Loiseau gathered up the cards, and remarked that he was hungry.

His wife thereupon produced a parcel tied with string, from which she extracted a piece of cold veal. This she cut into neat, thin slices, and both began to eat.

'We may as well do the same,' said the countess. The rest agreed, and she unpacked the provisions which had been prepared for herself, the count and the Carré-Lamadons. In one of those oval dishes, the lids of which are decorated with an earthenware hare by way of showing that a game pie lies within, was a succulent delicacy consisting of the brown flesh of the game, larded with streaks of bacon and flavoured with other meats chopped fine. A solid wedge of Gruyère cheese, which had been wrapped in newspaper, bore the imprint 'Items of News' on its rich, oily surface.

The two good sisters brought to light a hunk of sausage smelling strongly of garlic; and Cornudet, plunging both hands at once into the capacious pockets of his loose overcoat, produced from one four hard-boiled eggs and from the other a crust of bread. He removed the shells, threw them into the straw beneath his feet, and began to devour the eggs, letting morsels of the bright yellow yolk fall in his mighty beard, where they looked like stars.

Boule de Suif, in the haste and confusion of her departure, had not thought of anything, and, stifling with rage, she watched all these people placidly eating. At first, ill-suppressed wrath shook her whole person, and she opened her lips to shriek the truth at them, to overwhelm them with a volley of insults; but she could not utter a word, so choked was she with indignation.

No one looked at her, no one thought of her. She felt herself swallowed up in the scorn of these virtuous creatures, who had first sacrificed then rejected her as a thing useless and unclean. Then she remembered her big basket full of the good things they had so greedily devoured: the two chickens coated in jelly, the pies, the pears, the four bottles of claret; and her fury broke like a cord that is over-stretched, and she was on the verge of tears. She made terrible efforts at self-control, drew herself up, swallowed the sobs which choked her; but the tears rose nevertheless, shone at the brink of her eyelids, and soon two heavy drops coursed slowly down her cheeks. Others followed more quickly, like water filtering from a rock, and fell, one after another, on her rounded bosom. She sat upright, with a fixed expression, her face pale and rigid, hoping desperately that no one saw her give way.

But the countess noticed that she was weeping, and with a sign drew her husband's attention to the fact. He shrugged his shoulders, as if to say: 'Well, what of it? It's not my fault.'

Madame Loiseau chuckled triumphantly, and murmured: 'She's weeping for shame.'

The two nuns had betaken themselves once more to their prayers, first wrapping the remainder of their sausage in paper.

Then Cornudet, who was digesting his eggs, stretched his long legs under the opposite seat, threw himself back, folded his arms, smiled like a man who had just thought of a good joke, and began to whistle 'The Marseillaise'.

The faces of his neighbours clouded; the popular air evidently did not find favour with them; they grew nervous and irritable, and seemed ready to howl as a dog does at the sound of a barrel-organ. Cornudet saw the discomfort he was creating, and whistled the louder; sometimes he even hummed the words:

> Sacred love of the motherland,
> Lend support to our avenging arms.
> Liberty, cherished Liberty,
> Fight with your defenders!

The coach progressed more swiftly, the snow being harder now; and all the way to Dieppe, during the long, dreary hours of the journey, first in the gathering dusk, then in the thick darkness, raising his voice above the rumbling of the vehicle, Cornudet continued with fierce obstinacy his vengeful and monotonous whistling, forcing his weary and exasperated hearers to follow the song from end to end, to recall every word of every line, as each was repeated over and over again with untiring persistency.

And Boule de Suif still wept, and sometimes a sob she could not restrain was heard in the darkness between two couplets of the song.

Two Friends

Besieged Paris was in the throes of famine. Even the sparrows on the roofs and the rats in the sewers were growing scarce. People were eating anything they could get.

As Monsieur Morissot, watchmaker by profession and idler for the nonce, was strolling along the boulevard one bright January morning, his hands in his trouser pockets and his stomach empty, he suddenly came face to face with a friend – Monsieur Sauvage, a fishing companion.

Before the war broke out, Morissot had been in the habit, every Sunday morning, of setting forth with a bamboo rod in his hand and a tin box on his back. He took the Argenteuil train, got out at Colombes, and walked thence to the Ile Marante. The moment he arrived at this place of his dreams he began fishing and remained till nightfall.

Every Sunday he met at this spot Monsieur Sauvage, a stout, jolly, little man, a draper in the Rue Notre Dame de Lorette, and also an ardent fisherman. They often spent half the day side by side, rod in hand and feet dangling over the water, and a sincere friendship had sprung up between the two.

Some days they did not speak; at other times they chatted; but they understood each other perfectly without the aid of words, having similar tastes and feelings.

In the spring, about ten o'clock in the morning, when the early sun caused a light mist to float on the water and gently warmed the backs of the two enthusiastic anglers, Morissot would occasionally remark to his neighbour: 'Isn't it pleasant here?'

To which the other would reply: 'I can't imagine anything better!'

And these few words sufficed to make them understand and appreciate each other.

In the autumn, towards the close of day, when the setting sun shed a blood-red colour over the western sky, and the reflection of the crimson clouds tinged the whole river, brought a glow to the faces of the two friends and gilded the trees, whose leaves were already turning at the first chill touch of winter, Monsieur Sauvage would sometimes smile at Morissot, and say: 'What a glorious spectacle!'

And Morissot would answer, without taking his eyes from his float: 'This is much better than the boulevard, isn't it?'

As soon as they recognised each other they shook hands cordially, affected at the thought of meeting in such changed circumstances.

Monsieur Sauvage, with a sigh, murmured: 'These are sad times!'

Morissot shook his head mournfully.

'And such weather! This is the first fine day of the year.'

The sky was, in fact, of a bright, cloudless blue. They walked along, side by side, reflective and sad. 'And to think of the fishing!' said Morissot. 'What good times we used to have!'

'When shall we be able to fish again?' asked Monsieur Sauvage.

They entered a small café, took an absinthe together, and then resumed their walk along the pavement.

Morissot stopped suddenly.

'Shall we have another absinthe?' he said.

'If you like,' agreed Monsieur Sauvage.

And they entered a wine shop.

They were quite unsteady when they came out, owing to the effect of the alcohol on their empty stomachs. It was a fine, mild day, and a gentle breeze fanned their faces.

The fresh air completed the effect of the alcohol on Monsieur Sauvage. He stopped suddenly, saying: 'Suppose we go there?'

'Where?'

'Fishing.'

'But where?'

'Why, to the old place. The French outposts are close to Colombes. I know Colonel Dumoulin, and we shall easily get leave to pass.'

Morissot trembled with desire.

'Very well. I agree.'

And they separated, to fetch their rods and lines.

An hour later they were walking side by side on the high road. Presently they reached the villa occupied by the colonel. He smiled at their request, and granted it. They resumed their walk, furnished with a password.

Soon they left the outposts behind them, made their way through deserted Colombes, and found themselves on the outskirts of the small vineyards which border the Seine. It was about eleven o'clock.

Before them lay the village of Argenteuil, apparently lifeless. The heights of Orgemont and Sannois dominated the landscape. The great plain, extending as far as Nanterre, was empty, quite empty – a waste of dun-coloured soil and bare cherry trees.

Monsieur Sauvage, pointing to the heights, murmured: 'The Prussians are up yonder!'

And the sight of the deserted country filled the two friends with vague misgivings.

The Prussians! They had never seen them as yet, but they had felt their presence in the neighbourhood of Paris for months past – ruining France, pillaging, massacring and starving the people. And a kind of superstitious terror was added to the hatred they already felt towards this unknown, victorious nation.

'Suppose we were to meet any of them?' said Morissot.

'We'd offer them some fish,' replied Monsieur Sauvage, with that Parisian light-heartedness which nothing can wholly quench.

Still, they hesitated to show themselves in the open country, overawed by the utter silence which reigned around them.

At last Monsieur Sauvage said boldly: 'Come, we'll make a start; only let us be careful!'

And they made their way through one of the vineyards, bent double, creeping along beneath the cover afforded by the vines, with eye and ear alert.

A strip of bare ground remained to be crossed before they could gain the river bank. They ran across this, and, as soon as they were at the water's edge, concealed themselves among the dry reeds.

Morissot placed his ear to the ground, to ascertain, if possible, whether footsteps were coming their way. He heard nothing. They seemed to be utterly alone.

Their confidence was restored, and they began to fish.

Before them the deserted Ile Marante hid them from the farther shore. The little restaurant was closed, and looked as if it had been deserted for years.

Monsieur Sauvage caught the first gudgeon, Monsieur Morissot the second, and almost every moment one or other raised his line with a little, glittering, silvery fish wriggling at the end; they were having excellent sport.

They slipped their catch gently into a close-meshed bag lying at their feet; they were filled with joy – the joy of once more indulging in a pastime of which they had long been deprived.

The sun poured its rays on their backs; they no longer heard anything or thought of anything. They ignored the rest of the world; they were fishing.

But suddenly a rumbling sound, which seemed to come from the bowels of the earth, shook the ground beneath them: the cannon were resuming their thunder.

Morissot turned his head and could see towards the left, beyond the banks of the river, the formidable outline of Mont-Valérien, from whose summit arose a white puff of smoke.

The next instant a second puff followed the first, and in a few moments a fresh detonation made the earth tremble.

Others followed, and minute by minute the mountain gave forth its deadly breath and a white puff of smoke, which rose slowly into the peaceful heaven and floated above the summit of the cliff.

Monsieur Sauvage shrugged his shoulders.

'They are at it again!' he said.

Morissot, who was anxiously watching his float bobbing up and down, was suddenly seized with the angry impatience of a peaceful man towards the madmen who were firing thus, and remarked indignantly: 'What fools they are to kill one another like that!'

'They're worse than animals,' replied Monsieur Sauvage.

And Morissot, who had just caught a bleak, declared: 'And to think that it will be just the same so long as there are governments!'

'The Republic would not have declared war,' interposed Monsieur Sauvage.

Morissot interrupted him: 'Under a king we have foreign wars; under a republic we have civil war.'

And the two began placidly discussing political problems with the sound common sense of peaceful, matter-of-fact citizens – agreeing on one point: that they would never be free. And Mont-Valérien thundered ceaselessly, demolishing the houses of the French with its cannon balls, grinding lives of men to powder, destroying many a dream, many a cherished hope, many a prospective happiness; ruthlessly causing endless woe and suffering in the hearts of wives, of daughters, of mothers, in other regions.

'Such is life!' declared Monsieur Sauvage.

'Say, rather, such is death!' replied Morissot, laughing.

But they suddenly trembled with alarm at the sound of footsteps behind them, and, turning round, they perceived close at hand four tall, bearded men, dressed after the manner of liveried servants and wearing flat caps on their heads. They were covering the two anglers with their rifles.

The rods slipped from their owners' grasp and floated away down the river.

In the space of a few seconds they were seized, bound, thrown into a boat, and taken across to the Ile Marante.

And behind the house they had thought deserted were about a score of German soldiers.

A shaggy-looking giant, who was bestriding a chair and smoking a long clay pipe, addressed them in excellent French with the words: 'Well, gentlemen, have you had good luck with your fishing?'

Then a soldier deposited at the officer's feet the bag full of fish, which he had taken care to bring away.

The Prussian smiled. 'Not bad, I see. But we have something else to talk about. Listen to me, and don't be alarmed.

'You must know that, in my eyes, you are two spies sent to report my movements. Naturally, I capture you and I shoot you. You pretend to be fishing, the better to disguise your real errand. You have fallen into my hands, and must take the consequences. Such is war.

'But as you came here through the outposts you must have a password for your return. Tell me that password and I will let you go.'

The two friends, pale as death, stood silently side by side, a slight fluttering of the hands alone betraying their emotion.

'No one will ever know,' continued the officer. 'You will return peacefully to your homes, and the secret will disappear with you. If you refuse, it means death – instant death. Choose!'

They stood motionless, and did not open their lips.

The Prussian, perfectly calm, went on, with hand outstretched towards the river: 'Just think that in five minutes you will be at the bottom of that water. In five minutes! You have relations, I presume?'

Mont-Valérien still thundered.

The two fishermen remained silent. The German turned and gave an order in his own language. Then he moved his chair a little way off, that he might not be so near the prisoners, while a dozen men stepped forward, rifles at the ready, and took up a position twenty paces off.

'I give you one minute,' said the officer; 'not a second longer.'

Then he rose quickly, went over to the two Frenchmen, took Morissot by the arm, led him a short distance off, and said in a low voice: 'Quick! the password! Your friend will know nothing. I will pretend to relent.'

Morissot answered not a word.

Then the Prussian took Monsieur Sauvage aside in like manner, and made him the same proposal.

Monsieur Sauvage made no reply.

Again they stood side by side.

The officer issued his orders; the soldiers raised their rifles.

Then by chance Morissot's eyes fell on the bag full of gudgeon lying in the grass a few feet from him.

A ray of sunlight made the still quivering fish glisten like silver. And

Morissot's heart sank. Despite his efforts at self-control his eyes filled with tears.

'Goodbye, Monsieur Sauvage,' he faltered.

'Goodbye, Monsieur Morissot,' replied Sauvage.

They shook hands, trembling from head to foot with a dread beyond their mastery.

The officer cried: 'Fire!'

The twelve shots were as one.

Monsieur Sauvage fell forward instantaneously. Morissot, being the taller, swayed slightly and fell across his friend with face turned skyward and blood oozing from a rent in the breast of his coat.

The German issued fresh orders.

His men dispersed, and presently returned with ropes and large stones, which they attached to the feet of the two friends; then they carried them to the river bank.

Mont-Valérien, its summit now enshrouded in smoke, continued to thunder.

Two soldiers took Morissot by the head and the feet; two others did the same with Sauvage. The bodies, swung vigorously by strong hands, were cast to a distance, and, describing a curve, fell feet foremost into the stream.

The water splashed high, foamed, eddied, and then was still again; tiny waves lapped the shore.

A few streaks of blood flecked the surface of the river.

The officer, calm throughout, remarked, with grim humour: 'It's the fishes' turn now!'

Then he retraced his way to the house.

Suddenly he caught sight of the net full of gudgeon, lying forgotten in the grass. He picked it up, examined it, smiled, and called: 'Wilhelm!'

A white-aproned soldier responded to the summons, and the Prussian, tossing him the catch of the two dead men, said: 'Have these fish fried for me at once, while they are still alive; they'll make an excellent dish.'

Then he relit his pipe.

Madame Tellier's Establishment

I

They went there every evening about eleven o'clock, just as they would go to the club. Six or eight of them; always the same set, not fast men, but respectable tradesmen, and young men in government or some other employ. They would drink their Chartreuse, and laugh with the girls, or else talk seriously with Madame Tellier, whom everybody respected, and then they would go home at twelve o'clock! The younger men would sometimes stay later.

It was a small, comfortable house painted yellow, at the corner of a street behind Saint Etienne's Church, and from the windows one could see the docks full of ships being unloaded, the big salt marsh, and, rising beyond it, the Virgin's Hill with its old grey chapel.

Madame Tellier, who came of a respectable family of peasant proprietors in the Department of the Eure, had taken up her profession just as she would have become a milliner or dressmaker. The prejudice which is so violent and deeply rooted in large towns does not exist in the country places in Normandy. The peasant says: 'It is a paying business,' and he sends his daughter to keep an establishment of this character just as he would send her to keep a girls' school.

She had inherited the house from an old uncle, to whom it had belonged. Monsieur and Madame Tellier, who had formerly been innkeepers near Yvetot, had immediately sold their house, as they thought that the business at Fécamp was more profitable, and they arrived one fine morning to assume the direction of the enterprise, which was declining on account of the absence of the proprietor. They were good people in their way, and soon made themselves liked by their staff and their neighbours.

Monsieur died of apoplexy two years later, for as the new place kept him in idleness and without any exercise, he had grown excessively stout, and his health had suffered. Since Madame had been a widow, all the frequenters of the establishment made much of her; but people said that, personally, she was quite virtuous, and even the girls in the house could not discover anything against her. She was tall, stout and affable, and her complexion, which had become pale in the dimness of her house, the shutters of which were scarcely ever opened, shone as if it had been varnished. She had a fringe of curly false hair, which gave her a juvenile look that contrasted strongly with the ripeness of her figure. She was always smiling and cheerful, and was fond of a joke, but there was a shade of reserve about her which her occupation had not quite made her lose. Coarse words always shocked her, and when any young fellow who had been badly brought up called her establishment a hard name, she was angry and disgusted.

In a word, she had a refined mind, and although she treated her women as friends, yet she very frequently used to say that 'she and they were not made of the same stuff'.

Sometimes during the week she would hire a carriage and take some of her girls into the country, where they used to enjoy themselves on the grass by the side of the little river. They were like a lot of girls let out from school, and would run races and play childish games. They had a cold dinner on the grass, and drank cider, and went home at night with a delicious feeling of fatigue; in the carriage they kissed Madame Tellier as their kind mother, who was full of goodness and complaisance.

The house had two entrances. At the corner there was a sort of tap-room, which sailors and the lower orders frequented at night, and she had two girls whose special duty it was to wait on them with the assistance of Frédéric, a short, light-haired, beardless fellow, as strong as a horse. They set the half-bottles of wine and the jugs of beer on the shaky marble tables before the customers, and then urged the men to drink.

The three other girls – there were only five of them – formed a kind of aristocracy; they remained with the company on the first floor, unless they were wanted downstairs and there was nobody on the first floor.

The Jupiter drawing-room, where the tradesmen used to meet, was papered in blue, and embellished with a large representation of Leda and the swan. The room was reached by a winding staircase, through a narrow door opening on the street, and above this door a lantern enclosed in wire, such as one still sees in some towns at the foot of the shrine of some saint, burned all night long.

The house, which was old and damp, smelt slightly of mildew. At times there was an odour of eau de Cologne in the passages, or sometimes from a half-open door downstairs the noisy mirth of the common men sitting and drinking rose to the first floor, much to the disgust of the gentlemen who were there. Madame Tellier, who was on friendly terms with her customers, did not leave the room, and as she took much interest in what was going on in the town, they regularly told her all the news. Her serious conversation was a change from the ceaseless chatter of the three women; it was a rest from the obscene jokes of those stout persons who every evening indulged in the commonplace debauchery of drinking a glass of liqueur in company with common women.

The names of the girls on the first floor were Fernande, Raphaële and Rosa the Jade. As the staff was limited, Madame had contrived that each member of it should be a pattern, an epitome of a feminine type, so that every customer might find as nearly as possible the realisation of his ideal.

Fernande represented the handsome blonde; she was very tall, rather fat, and lazy; a country girl, who could not get rid of her freckles, and whose short, light, almost colourless, tow-like hair, like combed-out hemp, barely covered her head.

Raphaële, who came from Marseilles, played the indispensable part of the handsome Jewess, and was thin, with high cheekbones, which were covered with rouge, and black hair, shiny with pomatum, which curled on her forehead. Her eyes would have been handsome, if the right one had not had a speck in it. Her Roman nose came down over a square jaw, where two false upper teeth contrasted strangely with the bad colour of the rest.

Rosa was a little roll of fat, nearly all body, with very short legs; from morning till night she sang songs, which were alternately risqué or sentimental, in a harsh voice; told silly, interminable tales, and only stopped talking in order to eat, and left off eating in order to talk; she was never still, and was active as a squirrel, in spite of her embonpoint and her short legs; her laugh, which was a torrent of shrill cries, resounded here and there, ceaselessly, in a bedroom, in the attic, in the café, everywhere, and all about nothing.

The two women on the ground floor, Louise, who was nicknamed La Cocotte, and Flora, whom they called the Seesaw, because she limped a little – the former always dressed as the Goddess of Liberty, with a tri-coloured sash, and the other as a Spanish woman, with a string of copper coins in her carroty hair, which jingled at every uneven step – looked like cooks dressed up for the carnival. They were like all other women of the lower orders, neither uglier nor better looking than they usually are. They looked just like servants at an inn, and were generally called 'the Beer Pumps'.

A jealous peace, which was very rarely disturbed, reigned among these five women, thanks to Madame Tellier's conciliatory wisdom and to her constant good humour, and the establishment, which was the only one of the kind in the little town, was very much frequented. Madame Tellier had succeeded in giving it such a respectable appearance, she was so amiable and obliging to everybody, her good heart was so well known, that she was treated with a certain amount of consideration. The regular customers spent money on her, and were delighted when she was especially friendly towards them. When they met during the day, they would say: 'Until this evening, you know where,' just as men say: 'At the club, after dinner.' In a word, Madame Tellier's house was somewhere to go to, and they very rarely missed their daily meetings there.

One evening towards the end of May, the first arrival, Monsieur Poulin, who was a timber merchant, and had been mayor, found the door shut. The lantern behind the grating was not alight; there was not a sound in the house; everything seemed dead. He knocked, gently at first, then more loudly, but nobody answered the door. Then he went slowly up the street, and when he got to the market place he met Monsieur Duvert, the gun-maker, who was going to the same place, so they went back together, but did not meet with any better success. But suddenly they heard a commotion, and on going round the house, they saw a number of English and French sailors, who were hammering at the closed shutters of the tap-room with their fists.

The two tradesmen immediately turned to flee, but a low 'Pst!' stopped them; it was Monsieur Tournevau, the fish-curer, who had recognised them, and was trying to attract their attention. They told him what had happened, and he was all the more annoyed as he was a married man and father of a family, and only went on Saturdays. That was his regular evening, and now he would be deprived of this dissipation for the whole week.

The three men went as far as the quay together, and on the way they met young Monsieur Philippe, the banker's son, who frequented the place regularly, and Monsieur Pinipesse, the collector. They all returned to the Rue aux Juifs together, to make a last attempt. But the exasperated sailors were besieging the house, throwing stones at the shutters and shouting, so the five first-floor customers went away as quickly as possible, and walked aimlessly about the streets.

Presently they met Monsieur Dupuis, the insurance agent, and then Monsieur Vasse, the Judge of the Tribunal of Commerce, and they took a long walk, going to the pier first of all. Here they sat down in a row on the granite parapet and watched the rising tide, and when they had remained there for some time, Monsieur Tournevau said: 'This is not very amusing!'

'Decidedly not,' Monsieur Pinipesse replied, and they started off to walk again.

After going through the street alongside the hill, they returned over the wooden bridge which crosses the Retenue, passed close to the railway, and came out again on the marketplace, when, suddenly, a quarrel arose between Monsieur Pinipesse, the collector, and Monsieur Tournevau about an edible mushroom which one of them declared he had found in the neighbourhood.

As they were out of temper already from having nothing to do, they would very probably have come to blows if the others had not interfered. Monsieur Pinipesse went off furious, and soon another altercation arose between the ex-mayor, Monsieur Poulin, and Monsieur Dupuis, the insurance agent, on the subject of the tax collector's salary and the profits which he might make. Insulting remarks were freely passing between them, when a torrent of formidable cries was heard, and the body of sailors, who were tired of waiting so long outside a closed house, came into the square. They were walking arm in arm, two and two, forming a long procession, and were shouting furiously. The townsmen hid themselves in a doorway, and the yelling crew disappeared in the direction of the abbey. For a long time they still heard the noise, which diminished like a storm in the distance, and then silence was restored. Monsieur Poulin and Monsieur Dupuis, who were angry with each other, went in different directions without wishing each other goodbye.

The other four set off again, and instinctively went in the direction of Madame Tellier's establishment, which was still closed, silent, impenetrable. A quiet but obstinate drunken man was knocking at the door of the lower room, and then stopped and called Frédéric in a low voice, but finding that he got no answer, he sat down on the doorstep, and waited the course of events.

The others were just going to retire, when the noisy band of sailors reappeared at the end of the street. The French sailors were shouting 'The Marseillaise' and the Englishmen 'Rule Britannia'. There was a general lurching against the wall, and then the drunken fellows went on their way towards the quay, where a fight broke out between the two nations, in the course of which an Englishman had his arm broken and a Frenchman his nose split.

The drunken man who had waited outside the door was crying by that time, as drunken men and children cry when they are vexed, and the others went away. By degrees calm was restored in the noisy town; here and there, at moments, the far-off sound of voices could be heard, and then died away in the distance.

One man only was still wandering about, Monsieur Tournevau, the fish-curer, who was annoyed at having to wait until the following

Saturday. He hoped something would turn up, he did not know what; but he was exasperated at the police for thus allowing an establishment of such public utility, which they had under their control, to be closed.

He went back to it and examined the walls, trying to find some explanation, and on the shutter he saw a notice stuck up. He struck a wax match and read the following, written in a large, uneven hand: 'Closed for First Communion.'

Then he went away, as he saw it was useless to remain, and left the drunken man lying on the pavement fast asleep, outside that inhospitable door.

The next day, all the regular customers, one after the other, found some reason for going through the street, with bundles of papers under their arms to keep them in countenance, and with a furtive glance they all read that mysterious notice: 'Closed for First Communion.'

II

Madame Tellier had a brother, who was a carpenter in their native place, Virville, in the Department of Eure. When she still kept the inn at Yvetot, she had stood godmother to that brother's daughter, who had received the name of Constance – Constance Rivet; Madame herself being a Rivet on her father's side. The carpenter, who knew that his sister was in a good position, did not lose sight of her although they did not meet often, for they were both kept at home by their occupations and lived a long way from each other. But as the girl was twelve years old, and going to be making her First Communion, he seized that opportunity to write to his sister, asking her to come and be present at the ceremony. Their old parents were dead, and as she could not well refuse, she accepted the invitation. Her brother, whose name was Joseph, hoped that by dint of showing his sister attention, she might be induced to make her will in the girl's favour, as she had no children of her own.

His sister's occupation did not trouble his scruples in the least, and, besides, nobody knew anything about it at Virville. When they spoke of her, they only said: 'Madame Tellier is living at Fécamp,' which might mean that she was living on her own private income. It was quite twenty leagues from Fécamp to Virville, and for a peasant, twenty leagues on land is as long a journey as crossing the ocean would be to city people. The inhabitants of Virville had never been farther than Rouen, and nothing attracted the people from Fécamp to a village of five hundred houses in the middle of a plain, and situated in another department; at any rate, nothing was known about her business.

But the Communion was coming on, and Madame Tellier was in great embarrassment. She had no substitute, and did not at all care to leave her house, even for a day; for all the rivalries between the girls upstairs and those downstairs would infallibly break out. No doubt Frédéric would get drunk, and when he was in that state, he would knock anybody down for a mere word. At last, however, she made up her mind to take them all with her, with the exception of the man, to whom she gave a holiday until the next day but one.

When she asked her brother, he made no objection, and undertook to put them all up for a night, and so on Saturday morning the eight o'clock express carried off Madame Tellier and her companions in a second-class carriage. As far as Beuzeville they were alone, and chattered like magpies, but at that station a couple got in. The man, an old peasant, dressed in a blue blouse with a turned-down collar, wide sleeves tight at the wrist, ornamented with white embroidery, wearing an old high hat with long nap, held an enormous green umbrella in one hand and a large basket in the other, from which the heads of three frightened ducks protruded. The woman, who sat up stiffly in her rustic finery, had a face like a fowl, with a nose that was as pointed as a bill. She sat down opposite her husband and did not stir, as she was startled at finding herself in such smart company.

There was certainly an array of striking colours in the carriage. Madame Tellier was dressed in blue silk from head to foot, and had on a dazzling red imitation French cashmere shawl. Fernande was puffing in a Scotch plaid dress, of which her companions had laced the bodice as tight as they could, forcing up her full bust. Raphaële, with a bonnet covered with feathers, so that it looked like a bird's nest, had on a lilac dress with gold sequins on it, and there was something Oriental about it that suited her Jewish face. Rosa wore a pink skirt with large flounces, and looked like a very fat child, an obese dwarf; while the Beer Pumps looked as if they had cut their dresses out of old flowered curtains dating from the Restoration.

As soon as they were no longer alone in the compartment, the ladies put on staid looks, and began to talk of subjects which might give others a high opinion of them. But at Bolbec a gentleman with light whiskers, a gold chain, and wearing two or three rings, got in, and put several parcels wrapped in oilcloth on the rack over his head. He looked inclined for a joke, and seemed a good-hearted fellow.

'Are you ladies changing your quarters?' he asked, and that question embarrassed them all considerably. Madame Tellier, however, quickly regained her composure, and said sharply, to avenge the honour of her corps: 'I think you might try to be polite!'

He excused himself, and said: 'I beg your pardon, I ought to have said your nunnery.'

She could not think of a retort, so, perhaps thinking she had said enough, Madame gave him a dignified bow and compressed her lips.

Then the gentleman, who was sitting between Rosa and the old peasant, began to wink knowingly at the ducks whose heads were sticking out of the basket, and when he felt that he had fixed the attention of his public, he began to tickle them under the bills and spoke funnily to them to make the company smile.

'We have left our little pond, quack! quack! to make the acquaintance of the little spit, qu–ack! qu–ack!'

The unfortunate creatures turned their necks away, to avoid his caresses, and made desperate efforts to get out of their wicker prison, and then, suddenly, all at once, uttered the most lamentable quacks of distress. The women exploded with laughter. They leaned forward and pushed each other, so as to see better; they were very much interested in the ducks, and the gentleman redoubled his airs, his wit and his teasing.

Rosa joined in, and leaning over her neighbour's legs, she kissed the three animals on the head, and immediately all the girls wanted to kiss them, in turn, and as they did so the gentleman took them on his knee, jumped them up and down and pinched their arms. The two peasants, who were even in greater consternation than their poultry, rolled their eyes as if they were possessed, without venturing to move, and their old wrinkled faces had not a smile, not a twitch.

Then the gentleman, who was a commercial traveller, offered the ladies suspenders by way of a joke, and taking up one of his packages, he opened it. It was a joke, for the parcel contained garters. There were blue silk, pink silk, red silk, violet silk, mauve silk garters, and the buckles were made of two gilt metal cupids embracing each other. The girls uttered exclamations of delight and looked at them with that gravity natural to all women when they are considering an article of dress. They consulted one another by their looks or in a whisper, and replied in the same manner, and Madame Tellier was longingly handling a pair of orange garters that were broader and more imposing-looking than the rest; really fit for the mistress of such an establishment.

The gentleman waited, for he had an idea.

'Come, my dears,' he said, 'you must try them on.'

There was a torrent of exclamations, and they squeezed their petticoats between their legs, but he quietly bided his time and said: 'Well, if you will not try them on I shall pack them up again.'

And he added cunningly: 'I offer any pair they like to those who will try them on.'

But they would not, and sat up very straight and looked dignified.

But the Beer Pumps looked so distressed that he renewed his offer to them; Flora, especially, visibly hesitated, and he insisted: 'Come, my dear, a little courage! Just look at that lilac pair; it will suit your dress admirably.'

That decided her, and pulling up her dress she showed a thick leg fit for a milkmaid, in a badly fitting, coarse stocking. The commercial traveller stooped down and fastened the garter. When he had done this, he gave her the lilac pair and asked: 'Who next?'

'I! I!' they all shouted at once, and he began on Rosa, who uncovered a shapeless, round thing without any ankle, a regular 'sausage of a leg', as Raphaële used to say.

Lastly, Madame Tellier herself put out her leg, a handsome, muscular Norman leg, and in his surprise and pleasure, the commercial traveller gallantly took off his hat to salute that master calf, like a true French cavalier.

The two peasants, who were speechless from surprise, glanced sideways out of the corners of their eyes, and they looked so exactly like fowls that the man with the light whiskers, when he sat up, said: 'Co–co–ri–co,' under their very noses, and that gave rise to another storm of amusement.

The old people got out at Motteville with their basket, their ducks and their umbrella, and they heard the woman say to her husband as they went away: 'They are no good and are off to that cursed place, Paris.'

The funny commercial traveller himself got out at Rouen, after behaving so coarsely that Madame Tellier was obliged sharply to put him in his place, and she added, as a moral: 'This will teach us not to talk to the first comer.'

At Oissel they changed trains, and at a little station farther on Monsieur Joseph Rivet was waiting for them with a large cart with a number of chairs in it, drawn by a white horse.

The carpenter politely kissed all the ladies and then helped them into his conveyance.

Three of them sat on three chairs at the back, Raphaële, Madame Tellier and her brother on the three chairs in front, while Rosa, who had no seat, settled herself as comfortably as she could on tall Fernande's knees, and then they set off.

But the horse's jerky trot shook the cart so terribly that the chairs began to dance and threw the travellers about, to the right and to the left, as if they were helpless puppets, which made them scream and pull horrible grimaces. They clung on to the sides of the vehicle, their bonnets fell on their backs, over their faces and on their shoulders, and the white horse went on stretching out his head and holding out his little tail, which was hairless like a rat's, and with which he whisked his buttocks from time to time.

Joseph Rivet, with one leg on the shafts and the other doubled under him, held the reins with his elbows very high, and kept uttering a kind of clucking sound, which made the horse prick up its ears and go faster.

The green country extended on either side of the road, and here and there the rape in flower presented a waving expanse of yellow. The wind carried its strong, wholesome, sweet and penetrating odour to some distance. The cornflowers showed their little blue heads amid the rye, and the women wanted to pick them, but Monsieur Rivet refused to stop. Then, sometimes, a whole field appeared to be covered with blood, so thick were the poppies; and the cart, which looked as if it were filled with flowers of more brilliant hue, jogged on through fields bright with wild flowers; often it disappeared behind the trees of a farm, only to reappear and to go on again through the yellow or green standing crops studded with red and blue.

One o'clock struck as they drove up to the carpenter's door. They were tired out and pale with hunger, as they had eaten nothing since they left home. Madame Rivet ran out and made them alight, one after another, and kissed them as soon as they were on the ground, and she seemed as if she would never tire of kissing her sister-in-law, whom she apparently wanted to monopolise. They had lunch in the workshop, which had been cleared out for the next day's dinner.

The capital omelette, followed by boiled chitterlings and washed down with good hard cider, made them all feel comfortable.

Rivet had taken a glass so that he might drink with them, and his wife cooked, waited on them, brought in the dishes, took them out and asked each of them in a whisper whether they had everything they wanted. A number of boards standing against the walls and heaps of shavings that had been swept into the corners gave out a smell of planed wood – the scent of a carpenter's shop, that resinous odour which penetrates to the lungs.

They wanted to see the little girl, but she had gone to church and would not be back again until evening, so they all went out for a stroll in the country.

It was a small village, through which the high road passed. Ten or a dozen houses on either side of the single street were inhabited by the butcher, the grocer, the carpenter, the innkeeper, the shoemaker, the baker and other tradesmen. The church was at the end of the street and was surrounded by a small graveyard; four immense lime-trees, which stood just outside the porch, shaded it completely. It was built of flint, in no particular style, and had a slate-clad steeple. When you got past it, you were again in the open country, which was studded here and there by clumps of trees which hid the homesteads.

Rivet had given his arm to his sister, out of politeness, although he was in his working clothes, and was walking with her in a dignified manner. His wife, who was overwhelmed by Raphaële's gold-sequinned dress, walked between her and Fernande, and Rosa was trotting behind with Louise and Flora, the Seesaw, who was limping along, quite tired out.

The inhabitants came to their doors, the children left off playing, many a window curtain was raised, to reveal a muslin cap, while an old woman with a crutch, who was almost blind, crossed herself as if it were a religious procession, and they all gazed for a long time at those handsome ladies from town, who had come so far to be present at the First Communion of Joseph Rivet's little girl, and the carpenter rose very much in the public estimation.

As they passed the church they heard some children singing. Little shrill voices were singing a hymn, but Madame Tellier would not let them go in, for fear of disturbing the little cherubs.

After the walk, during which Joseph Rivet enumerated the principal landed proprietors and spoke about the yield of the land and the productiveness of the cows and sheep, he took his tribe of women home and installed them in his house, but as it was very small he had to put them into the rooms two and two.

Just for once Rivet would sleep in the workshop on the shavings; his wife was to share her bed with her sister-in-law, and Fernande and Raphaële were to sleep together in the next room. Louise and Flora were put into the kitchen, where they had a mattress on the floor, and Rosa had a little dark cupboard to herself at the top of the stairs, close to the loft, where the candidate for First Communion was to sleep.

When the little girl came in she was overwhelmed with kisses; all the women wished to caress her with that need for tender expansion, that habit of professional affection which had made them kiss the ducks in the railway carriage.

They each of them took her on their knees, stroked her soft, light hair and pressed her in their arms with vehement and spontaneous outbursts of affection, and the child, who was very good and religious, bore it all patiently.

As the day had been a fatiguing one for everybody, they all went to bed soon after dinner. The whole village was wrapped in that perfect stillness of the country, which is almost like a religious silence, and the girls, who were accustomed to the noisy evenings of their establishment, felt rather impressed by the perfect repose of the sleeping village, and they shivered, not with cold, but with those little shivers of loneliness which come over uneasy and troubled hearts.

As soon as they were in bed, two and two together, they clasped each other in their arms, as if to protect themselves against this feeling of the calm and profound slumber of the earth. But Rosa, who was alone in her little dark cupboard, felt a vague and painful emotion come over her.

She was tossing about in bed, unable to get to sleep, when she heard the faint sobs of a crying child close to her head, through the partition. She was frightened, and called out, and was answered by a weak voice, broken by sobs. It was the little girl, who was used always to sleeping in her mother's room, and who was afraid in her small attic.

Rosa was delighted, got up softly so as not to awaken anyone, and went and fetched the child. She took her into her warm bed, kissed her and pressed her to her bosom, lavished exaggerated manifestations of tenderness on her, and at last grew calmer herself and went to sleep. And till morning the candidate for First Communion slept with her head on Rosa's bosom.

At five o'clock the little church bell, ringing the Angelus, woke the women, who usually slept the whole morning long.

The villagers were up already, and women went busily from house to house, carefully carrying short, starched muslin dresses or very long wax tapers tied in the middle with a bow of silk fringed with gold, and with dents in the wax for the fingers.

The sun was already high in the blue sky, which still had a rosy tint towards the horizon, like a faint remaining trace of dawn. Families of fowls were walking about outside the houses, and here and there a black cock, with a glistening breast, raised his red comb, flapped his wings and uttered his shrill crow, which the other cocks repeated.

Vehicles of all sorts came from neighbouring parishes, stopping at the different houses, and tall Norman women dismounted, wearing dark dresses, with kerchiefs crossed over at the bosom and fastened with silver brooches a hundred years old. The men had put on their blue smocks over their new frock-coats or over their old dress-coats of green cloth, the two tails of which hung down below their blouses. When the horses were in the stables there was a double line of rustic conveyances along the road: carts, cabriolets, tilburies, wagonettes, traps of every shape and age, tipping forward on their shafts or else tipping backwards with the shafts up in the air.

The carpenter's house was as busy as a beehive. The women, in dressing-jackets and petticoats, with their thin, loose hair, which looked faded and worn, hanging down their backs, were busy dressing the child, who was standing quietly on a table, while Madame Tellier was directing the movements of her battalion. They washed her, did her hair, dressed her, and with the help of a number of pins, they arranged the folds of her dress and took in the waist, which was too large.

Then, when she was ready, she was told to sit down and not to move, and the women hurried off to get ready themselves.

The church bell began to ring again, and its tinkle was lost in the air, like a feeble voice which is soon drowned in space. The candidates came out of the houses and went towards the parochial building, which contained the two schools and the mansion house, and which stood quite at one end of the village, while the church was situated at the other.

The parents, in their very best clothes, followed their children, with embarrassed looks, and those clumsy movements of a body bent by toil.

The little girls disappeared in a cloud of muslin, as if enveloped in whipped cream, while the lads, who looked like embryo waiters in a café and whose heads shone with pomatum, walked with their legs apart, so as not to get any dust or dirt on their black trousers.

It was something for a family to be proud of when a large number of relatives, who had come from a distance, surrounded a child, so the carpenter's triumph was complete.

Madame Tellier's regiment with its leader at its head followed Constance; her father gave his arm to his sister, her mother walked by the side of Raphaële, Fernande with Rose, and Louise and Flora brought up the rear, and thus they proceeded majestically through the village, like a general's staff in full uniform, while the effect on the village was startling.

At the school the girls ranged themselves under the Sister of Mercy and the boys under the schoolmaster, and they started off, singing a hymn as they went. The boys led the way, in two files, between the two rows of vehicles, from which the horses had been taken out, and the girls followed in the same order; and as all the people in the village had given the town ladies precedence out of politeness, they came immediately behind the girls, and lengthened the double line of the procession still more, three on the right and three on the left, while their dresses were as striking as a display of fireworks.

When they went into the church the congregation grew quite excited. They pressed against each other, turned round and jostled one another in order to see, and some of the devout ones exclaimed out loud, for they were so astonished at the sight of those ladies whose dresses were more elaborate than the priest's vestments.

The mayor offered them his pew, the first one on the right, close to the choir, and Madame Tellier sat there with her sister-in-law. Fernande and Raphaële, Rosa, Louise and Flora occupied the second seat, in company with the carpenter.

The choir was full of kneeling children, the girls on one side and the boys on the other, and the long wax tapers which they held looked like lances pointing in all directions. Three men were standing in front of the lectern, singing as loud as they could. They prolonged the syllables of the sonorous Latin indefinitely, holding on to 'Amens' with interminable 'A–a's', which the reed stop of the organ sustained in a monotonous, long-drawn-out tone. A child's shrill voice took up the reply, and from time to time a priest sitting in a stall and wearing a biretta got up, muttered something and sat down again, while the three singers continued, their eyes fixed on the big book of plainchant lying open before them on the outstretched wings of a wooden eagle.

Then silence ensued until a bell tinkled and the holy office began. Towards the close Rosa, with her head in both hands, suddenly thought of her mother, her village church and her First Communion. She almost fancied that that day had returned, when she was so small and was almost hidden in her white dress, and she began to cry.

First of all she wept silently, and the tears dropped slowly from her eyes, but her emotion increased with her recollections, and she began to sob. She took out her pocket handkerchief, wiped her eyes and held it to her mouth, so as not to scream, but it was in vain. A sort of rattle escaped her throat, and she was answered by two other profound, heartbreaking sobs, for her two neighbours, Louise and Flora, who were kneeling near her, overcome by similar recollections, were sobbing by her side, amid a flood of tears; and as tears are contagious, Madame Tellier soon in turn found that her eyes were wet, and on turning to her sister-in-law, she saw that all the occupants of her pew were also crying.

Soon, throughout the church, here and there, a wife, a mother, a sister, seized by the strange sympathy of poignant emotion, and affected at the sight of those handsome ladies on their knees, shaken with sobs, was moistening her cambric pocket handkerchief and pressing her beating heart with her left hand.

Just as the sparks from an engine will set fire to dry grass, so the tears of Rosa and of her companions infected the whole congregation in a moment. Men, women, old men and lads in new smocks were soon all sobbing, a supernatural presence seemed to be hovering over their heads – a spirit, the powerful breath of an invisible and all-powerful Being. The children drew near the holy table and the old priest administered the sacrament

Suddenly a species of madness seemed to pervade the church, the noise of a crowd in a state of frenzy, a tempest of sobs and stifled cries. It came like gusts of wind which blow the trees in a forest, and the priest, paralysed by emotion, stammered out incoherent prayers, a jumble of words, the ardent prayers of a soul straining towards heaven.

The people behind him gradually grew calmer. The cantors, in all the dignity of their white surplices, went on in somewhat uncertain voices, and the reed stop itself seemed hoarse, as if the instrument had been weeping; the priest, however, raised his hand to command silence and went and stood on the chancel steps, when everybody was silent at once.

After a few remarks on what had just taken place, which he attributed to a miracle, he continued, turning to the seats where the carpenter's guests were sitting: 'I especially thank you, my dear sisters, who have come from such a distance, and whose presence among us, whose evident faith and ardent piety have set such a salutary example to all. You have edified my parish; your emotion has warmed all hearts; without you, this great day would not, perhaps, have had this really divine character. It is sufficient, at times, that there should be one chosen lamb, for the Lord to descend on His flock.'

His voice failed him again, from emotion, and he said no more, but concluded the service.

They now left the church as quickly as possible; the children themselves were restless and tired with such prolonged tension of the mind. The parents were anxious to see about dinner.

There was a crowd outside, a noisy crowd, a babel of loud voices, where the shrill Norman accent was discernible. The villagers formed two ranks, and when the children appeared, each family took possession of its own.

The whole houseful of women caught hold of Constance, surrounded her and kissed her, and Rosa was especially demonstrative. At last she took hold of one hand, while Madame Tellier took the other, and Raphaële and Fernande held up her long muslin skirt, so that it might not drag in the dust; Louise and Flora brought up the rear with Madame

Rivet; and the child, who was very silent and thoughtful, set off for home in the midst of this guard of honour.

Dinner was served in the workshop on long boards supported by trestles, and through the open door they could see all the enjoyment that was going on in the village. Everywhere they were feasting. Through every window were to be seen tables surrounded by people in their Sunday best, and a cheerful noise was heard in every house, while the men sat in their shirt-sleeves, drinking glass after glass of cider.

In the carpenter's house the gaiety maintained more or less an air of reserve, the consequence of the emotion of the girls in the morning; Rivet was the only one who was in a jolly mood, and he was drinking to excess. Madame Tellier looked at the clock every moment, for, in order not to lose two days running, they must take the 3.55 train, which would bring them to Fécamp by dark.

The carpenter tried very hard to distract her attention, so as to keep his guests until the next day, but he did not succeed, for she never joked when there was business on hand, and as soon as they had had their coffee she ordered her girls to make haste and get ready; then, turning to her brother, she said: 'You must put in the horse immediately,' and she herself went to finish her last preparations.

When she came down again, her sister-in-law was waiting to speak to her about the child, and a long conversation took place, in which, however, nothing was settled. The carpenter's wife was artful and pretended to be very much affected, and Madame Tellier, who was holding the girl on her knee, would not pledge herself to anything definite, but merely gave vague promises – she would not forget her, there was plenty of time, and besides, they would meet again.

But the conveyance did not come to the door and the women did not come downstairs. Upstairs they even heard loud laughter, romping, little screams and much clapping of hands, and so, while the carpenter's wife went to the stable to see whether the cart was ready, Madame went upstairs.

Rivet, who was very drunk, was plaguing Rosa, who was half choking with laughter. Louise and Flora were holding him by the arms and trying to calm him, as they were shocked at his levity after that morning's ceremony; but Raphaële and Fernande were urging him on, convulsed and holding their sides with laughter, and they uttered shrill cries at every rebuff the drunken fellow received.

Rivet was furious, his face was red, and he was trying to shake off the two women who were clinging to him, while he was pulling Rosa's skirt with all his might and stammering incoherently.

But Madame Tellier, who was very indignant, went up to her brother, seized him by the shoulders, and threw him out of the room with such violence that he fell against the wall in the passage, and a minute afterwards they heard him pumping water on his head in the yard, and when he reappeared with the cart he was quite calm.

They went back the same way that they had come the day before, and the little white horse started off with his quick, dancing trot. Under the hot sun, their fun, which had been checked during dinner, broke out again. The girls now were amused at the jolting of the cart; they pushed their neighbours' chairs and burst out laughing every moment.

There was a glare of light over the country which dazzled their eyes, and the wheels raised two trails of dust along the high road. Presently, Fernande, who was fond of music, asked Rosa to sing something, and she boldly struck up the 'Gros Curé de Meudon', but Madame Tellier made her stop immediately, as she thought it a very unsuitable song for such a day, and she added: 'Sing us something of Béranger's.' And so, after a moment's hesitation, Rosa began Beranger's song 'The Grand-mother' in her worn-out voice, and all the girls, and even Madame Tellier herself, joined in the chorus:

> 'My leg was trim to see,
> So soft and plump my arm;
> I wasted youth, ah me!
> What use was all my charm?'

'That is first-rate,' Rivet declared, carried away by the rhythm, and they shouted the refrain to every verse, while Rivet beat time on the shaft with his foot and with the reins on the back of the horse, who, as if he himself were carried away by the rhythm, broke into a wild gallop, and threw all the women in a heap, one on top of the other, on the bottom of the conveyance.

They got up, laughing as if they were mad, and the song went on, shouted at the top of their voices, beneath the burning sky, among the ripening corn, to the rapid gallop of the little horse, who set off every time the refrain was sung, and galloped a hundred yards, to their great delight, while occasionally a stone-breaker by the roadside sat up and looked at the load of shouting females through his wire spectacles.

When they got out at the station, the carpenter said: 'I am sorry you are going; we might have had some good times together.'

But Madame Tellier replied very sensibly: 'Everything has its right time, and we cannot always be enjoying ourselves.'

And then he had a sudden inspiration: 'Look here, I will come and see you at Fécamp next month.' And he gave Rosa a roguish and knowing look.

'You may come if you like', his sister replied, 'but you are not to be up to any of your tricks.'

He did not reply, and as they heard the whistle of the train, he immediately began to kiss them all. When it came to Rosa's turn, he tried to get to her mouth, which she, however, smiling with her lips closed, turned away from him each time by a rapid movement of her head to one side. He held her in his arms, but he could not attain his object, as his large whip, which he was holding in his hand and waving behind the girl's back in desperation, interfered with his movements.

'Passengers for Rouen, take your seats!' a guard cried, and they got in. There was a slight whistle, followed by a loud whistle from the engine, which noisily puffed out its first jet of steam, while the wheels began to turn a little with visible effort, and Rivet left the station and ran along by the track to get another look at Rosa; and as the carriage passed him, he began to crack his whip and to jump, while he sang at the top of his voice:

> 'My leg was trim to see,
> So soft and plump my arm;
> I wasted youth, ah me!
> What use was all my charm?'

And then he watched a white pocket-handkerchief, which somebody was waving, as it disappeared in the distance.

III

They slept the peaceful sleep of a quiet conscience until they got to Rouen, and when they returned to the house, refreshed and rested, Madame Tellier could not help saying: 'It was all very well, but I was longing to get home.'

They hurried over their supper, and then, when they had put on their usual evening costume, waited for their regular customers. The little coloured lamp outside the door told the passers-by that Madame Tellier had returned, and in a moment the news spread, nobody knew how or through whom.

Monsieur Philippe, the banker's son, even carried his friendliness so far as to send a special messenger to Monsieur Tournevau, who was in the bosom of his family.

The fish-curer had several cousins to dinner every Sunday, and they were having coffee, when a man came in with a letter in his hand. Monsieur Tournevau was much excited; he opened the envelope and grew pale; it contained only these words in pencil:

The cargo of cod has been found; the ship has come into port; good business for you. Come immediately.

He felt in his pockets, gave the messenger two sous, and suddenly blushing to his ears, he said: 'I must go out.' He handed his wife the laconic and mysterious note, rang the bell, and when the servant came in, he asked her to bring him his hat and overcoat immediately. As soon as he was in the street, he began to hurry, and the way seemed to him to be twice as long as usual, in consequence of his impatience.

Madame Tellier's establishment had put on quite a holiday look. On the ground floor, a number of sailors were making a deafening noise, and Louise and Flora were being called for in every direction at once. The upstairs room was full by nine o'clock. Monsieur Vasse, the Judge of the Tribunal of Commerce, Madame Tellier's regular but Platonic wooer, was talking to her in a corner in a low voice, and they were both smiling, as if they were about to come to an understanding. Monsieur Poulin, the ex-mayor, was talking to Rosa, and she was running her hands through the old gentleman's white whiskers. Tall Fernande was on the sofa, her feet on the coat of Monsieur Pinipesse, the tax collector, and leaning back against young Monsieur Philippe, her right arm around his neck, while she held a cigarette in her left hand. Raphaële appeared to be talking seriously with Monsieur Dupuis, the insurance agent, and she finished by saying: 'Yes, I will, this evening.'

Just then the door opened suddenly and Monsieur Tournevau came in and was greeted with enthusiastic cries of 'Long live Tournevau!' And Raphaële, who was dancing alone up and down the room, went and threw herself into his arms. He seized her in a vigorous embrace and, without saying a word, lifted her up as if she had been a feather, crossed the drawing-room with her and disappeared through the door opening on to the staircase which led to the bedrooms.

Rosa was chatting to the ex-mayor, kissing him and pulling both his whiskers at the same time, in order to keep his head straight.

'Come along,' she said to him. 'Monsieur Tournevau has set us an example;' and the good-natured man followed Rosa from the room.

Fernande and Madame Tellier remained with the four men, and Monsieur Philippe exclaimed: 'I will pay for some champagne; get three bottles, Madame Tellier.' And Fernande gave him a hug, and whispered to him: 'Play us a waltz, will you?' So he rose and sat down at the old piano in the corner, and managed to get a hoarse waltz out of the depths of the instrument.

The tall girl put her arms round the tax collector, Madame Tellier let Monsieur Vasse take her round the waist, and the two couples turned round, kissing as they danced. Monsieur Vasse, who had formerly danced in good society, waltzed with such elegance that Madame Tellier was quite captivated, and regarded him with eyes that answered 'Yes' more eloquently than any spoken word.

Frédéric brought the champagne; the first cork popped, and Monsieur Philippe played the introduction to a quadrille, through which the four dancers walked in society fashion, decorously, with propriety, deportment, bows and curtsies, and then they began to drink.

Monsieur Philippe next struck up a lively polka, and Monsieur Tournevau, who had returned, started off with the handsome Jewess, whom he held without letting her feet touch the ground. Monsieur Pinipesse and Monsieur Vasse resumed with renewed vigour, and from time to time one or other couple would stop to toss off a long draught of sparkling wine. The dance was threatening to become never-ending, when Rosa reappeared, having left Monsieur Poulin sleeping. 'I want to dance,' she exclaimed. She caught hold of Monsieur Dupuis, who was sitting idly on the couch, and the dance began again.

But the bottles were empty. 'I will pay for one,' Monsieur Tournevau said. 'So will I,' Monsieur Vasse declared. 'And I will do the same,' Monsieur Dupuis chimed in.

They all began to clap their hands, and it soon became a regular ball; from time to time Louise and Flora ran upstairs quickly and had a few turns, until their customers downstairs grew impatient, and then they returned regretfully to the tap-room. At midnight they were still dancing.

Madame Tellier let them amuse themselves while she had long private talks in corners with Monsieur Vasse, as if to settle the final details of something that had already been arranged.

At last, at one o'clock, the two married men, Monsieur Tournevau and Monsieur Pinipesse, declared that they were going home, and wanted to pay. Nothing was charged for except the champagne, and that cost only six francs a bottle, instead of ten, which was the usual price, and when they expressed their surprise at such generosity, Madame Tellier, who was beaming, said to them: 'We don't have a holiday every day.'

Mademoiselle Fifi

Major Count von Farlsberg, the Prussian commandant, was reading his newspaper as he lay back in a great easy-chair, with his booted feet on the beautiful marble mantelpiece where his spurs had made two holes, which had grown deeper every day during the three months that he had been in the château of Uville.

A cup of coffee was steaming on a small inlaid table, which was stained with liquids, charred by cigar ends, and notched by the penknife of the victorious officer, who occasionally would stop while sharpening a pencil to jot down figures or to make a drawing on it, just as it took his fancy.

When he had read his letters and the German newspapers, which his orderly had brought him, he got up, and after throwing three or four enormous pieces of green wood on the fire, for these gentlemen were gradually cutting down all the trees in the park in order to keep themselves warm, he went to the window. The rain was descending in torrents, a regular Normandy rain, which looked as if it were being poured out by some furious person, a slanting rain, opaque as a curtain, which formed a kind of wall with diagonal stripes, and deluged everything, a rain such as one frequently experiences in the neighbourhood of Rouen, which is the watering-pot of France.

For a long time the officer looked at the sodden turf and at the swollen Andelle beyond it, which was overflowing its banks; he was drumming a waltz with his fingers on the window-panes, when a noise made him turn round. It was his second in command, Captain Baron von Kelweinstein.

The major was a giant, with broad shoulders and a long, fan-like beard which covered his chest. His whole solemn person suggested the idea of a military peacock, a peacock who was carrying his tail spread out on his breast. He had cold but gentle blue eyes, and a scar from a sword-cut, which he had received in the war with Austria; he was said to be an honourable man, as well as a brave officer.

The captain, a short, red-faced man, was tightly belted in at the waist; his red hair was cropped quite close to his head, and in certain lights he almost looked as if he had been rubbed over with phosphorus. He had broken two front teeth one night – he could not quite remember how –

and this sometimes made him speak unintelligibly, and he had a bald patch on the top of his head surrounded by a fringe of bright ginger hair, which made him look like a monk.

The commandant shook hands with him and drank his cup of coffee (the sixth that morning) while he listened to his subordinate's report of what had occurred; and then they both went to the window and declared that it was a very unpleasant outlook. The major, who was a quiet man, with a wife at home, could accommodate himself to everything; but the captain, who was in the habit of frequenting low resorts, and enjoyed women's society, was angry at having to be shut up for three months in that wretched hole.

There was a knock at the door, and when the commandant said, 'Come in,' one of the orderlies appeared, and by his mere presence announced that luncheon was ready. In the dining-room they met three other officers of lower rank – a lieutenant, Otto von Grossling, and two sub-lieutenants, Fritz Scheuneberg and the Marquis von Eyrick, a very short, fair-haired man, who was proud and brutal towards men, harsh towards prisoners, and as explosive as gunpowder. Since he had been in France his comrades had called him nothing but Mademoiselle Fifi. They had given him that nickname on account of his dandified style and small waist, which looked as if he wore corsets, of his pale face, on which his budding moustache scarcely showed, and on account of the habit he had acquired of employing the French expression *Fi, fi donc*, which he pronounced with a slight whistle when he wished to express his supreme contempt for persons or things.

The dining-room of the château was a long and magnificent room, whose fine old mirrors, that were cracked by pistol bullets, and whose Flemish tapestry, which was cut to ribbons and hanging in rags in places from sword-cuts, told too well what Mademoiselle Fifi's occupation was during his spare time.

There were three family portraits on the walls: a steel-clad knight, a cardinal and a judge, who were all smoking long porcelain pipes, which had been inserted into holes in the canvas, while a lady with a tight-laced bodice proudly exhibited a pair of enormous moustaches, drawn with charcoal. The officers ate their luncheon almost in silence in that mutilated room, which looked dull in the rain and melancholy in its dilapidated condition, although its old oak floor had become as solid as the stone floor of an inn.

When they had finished eating and were smoking and drinking, they began, as usual, to grumble at the dull life they were leading. The bottles of brandy and of liqueur passed from hand to hand, and all sat back in their chairs and took repeated sips from their glasses, scarcely removing from their mouths the long, curved stems, which terminated in china bowls, painted in a manner that might have pleased a Hottentot.

As soon as their glasses were empty they filled them again, with a gesture of resigned weariness, but Mademoiselle Fifi emptied his every minute, and a soldier immediately gave him another. They were enveloped in a cloud of strong tobacco smoke, and seemed to be sunk in a state of drowsy, stupid intoxication, that condition of stupid intoxication of men who have nothing to do, when suddenly the baron sat up and said: 'Heavens! This cannot go on; we must think of something to do.' And on hearing this, Lieutenant Otto and Sub-Lieutenant Fritz, who pre-eminently possessed the serious, heavy German countenance, said: 'What, captain?'

He thought for a few moments and then replied: 'What? Why, we must get up some entertainment if the commandant will allow us.'

'What sort of an entertainment, captain?' the major asked, taking his pipe out of his mouth.

'I will arrange all that, commandant,' the baron replied. 'I will send Le Devoir to Rouen, and he will bring back some ladies. I know where they can be found. We will have supper here, as all the materials are at hand, and, at least, we shall have a jolly evening.'

Count von Farlsberg shrugged his shoulders and said with a smile: 'You must be mad, my friend.'

But all the other officers had risen and surrounded their chief, saying: 'Let the captain have his way, commandant; it is terribly dull here.' And the major ended by yielding. 'Very well,' he replied, and the baron immediately sent for Le Devoir. He was an old non-commissioned officer, who had never been seen to smile, but who carried out all the orders of his superiors to the letter, no matter what they might be. He stood there, with an impassive face, while he received the baron's instructions, and then went out, and five minutes later a large military wagon, covered with tarpaulin, galloped off as fast as four horses could draw it in the pouring rain. The officers all seemed to awaken from their lethargy, their looks brightened and they began to talk.

Although it was raining as hard as ever, the major declared that it was not so dark, and Lieutenant von Grossling said with conviction that the sky was clearing up, while Mademoiselle Fifi did not seem to be able to keep still. He got up and sat down again, and his bright eyes seemed to be looking for something to destroy. Suddenly, looking at the lady with the moustaches, the young fellow pulled out his revolver and said: 'You shall not see it.' And without leaving his seat he aimed, and with two successive bullets cut out both the eyes of the portrait.

'Let us make a mine!' he then exclaimed, and the conversation was suddenly interrupted, as if they had found some fresh and powerful subject of interest. The mine was his invention, his method of destruction, and his favourite amusement.

When he left the château, the lawful owner, Comte Fernand d'Amoys d'Uville, had not had time to carry away or to hide anything except the plate, which had been stowed in a cavity made in one of the walls. As he was very rich and had good taste, the large drawing-room, which opened into the dining-room, remained like a gallery in a museum, after his precipitate flight. Expensive oil paintings, watercolours and drawings hung on the walls, while on the tables, on the hanging shelves and in elegant glass cupboards there were a thousand ornaments: small vases, statuettes, groups of Dresden figurines and grotesque Chinese carvings, old ivory and Venetian glass, which filled the large room with their costly and fantastic array.

Scarcely anything was left now; not that the things had been stolen, for the major would not have allowed that, but Mademoiselle Fifi would every now and then have a mine, and on those occasions all the officers thoroughly enjoyed themselves for five minutes. The little marquis now went into the drawing-room to get what he wanted, and returned with a small, delicate china teapot, which he filled with gunpowder. He then carefully pushed a fuse through the spout. This he lighted and took his infernal machine into the next room, after which he came back immediately and shut the door. The Germans stood expectant, their faces full of childish, smiling curiosity, and as soon as the explosion had shaken the château, they all rushed in at once.

Mademoiselle Fifi, who got in first, clapped his hands in delight at the sight of a terracotta Venus, whose head had been blown off, and each picked up pieces of porcelain and wondered at the strange shapes of the fragments, while the major was looking with a paternal eye at the large drawing-room, which had been wrecked after the fashion of a Nero, and was strewn with the remains of works of art. He went out first and said with a smile: 'That was a great success this time.'

But there was such a cloud of smoke in the dining-room, mingled with the tobacco smoke, that they could not breathe, so the commandant opened the window, and all the officers, who had returned for a last glass of cognac, went up to it.

The moist air blew into the room, bringing with it a sort of powdery spray, which sprinkled their beards. They looked at the tall trees which were dripping with rain, at the broad valley which was covered with mist, and at the church spire in the distance, a grey point in the driving rain.

The bells had not rung since their arrival. That was the only resistance which the invaders had met with in the neighbourhood. The parish priest had not refused to provide lodging and food for the Prussian soldiers; he had several times even drunk a bottle of beer or claret with the hostile commandant, who often employed him as a benevolent intermediary; but it was no use asking him to ring the bells; he would sooner have allowed himself to be shot. That was his way of protesting against the invasion, a peaceful and silent protest, the only one, he said, which was suitable to a priest, who was a man of mildness, and not of blood; and everyone, for twenty-five miles round, praised Abbé Chanta-voine's firmness and heroism in venturing to proclaim the public mourning by the obstinate silence of his church bells.

The whole village, enthusiastic at his resistance, was ready to back up their pastor and to risk anything, for they looked upon that silent protest as the safeguard of the national honour. It seemed to the peasants that they had set a greater example to their country than Belfort or Strassburg, and that the name of their little village would thus become immortalised; but, with that exception, they refused their Prussian conquerors nothing.

The commandant and his officers laughed among themselves at this inoffensive courage, and as the people in the whole country round showed themselves obliging and complaisant towards them, they willingly tolerated their silent patriotism. Little Wilhelm alone would have liked to have forced them to ring the bells. He was very angry at his superior's politic compliance with the priest's scruples, and every day begged the commandant to allow him to sound 'ding-dong, ding-dong', just once, only just once, just by way of a joke. And he asked it in the coaxing, tender voice of some loved woman who is bent on obtaining her wish, but the commandant would not yield, and, to console himself, Mademoiselle Fifi made a mine in the Château d'Uville.

The five men stood there together for five minutes, breathing in the moist air, and at last Lieutenant Fritz said with a laugh: 'The ladies will certainly not have fine weather for their drive.' Then they separated, each to his duty, while the captain had plenty to do in arranging for the dinner.

When they met again towards evening they began to laugh at seeing each other as spick and span and smart as on the day of a grand review. The commandant's hair did not look so grey as it was in the morning, and the captain had shaved, leaving only his moustache, which made him look as if he had a streak of fire under his nose.

In spite of the rain, they left the window open, and one of them went to listen from time to time; and at a quarter past six the baron said he heard a rumbling in the distance. They all rushed down, and presently the wagon drove up at a gallop, with its four horses steaming and blowing and splashed with mud to their girths. Five women dismounted, five handsome girls whom a comrade of the captain to whom Le Devoir had presented his card had selected with care.

They had not required much pressing, as they had got to know the Prussians in the three months during which they had had to do with them, and so they resigned themselves to the men as they did to the state of affairs.

They went at once into the dining-room, which looked more dismal in its dilapidated condition when it was lighted up; while the table, covered with choice dishes, the beautiful china and glass and the plate, which had been found in the hole in the wall where its owner had hidden it, gave it the appearance of a bandits' inn, where they were supping after committing a robbery in the place. The captain was radiant, and put his arm round the women as if he were familiar with them; and when the three young men wanted to appropriate one each, he opposed them authoritatively, reserving to himself the right to apportion them justly, according to their several ranks, so as not to offend the higher powers. Therefore, to avoid discussion, jarring and suspicion of partiality, he placed them all in a row according to height, and addressing the tallest, he said in a voice of command: 'What is your name?'

'Pamela,' she replied in a bold voice.

And then he said: 'Number One, called Pamela, is adjudged to the commandant.' Then, having kissed Blondina, the second, as a sign of proprietorship, he proffered stout Amanda to Lieutenant Otto; Eva, 'the Tomato', to Sub-Lieutenant Fritz, and Rachel, the shortest of them all, a very young, dark girl, with eyes as black as ink, a Jewess, whose nose proved the rule which allots hooked noses to all her race, to the youngest officer, the Marquis Wilhelm von Eyrick.

They were all plump and pretty, without any distinctive features, and each had a similarity of complexion and figure.

The three young men wished to carry off their prizes immediately, under the pretext that they might wish to freshen their toilets; but the captain wisely opposed this, for he said they were quite fit to sit down to dinner, and his experience in such matters carried the day, so there were only many kisses – expectant kisses.

Suddenly Rachel choked, and began to cough until the tears came into her eyes, while smoke came through her nostrils. Under the pretence of kissing her, the marquis had blown tobacco smoke into her mouth. She did not fly into a rage, and did not say a word, but she looked at her tormentor with latent hatred in her dark eyes.

They sat down to dinner. The commandant seemed delighted; he made Pamela sit on his right, and Blondina on his left, and said, as he unfolded his table napkin: 'That was a delightful idea of yours, captain.'

Lieutenants Otto and Fritz, who were as polite as if they had been with fashionable ladies, rather intimidated their guests, but Baron von Kelweinstein beamed, made obscene remarks and seemed on fire with his crown of red hair. He paid the women compliments in French of the Rhine, and sputtered out gallant remarks, only fit for a low tavern, from between his two broken teeth.

They did not understand him, however, and their intelligence did not seem to be awakened until he uttered foul words and broad expressions, which were mangled by his accent. Then they all began to laugh at once like crazy women and fell against each other, repeating the words, which the baron now purposely mispronounced, in order that he might have the pleasure of hearing them utter obscenities. They gave him as much as he wanted, for they were drunk after the first bottle of wine, and resuming their usual habits and manners, they kissed the officers to right and left of them, pinched their arms, uttered wild cries, drank out of every glass and sang French couplets and bits of German songs which they had picked up in their daily intercourse with the enemy.

Soon the men themselves became very unrestrained, shouted and broke the plates and dishes, while the soldiers standing behind waited on them stolidly. The commandant was the only one who kept himself under control.

Mademoiselle Fifi had taken Rachel on his knee, and, getting excited, at one moment he kissed the little black curls on her neck and at another he pinched her furiously and made her scream, for he was seized by a species of ferocity fuelled by his desire to hurt her. He often held her close to him and pressed a long kiss on the Jewess's rosy mouth until she lost her breath, and at last he bit her until a stream of blood ran down her chin and on to her dress.

For the second time she looked him full in the face, and as she wiped away the blood, she said: 'You will have to pay for that!' But he merely laughed and replied: 'I will pay.'

At dessert, champagne was served, and the commandant rose, and in the same voice in which he would have proposed the health of the Empress Augusta, he drank: 'To our ladies!' And a series of toasts began, toasts worthy of the lowest soldiers and of drunkards, mingled with obscene jokes, which were made still more brutal by their ignorance of the language. They got up, one after the other, trying to say something witty, forcing themselves to be funny, and the women, who were so drunk that they almost fell off their chairs, applauded madly each time.

The captain, who no doubt wished to impart an appearance of gallantry to the orgy, raised his glass again and said: 'To our victories over hearts!' And, thereupon, Lieutenant Otto, who was a species of bear from the Black Forest, jumped up, inflamed with drink, and suddenly seized by an access of alcoholic patriotism, he cried: 'To our victories over France!'

Drunk as they were, the women were silent, except Rachel who turned round, trembling, and said: 'I know some Frenchmen in whose presence you would not dare say that.' But the little marquis, still holding her on his knee, began to laugh, for the wine had made him very merry, and said: 'Ha! ha! ha! I have never met any of them myself. As soon as we show ourselves, they run away!' The girl, who was in a terrible rage, shouted into his face: 'You are lying, you dirty scoundrel!'

For a moment he looked at her steadily with his bright eyes upon her, as he had looked at the portrait before he destroyed it with bullets from his revolver, and then he began to laugh: 'Ah! yes, talk about them, my dear! Should we be here now if they were brave?' And, getting excited, he exclaimed: 'We are the masters! France belongs to us!' She made one spring from his knee and threw herself into her chair while he arose, held out his glass over the table and repeated: 'France and the French, the woods, the fields and the houses of France belong to us!'

The others, who were quite drunk, and who were suddenly seized by military enthusiasm, the enthusiasm of brutes, seized their glasses, and shouting, 'Long live Prussia!' they emptied them at a draught.

The girls did not protest, for they were reduced to silence and were afraid. Even Rachel did not say a word, as she had no reply to make. Then the little marquis put his champagne glass, which had just been refilled, on the head of the Jewess and exclaimed: 'All the women in France belong to us also!'

At that she got up so quickly that the glass upset, spilling the amber-coloured wine on her black hair as if to baptise her, and broke into a hundred fragments as it fell to the floor. Her lips trembling, she defied the looks of the officer, who was still laughing, and stammered out in a voice choked with rage: 'That – that – that – is not true – for you shall not have the women of France!'

He sat down again so as to laugh at his ease; and, trying to speak with the Parisian accent, he said: 'That is good, very good! But why did you come here, my dear?' She was thunderstruck and made no reply for a moment, for in her agitation she did not understand him at first, but as soon as she grasped his meaning she said to him indignantly and vehemently: 'I! I! I am not a woman, I am only a strumpet, and that is good enough for a Prussian.'

Almost before she had finished he slapped her full in the face; but as he was raising his hand, as if to strike her again, she seized a small dessert knife with a silver blade from the table and, almost mad with rage, stabbed him right in the hollow of his neck. Something that he was going to say died in his throat, and he sat there with his mouth half open and a terrible look in his eyes.

All the officers shouted in horror and jumped up tumultuously; but, throwing her chair between the legs of Lieutenant Otto, who fell down at full length, she ran to the window, opened it before they could seize her and jumped out into the night and the pouring rain.

In two minutes Mademoiselle Fifi was dead, and Fritz and Otto drew their swords and wanted to kill the women, who threw themselves at their feet and clung to their knees. With some difficulty the major stopped the slaughter and had the four terrified girls locked up in a room under the care of two soldiers, and then he organised the pursuit of the fugitive as carefully as if he were about to engage in a skirmish, feeling quite sure that she would be caught.

The table, which had been cleared immediately, now served as a bed on which to lay out the lieutenant, and the four officers stood at the windows, rigid and sobered, with the stern faces of soldiers on duty; and, through the steady torrent of rain, tried to penetrate the darkness of the night. Suddenly a shot was heard, and then another, a long way off; and for four hours they heard from time to time near or distant reports and rallying cries, and strange words of challenge, uttered in guttural voices.

In the morning the search-party returned. Two soldiers had been killed and three others wounded by their comrades in the ardour of that chase and in the confusion of that nocturnal pursuit; but they had not caught Rachel.

Then the inhabitants of the district were terrorised, the houses were turned topsy-turvy, the country was scoured over and over again, but the Jewess did not seem to have left a single trace of her flight behind her.

When the general was told of it he gave orders to hush up the affair, so as not to set a bad example to the army, but he severely censured the commandant, who in turn punished his inferiors. The general had said: 'One does not go to war in order to amuse oneself and to caress prostitutes.' Count von Farlsberg, in his exasperation, made up his mind to have his revenge on the district, but as he required a pretext for showing severity, he sent for the priest and ordered him to have the bell tolled at the funeral of the Marquis von Eyrick.

Contrary to all expectation, the priest showed himself humble and most respectful, and when Mademoiselle Fifi's body left the Château d'Uville on its way to the cemetery, carried by soldiers, preceded, surrounded and followed by soldiers who marched with loaded rifles, for the first time the bell sounded its funeral knell in a lively manner, as if a friendly hand were caressing it. At night it rang again, and the next day, and every day; it rang as much as anyone could desire. Sometimes even it would start at night and sound gently through the darkness, seized with a strange joy, awakened one could not tell why. All the peasants in the neighbourhood declared that it was bewitched, and nobody except the priest and the sacristan would now go near the church tower. And they went because a poor girl was living there in terror and solitude, provided for secretly by those two men.

She remained there until the German troops departed, and then one evening the priest borrowed the baker's cart and himself drove his young charge to Rouen. When they got there he embraced her, and she quickly went back on foot to her old establishment, where the proprietress, who thought that she was dead, was very glad to see her again.

A short time afterwards a patriot who had no prejudices, who liked her because of her bold deed, and who afterwards loved her for herself, married her and made of her a lady quite as good as many others so described.

Clair de Lune

Abbé Marignan's martial name suited him well. He was a tall, thin priest, fanatical, excitable, and yet upright. All his beliefs were fixed, never varying. He believed sincerely that he knew his God, understood His plans, desires and intentions.

When he walked with long strides across the garden walk of his little country parsonage, he would sometimes ask himself the question: 'Why has God done this?' And he would dwell on this continually, putting himself in the place of God, and he almost invariably found an answer. He would never have cried out in an outburst of pious humility: 'Thy ways, O Lord, are inscrutable.'

He said to himself: 'I am the servant of God; it is right for me to know the reason for His deeds, or to guess it if I do not know it.'

Everything in nature seemed to him to have been created in accordance with admirable and absolute logic. The 'whys' and 'becauses' always balanced. Dawn was given to make our awakening pleasant, the days to ripen the harvest, the rains to moisten it, and the dark nights for sleep.

The four seasons corresponded perfectly to the needs of agriculture, and no suspicion had ever come to the priest that nature in fact has no intentions; that, on the contrary, everything which exists must conform to the hard demands of seasons, climates and matter.

But he hated women – hated them unconsciously, and despised them by instinct. He often repeated the words of Christ: 'Woman, what have I to do with thee?' and he would add: 'It seems as though God, Himself, were dissatisfied with this work of His.' She was the tempter who led the first man astray, and who since then had ever been busy with her work of damnation. And even more than their sinful bodies, he hated their loving hearts.

He had often felt their tenderness directed towards himself, and though he knew that he was invulnerable, he grew angry at this need of love that is always vibrating in them.

According to his belief, God had created woman for the sole purpose of tempting and testing man. One must not approach her without defensive precautions and fear of possible snares. She was, indeed, just like a snare, with her lips open and her arms stretched out to man.

He had no indulgence except for nuns, whom their vows had rendered inoffensive; but he was stern with them, nevertheless, because he felt that at the bottom of their fettered and humble hearts the everlasting tenderness was burning brightly – that tenderness which was shown even to him, a priest.

He felt this cursed tenderness, even in their docility, in the low tones of their voices when speaking to him, in their lowered eyes, and in their resigned tears when he reproved them roughly. And he would shake his cassock on leaving the convent doors, and walk off, lengthening his stride as though flying from danger.

He had a niece who lived with her mother in a little house near him. He was bent upon making her a sister of charity.

She was a pretty, brainless madcap. When the abbé preached she laughed, and when he was angry with her she would give him a hug, drawing him to her heart, while he sought unconsciously to release himself from this embrace which nevertheless filled him with a sweet pleasure, giving him the sensation of paternity which slumbers in every man.

Often, when walking by her side, along the country road, he would speak to her of God, of his God. She never listened to him, but looked about her at the sky, the grass and flowers, and one could see the joy of life sparkling in her eyes. Sometimes she would dart forward to catch some flying creature, crying out as she brought it back: 'Look, uncle, how pretty it is! I want to hug it!' And this desire to 'hug' flies or lilac blossoms disquieted, angered and roused the priest, who saw, even in this, the ineradicable tenderness that is always budding in women's hearts.

Then there came a day when the sexton's wife, who kept house for the Abbé Marignan, told him, with caution, that his niece had a lover.

Almost suffocated by the fearful emotion this news roused in him, he stood there, his face covered with soap, for he was in the act of shaving.

When he had sufficiently recovered to think and speak he cried: 'It is not true; you lie, Mélanie!'

But the peasant woman put her hand on her heart, saying: 'May our Lord judge me if I lie, Monsieur le Curé! I tell you, she goes there every night when your sister has gone to bed. They meet by the riverside; you have only to go there and see, between ten o'clock and midnight.'

He ceased scraping his chin, and began to walk up and down impetuously, as he always did when he was in deep thought. When he began shaving again he cut himself three times.

All day long he was silent, full of anger and indignation. To his priestly hatred of this invincible love was added the exasperation of a spiritual father, of a guardian and pastor, deceived and tricked by a child, and the selfish emotion shown by parents when their daughter announces that she has chosen a husband without them, and in spite of them.

After dinner he tried to read a little, but could not, growing more and more angry. When ten o'clock struck he seized a formidable oak stick, which he was accustomed to carry on his nocturnal walks when visiting the sick. And he smiled at the enormous club which he twirled in a threatening manner in his strong, country fist. Then he raised it suddenly and, clenching his teeth, brought it down on a chair, the broken back of which fell over on the floor.

He opened the door to go out, but stopped on the threshold, surprised by the splendid moonlight, of such brilliance as is seldom seen.

And, as he was gifted with an emotional nature, one such as had those poetic dreamers, the Fathers of the Church, he felt suddenly distracted and moved by all the grand and serene beauty of this pale night.

In his little garden, bathed in soft light, his fruit trees in a row cast on the ground the shadow of their slender branches, scarcely in full leaf, while the giant honeysuckle, clinging to the wall of his house, exhaled a delicious sweetness, filling the warm moonlit atmosphere with a kind of perfumed soul.

He began to take long breaths, drinking in the air as drunkards drink wine, and he walked along slowly, delighted, marvelling, almost forgetting his niece.

As soon as he was outside the garden, he stopped to gaze upon the plain all flooded with the caressing light, bathed in that tender, languishing charm of serene nights. At each moment was heard the short, metallic note of the cricket, and distant nightingales shook out their scattered notes – their light, vibrant music that sets one dreaming, without thinking, a music made for kisses, for the seduction of moonlight.

The abbé walked on again, his heart failing, though he knew not why. He seemed weakened, suddenly exhausted; he wanted to sit down, to rest there, to think, to admire God in His works.

Beyond, following the undulations of the little river, a great line of poplars wound in and out. A fine mist, a white haze through which the moonbeams passed, silvering it and making it gleam, hung around and above the mountains, covering all the tortuous course of the water with a kind of light and transparent cotton wool.

The priest stopped once again, his soul filled with a growing and irresistible tenderness.

And a doubt, a vague feeling of disquiet came over him; he was asking one of those questions that he sometimes put to himself.

'Why did God make this? Since the night is destined for sleep, unconsciousness, repose, forgetfulness of everything, why make it more charming than day, softer than dawn or evening? And why does this seductive planet, more poetic than the sun, that seems destined, so discreet is it, to illuminate things too delicate and mysterious for the light of day, make the darkness so transparent?

'Why does not the greatest of feathered songsters sleep like the others? Why does it pour forth its voice in the mysterious night?

'Why this half-veil cast over the world? Why these tremblings of the heart, this emotion of the spirit, this enervation of the body? Why this display of enchantments that human beings do not see, since they are lying in their beds? For whom is destined this sublime spectacle, this abundance of poetry cast from heaven to earth?'

And the abbé could not understand.

But out there, on the edge of the meadow, under the arch of trees bathed in a shining mist, two figures were walking side by side.

The man was the taller, and held his arm about his sweetheart's neck and kissed her brow every little while. They imparted life, all at once, to the placid landscape in which they were framed as by a heavenly hand. The two seemed but a single being, the being for whom was destined this calm and silent night, and they came towards the priest as a living answer, the response his Master sent to his questionings.

He stood still, his heart beating, all upset; and it seemed to him that he saw before him some biblical scene, like the love of Ruth and Boaz, the accomplishment of the will of the Lord, in some of those glorious stories of which the sacred books tell. The verses of the Song of Songs began to ring in his ears, the appeal of passion, all the poetry of this poem replete with tenderness.

And he said unto himself: 'Perhaps God has made such nights as these to idealise the love of man.'

He shrank back from the two who still advanced with arms intertwined. Yes, it was his niece. But he asked himself now if he would not be disobeying God. And does not God permit love, since He surrounds it with such visible splendour?

And he went back musing, almost ashamed, as if he had intruded into a temple where he had no right to enter.

Miss Harriet

There were seven of us on a drag, four women and three men; one of the latter sat on the box-seat beside the coachman. We were ascending, at a snail's pace, the winding road up the steep cliff along the coast.

Setting out from Étretat at break of day in order to visit the ruins of Tancarville, we were still half asleep, benumbed by the keen air of the morning. The women especially, who were little accustomed to these early excursions, let their eyelids fall every moment, nodding their heads or yawning, quite insensible to the beauties of the dawn.

It was autumn. On both sides of the road stretched the bare fields, yellowed by the stubble of wheat and oats which covered the soil like a beard that has been badly shaved. The moist earth seemed to steam. Larks were singing high up in the air, while other birds piped in the bushes.

The sun rose at length in front of us, bright red on the plane of the horizon, and in proportion as it ascended, growing clearer from minute to minute, the country seemed to awake, to smile, to shake itself in its white robe of vapour like a young girl leaving her bed.

The Comte d'Etraille, who was seated on the box, cried: 'Look! look! a hare!' and he extended his arm towards the left, pointing to a patch of clover. The animal scurried along, almost hidden by the clover, only its large ears showing. Then it swerved across a furrow, stopped, started off again at full speed, changed its course, stopped anew, uneasy, spying out every danger, uncertain what route to take; then suddenly it began to run with great bounds, disappearing finally in a large patch of beetroot. All the men roused themselves to watch its movements.

René Lamanoir exclaimed: 'We are not at all gallant this morning,' and, regarding his neighbour, the little Baronne de Sérennes, who struggled against sleep, he said to her in a low tone: 'You are thinking of your husband, baroness. Reassure yourself; he will not return before Saturday, so you have still four days.'

She answered with a sleepy smile: 'How stupid you are!' Then, shaking off her torpor, she added: 'Now, let somebody say something to make us laugh. You, Monsieur Chenal, who have the reputation of having had more love affairs than the Duc de Richelieu, tell us a love story in which you have played a part; anything you like.'

Léon Chenal, an old painter, who had once been very handsome, very strong, very proud of his physique and very popular with women, took his long white beard in his hand and smiled. Then, after a few moments' reflection, he suddenly became serious.

'Ladies, it will not be an amusing tale, for I am going to relate to you the saddest love affair of my life, and I sincerely hope that none of my friends may ever pass through a similar experience.'

'I was twenty-five years of age and was exploring the coast of Normandy. I call exploring wandering about, with a knapsack on one's back, from inn to inn, under the pretext of making studies and sketching landscapes. I know nothing more enjoyable than that happy-go-lucky wandering life, in which one is perfectly free, without shackles of any kind, without care, without preoccupation, without thinking even of the morrow. One goes in any direction one pleases, without any guide except one's fancy, without any counsellor except one's eyes. One stops because a running brook attracts one, because the smell of potatoes frying tickles one's nose on passing an inn. Sometimes it is the perfume of clematis that decides one in one's choice or the roguish glance of the servant at an inn. Do not despise me for my affection for these rustics. These girls have a soul as well as senses, not to mention firm cheeks and fresh lips; while their hearty and willing kisses have the flavour of wild fruit. Love is always love, come whence it may. A heart that beats at your approach, an eye that weeps when you go away are things so rare, so sweet, so precious, that they must never be despised.

'I have had meetings in fields full of primroses, and in barns among the straw, still warm from the heat of the day. I have recollections of coarse grey cloth covering supple peasant skin and regrets for simple, frank kisses, more delicate in their unaffected sincerity than the subtle favours of charming and distinguished women.

'But what one loves most amid all these varied adventures is the country, the woods, the rising of the twilight, the moonlight. These are, for the painter, honeymoon trips with nature. One is alone with her in that long and quiet association. You go to sleep in the fields, amid marguerites and poppies, and when you open your eyes in the full glare of the sunlight you descry in the distance the little village with its clock tower which sounds the hour of noon.

'You sit down by the side of a spring which gushes out at the foot of an oak, amid a growth of tall, slender weeds, glistening with life. You go down on your knees, bend forward and drink that cold, clear water which wets your face; you drink it with a physical pleasure, as though you kissed the spring, lip to lip. Sometimes, when you find a deep pool along the course of these tiny brooks, you plunge in quite naked, and you feel on your skin, from head to foot, as it were, an icy and delicious caress, the light and gentle quivering of the stream.

'You are gay on the hills, melancholy on the edge of ponds, and inspired when the sun is setting in an ocean of blood-red clouds. And at night, under the moon, you think of a thousand strange things which would never have passed through your mind under the brilliant light of day.

'So, in wandering through the same country where we are this year, I came to the little village of Bénouville, on the cliff between Yport and Étretat. I came from Fécamp, following the coast, a high coast as straight as a wall, with its projecting chalk cliffs descending perpendicularly into the sea. I had walked since early morning on the short grass, smooth and yielding as a carpet, that grows on the edge of the cliff. And, singing loudly, I walked with long strides, looking sometimes at the slow circling flight of a gull with its white curved wings outlined on the blue sky, sometimes at the brown sails of a fishing boat on the green sea. In short, I had passed a happy day, a day of liberty and of freedom from care.

'A little farmhouse where travellers were lodged was pointed out to me, a kind of inn, kept by a peasant woman, which stood in the centre of a Norman courtyard surrounded by a double row of beeches.

'Leaving the coast, I reached the hamlet, which was hemmed in by great trees, and presented myself at the house of Mother Lecacheur.

'She was an old, wrinkled and stern peasant woman, who seemed always to receive customers under protest.

'It was the month of May. The spreading apple trees covered the court with a shower of blossoms which rained unceasingly both upon people and upon the grass.

'I said: "Well, Madame Lecacheur, have you a room for me?"

'Astonished to find that I knew her name, she answered: "That depends; everything is let, but all the same I can find out."

'In five minutes we had come to an agreement, and I deposited my bag upon the earthen floor of a rustic room, furnished with a bed, two chairs, a table and a washbowl. The room looked into the large, smoky kitchen, where the lodgers took their meals with the people of the farm and the landlady, who was a widow.

'I washed my hands, and then I went into the kitchen. The old woman was making a chicken fricassee for dinner in the large fireplace in which hung the iron pot, black with smoke.

' "You have other visitors, then, at the present time?" said I to her.

'She answered in an offended tone of voice: "I have a lady, an English lady, who has reached years of maturity. She occupies the other room."

'I obtained, by means of an extra five sous a day, the privilege of dining alone out in the yard when the weather was fine.

'My place was set outside the door, and I was beginning to gnaw the lean limbs of the Normandy chicken, to drink the clear cider and to munch the hunk of white bread, which was four days old but excellent, when suddenly the wooden gate which gave on the highway was opened, and a strange lady directed her steps towards the house. She was very thin, very tall, so tightly enveloped in a red Scotch plaid shawl that one might have supposed she had no arms if one had not seen a long hand appear just above the hips, holding a white tourist umbrella. Her face was like that of a mummy, surrounded with curls of grey hair, which tossed about at every step she took and made me think, I know not why, of a pickled herring in curl papers. Lowering her eyes, she passed quickly in front of me and entered the house.

'That singular apparition cheered me. She undoubtedly was my neighbour, the English lady of mature years of whom my hostess had spoken.

'I did not see her again that day. The next morning, when I had settled myself to begin painting at the end of that beautiful valley which you know and which extends as far as Étretat, I perceived, on lifting my eyes suddenly, something singular standing on the crest of the cliff, something like a pole decked out with flags. It was she. On seeing me, she suddenly disappeared. I re-entered the house at midday for lunch and took my seat at the general table, so as to make the acquaintance of this odd character. But she did not respond to my polite advances, was insensible even to my little attentions. I poured out water for her persistently; I passed her the dishes with great eagerness. A slight, almost imperceptible, movement of the head and an English word, murmured so low that I did not understand it, were her only acknowledgments.

'I ceased occupying myself with her, although she had disturbed my thoughts.

'At the end of three days I knew as much about her as did Madame Lecacheur herself.

'She was called Miss Harriet. Seeking out a secluded village in which to pass the summer, she had been attracted to Bénouville some six months before and did not seem disposed to leave it. She never spoke at table, ate rapidly, reading all the while a small book of Protestant propaganda. She gave a copy of it to everybody. The curé himself had received no less than four copies, conveyed by an urchin to whom she had paid two sous for the errand. She said sometimes to our hostess abruptly, without preparing her in the least for the declaration: "I love the Saviour more than all. I admire Him in all creation; I adore Him in all nature; I carry Him always in my heart." And she would immediately present the old woman with one of her tracts which were destined to convert the universe.

'In the village she was not liked. In fact, the schoolmaster having pronounced her an atheist, there was a kind of stigma attached to her. The curé, who had been consulted by Madame Lecacheur, responded: "She is a heretic, but God does not wish the death of the sinner, and I believe her to be a person of pure morals."

'These words, "atheist", "heretic", words which no one can precisely define, threw doubts into some minds. It was asserted, however, that this Englishwoman was rich and that she had passed her life in travelling through every country in the world, because her family had cast her off. Why had her family cast her off? Because of her impiety, of course!

'She was, in fact, one of those people of exalted principles; one of those opinionated puritans, of which England produces so many; one of those good and insupportable old maids who haunt the *tables d'hôte* of every hotel in Europe, who spoil Italy, poison Switzerland, render the charming cities of the Mediterranean uninhabitable, carry everywhere their fantastic manias, their manners of petrified vestals, their indescribable toilets and a certain odour of india-rubber which makes one believe that at night they are slipped into a rubber casing.

'Whenever I caught sight of one of them in a hotel I fled like the birds who see a scarecrow in a field.

'This woman, however, appeared so very singular that she did not displease me.

'Madame Lecacheur, hostile by instinct to everything that was not rustic, felt in her narrow soul a kind of hatred for the ecstatic declarations of the old maid. She had found a phrase by which to describe her, a term of contempt that rose to her lips, called forth by I know not what confused and mysterious mental ratiocination. She said: "That woman is a demoniac." This epithet, applied to that austere and sentimental creature, seemed to me irresistibly droll. I myself never called her anything now but "the demoniac", experiencing a singular pleasure in pronouncing aloud this word on perceiving her.

'One day I asked Mother Lecacheur: "Well, what is our demoniac about today?"

'To which my rustic friend replied with a shocked air: "What do you think, sir? She picked up a toad which had had its paw crushed and carried it to her room and put it in her washbowl and bandaged it as if it were a man. If that is not profanation I should like to know what is!"

'On another occasion, when walking along the shore, she bought a large fish which had just been caught, simply to throw it back into the sea again. The sailor from whom she had bought it, although she paid him handsomely, now began to swear, more exasperated, indeed, than if she had put her hand into his pocket and taken his money. For more than a month he could not speak of the circumstance without becoming furious and denouncing it as an outrage. Oh, yes! She was indeed a demoniac, this Miss Harriet, and Mother Lecacheur must have had an inspiration in thus christening her.

'The stable-man, who was called Sapeur, because he had served in Africa in his youth, entertained other opinions. He said with a roguish air: "She is an old hag who has seen life."

'If the poor woman had but known!

'The little kind-hearted Céleste did not wait upon her willingly, but I was never able to understand why. Probably her only reason was that she was a stranger, of another race, of a different tongue and of another religion. She was, in fact, a demoniac!

'She passed her time wandering about the country, adoring and seeking God in nature. I found her one evening on her knees in a cluster of bushes. Having discovered something red through the leaves, I brushed aside the branches, and Miss Harriet at once rose to her feet, confused at having been found thus, fixing on me terrified eyes like those of an owl surprised in open day.

'Sometimes, when I was working among the rocks, I would suddenly descry her on the edge of the cliff like a lighthouse signal. She would be gazing in rapture at the vast sea glittering in the sunlight and the boundless sky with its golden tints. Sometimes I would distinguish her at the end of the valley, walking quickly with her elastic English step, and I would go towards her, attracted by I know not what, simply to see her dried-up, ineffable features, which seemed to glow with inward and profound happiness.

'I would often encounter her also in the corner of a field, sitting on the grass under the shadow of an apple tree, with her little religious booklet lying open on her knee while she gazed out at the distance.

'I could not tear myself away from that quiet country neighbourhood, to which I was attached by a thousand links of love for its wide and peaceful landscape. I was happy in this sequestered farm, far removed from everything, but in touch with the earth, the good, beautiful, green earth. And – must I avow it? – there was, besides, a little curiosity which kept me at Mother Lecacheur's farm. I wished to become acquainted a little with this strange Miss Harriet and to know what passes through the minds of those wandering old maids of England.'

'We became acquainted in a rather singular manner. I had just finished a study which appeared to me to be worth something, and so it was, as it sold for ten thousand francs fifteen years later. It was as simple, however, as two and two make four and was not according to academic rules. The whole right side of my canvas represented a rock, an enormous rock, covered with sea-wrack, brown, yellow and red, across which the sun poured like a stream of oil. The light from the sun, invisible behind me, fell on the rock, and turned it to fiery gold. That was all. A first bewildering study of blazing, gorgeous light.

'On the left was the sea, not the blue sea or the slate-coloured sea, but a sea of jade, greenish, milky and solid beneath the deep-coloured sky.

'I was so pleased with my work that I danced from sheer delight as I carried it back to the inn. I would have liked the whole world to see it at once. I can remember that I showed it to a cow that was browsing by the wayside, exclaiming as I did so: "Look at that, my old beauty; you will not often see its like again."

'When I had reached the house I immediately called out to Mother Lecacheur, shouting with all my might: "Hello, there! Come here and look at this."

'The rustic approached and looked at my work with her stupid eyes. which distinguished nothing and could not even tell whether the picture represented an ox or a house.

'Miss Harriet just then came in, and she passed behind me as I was holding out my canvas at arm's length, exhibiting it to our landlady. The demoniac could not help but see it, for I took care to exhibit the thing in such a way that it could not escape her notice. She stopped abruptly and stood motionless, astonished. It was her rock which was depicted, the one she was wont to climb, so that she could dream away her time undisturbed.

'She uttered a British, "Oh," which was at once so accentuated and so flattering that I turned round to her, smiling, and said: "This is my latest study, mademoiselle."

'She murmured rapturously, comically and tenderly: "Oh! monsieur, you understand nature as a living thing."

'I coloured and was more touched by that compliment than if it had come from a queen. I was captured, conquered, vanquished. I could have embraced her, upon my honour.

'I took my seat at table beside her as usual. For the first time she spoke, thinking aloud: "Oh! I do so love nature."

'I passed her some bread, some water, some wine. She now accepted these with the little smile of a mummy. I then began to talk about the scenery.

'After the meal we rose from the table together and walked leisurely across the courtyard; then, attracted doubtless by the fiery glow which the setting sun cast over the face of the sea, I opened the gate which led to the cliff, and we walked along side by side, as contented as two persons might be who have just learned to understand and penetrate each other's motives and feelings.

'It was one of those warm, soft evenings which impart a sense of ease to flesh and spirit alike. All is enjoyment, everything charms. The balmy air, laden with the perfume of grasses and the odour of seaweed, soothes one's sense of smell with its wild fragrance, soothes the palate with its sea savour, soothes the mind with its pervading sweetness.

'We were now walking along the edge of the cliff, high above the boundless sea with its little waves rolling in, three hundred feet below. And we inhaled with open mouths and expanded chests that fresh breeze, briny from kissing the waves, that came from the ocean and passed across our faces.

'Wrapped in her plaid shawl, with a look of inspiration as she faced the breeze, the Englishwoman gazed fixedly at the sun as it sank towards the horizon. Far off in the distance a three-master in full sail was outlined on the blood-red sky and a steamship, somewhat nearer, passed along, leaving behind it a trail of smoke on the horizon. The sun went down slowly lower and lower and presently touched the water just behind the motionless vessel, which, in its dazzling radiance, looked as though framed in flames of fire. We saw the sun plunge, grow smaller and disappear, swallowed up by the ocean.

'Miss Harriet gazed in rapture at the last gleams of the dying day. She seemed longing to embrace the sky, the sea, the whole landscape.

'She murmured: "Oh! I love – I love – " I saw a tear in her eye. She continued: "I wish I were a little bird, so that I could soar up to the sky."

'She remained standing as I had often before seen her, perched on the cliff, her face as glowing as her crimson shawl. I should have liked to have sketched her in my album. It would have been a caricature of ecstasy.

'I turned away so as not to laugh.

'I then spoke to her of painting as I would have done to a fellow artist, using the technical terms common among the devotees of the profession. She listened attentively, eagerly seeking to divine the meaning of the terms, so as to understand my thoughts. From time to time she would exclaim: "Oh! I understand, I understand. It is very interesting."

'We returned home.

'The next day, on seeing me, she approached me, cordially holding out her hand; and we at once became firm friends.

'She was a good creature who had a kind of soul on springs, which became enthusiastic at a bound. She lacked equilibrium like all women who are spinsters at the age of fifty. She seemed to be preserved in a pickle of innocence, but her heart still retained something very youthful and inflammable. She loved both nature and animals with a fervour, a love like old wine mellowed through age, with a sensuous love that she had never given to a man.

'One thing is certain, that the sight of a mare roaming in a meadow with a foal at its side, a bird's nest full of young ones, screaming, with their open mouths and their enormous heads, affected her perceptibly.

'Poor, solitary, sad, wandering souls haunting the *tables d'hôte*! I have loved you ever since I became acquainted with Miss Harriet!

'I soon discovered that she had something she would like to tell me, but dare not, and I was amused at her timidity. When I started out in the morning with my knapsack on my back, she would accompany me in silence as far as the end of the village, evidently struggling to find words with which to begin a conversation. Then she would leave me abruptly and walk away quickly with her springy step.

'One day, however, she plucked up courage: "I should like to see how you paint your pictures. Do you mind? I have been very curious."

'And she blushed as if she had said something audacious.

'I conducted her to the bottom of the Petit-Val, where I had begun a large picture.

'She remained standing behind me, following all my movements with concentrated attention. Then, suddenly, fearing perhaps that she was disturbing me, she said: "Thank you," and walked away.

'But she soon became more friendly, and accompanied me every day, her face exhibiting visible pleasure. She carried her camp stool under her arm, not permitting me to carry it. She would remain there for hours, silent and motionless, following with her eyes the point of my brush in its every movement. When I obtained unexpectedly just the effect I wanted by a dash of colour put on with the palette knife, she involuntarily uttered a little "Ah!" of astonishment, of joy, of admiration. She had the most tender respect for my canvases, an almost religious respect for that human reproduction of a part of nature's work divine. My studies were to her in a way sacred pictures, and sometimes she spoke to me of God, with the idea of converting me.

'Oh, He was a queer, good-natured being, this God of hers! He was a sort of village philosopher without any great resources and without great power, for she always pictured Him to herself as inconsolable over injustices committed under His eyes, as though He were powerless to prevent them.

'She was, however, on excellent terms with Him, affecting even to be the confidante of His secrets and of His troubles. She would say: "God wills," or, "God does not will," just like a sergeant announcing to a recruit: "The colonel has commanded."

'At the bottom of her heart she deplored my ignorance of the Divine Will, which she endeavoured to impart to me.

'Almost every day I found in my pockets, in my hat when I lifted it from the ground, in my paintbox, in my polished shoes, standing in front of my door in the morning, those little pious tracts which she, no doubt, received directly from Paradise.

'I treated her as one would an old friend, with unaffected cordiality. But I soon perceived that she had changed somewhat in her manner, though, for a while, I paid little attention to it.

'When I was painting, whether in the valley or in some country lane, I would see her suddenly appear with her rapid, springy walk. She would then sit down abruptly, out of breath, as though she had been running or were overcome by some profound emotion. Her face would be red, that English red which is denied to the people of all other countries; then, without any reason, she would turn ashy pale and seem about to faint away. Gradually, however, her natural colour would return and she would begin to speak.

'Then, without warning, she would break off in the middle of a sentence, spring up from her seat and walk away so rapidly and so strangely that I was at my wits' ends to discover whether I had done or said anything to displease or wound her.

'I finally came to the conclusion that those were her normal manners, somewhat modified no doubt in my honour during the first days of our acquaintance.

'When she returned to the farm, after walking for hours on the windy coast, her long curls often hung straight down, as if their springs had been broken. This had hitherto seldom given her any concern, and she would come to dinner without embarrassment all dishevelled by her sister, the breeze. But now she would go to her room and arrange the untidy locks, and when I would say, with familiar gallantry, which, however, always offended her: "You are as beautiful as a star today, Miss Harriet," a blush would immediately rise to her cheeks, the blush of a young girl, of a girl of fifteen.

'Then she would suddenly become quite reserved and cease coming to watch me paint. I thought, "This is only a fit of temper; it will blow over." But it did not always blow over, and when I spoke to her she would answer me either with affected indifference or with sullen annoyance.

'She became by turns rude, impatient and nervous. I never saw her now except at meals, and we spoke but little. I concluded at length that I must have offended her in some way, and, accordingly, I said to her one evening: "Miss Harriet, what have I done to displease you? You are causing me much pain!"

'She replied in a most comical tone of anger: "Nothing, nothing. It is not true, not true," and she ran off and shut herself up in her room.

'Occasionally she would look at me in a peculiar manner. I have often said to myself since then that those who are condemned to death must look thus when they are informed that their last hour has come. In her eye there lurked a species of insanity, an insanity at once mystical and violent; and even more, a fever, an aggravated longing, impatient and impotent, for the unattained and unattainable.

'Nay, it seemed to me as if there was also going on within her a struggle in which her heart wrestled with an unknown force that she sought to master, and even, perhaps, something else. How was I to know? . . . How was I to know?

'It was indeed a singular revelation.

'For some time I had begun to work, as soon as daylight appeared, on a picture the subject of which was as follows:

'A deep ravine, enclosed, surmounted by two thickets of trees and vines, extended into the distance and was lost, submerged in that milky mist, in that cloud like cotton down that sometimes floats over valleys at daybreak. And at the extreme end of that heavy, transparent haze one saw, or, rather, surmised, that a couple of human beings were approaching, a human couple, a youth and a maiden, their arms interlaced, embracing each other, their heads inclined towards each other, their lips meeting.

'A first ray of the sun, glistening through the branches, pierced that mist of the dawn, illuminated it with a rosy reflection just behind the rustic lovers, framing their vague shadows in a silvery background. It was well done; yes, indeed, well done.

'I was working on the slope which led to the Valley of Étretat. On this particular morning I had, by chance, the sort of floating vapour which I needed. Suddenly something rose up in front of me like a phantom; it was Miss Harriet. On seeing me she was about to flee. But I called after her, saying: "Come here, come here, mademoiselle. I have a nice little picture for you."

'She came forward, though with seeming reluctance. I handed her my sketch. She said nothing, but stood for a long time, motionless, looking at it, and suddenly she burst into tears. She wept spasmodically, like one who has striven hard to restrain her tears, but who can do so no longer and abandons herself to grief, though still resisting. I sprang to my feet, moved at the sight of a sorrow I did not comprehend, and I took her by the hands with an impulse of brusque affection, a true French impulse which acts before it reflects.

'She let her hands rest in mine for a few seconds, and I felt them quiver as if all her nerves were being wrenched. Then she withdrew her hands abruptly, or, rather, snatched them away.

'I recognised that tremor, for I had felt it, and I could not be deceived. Ah! the love tremor of a woman, whether she be fifteen or fifty years of age, whether she be of humble or gentle birth, goes so straight to your heart that you can never be mistaken about it.

'Her whole frail being had trembled, vibrated, been overcome. I knew it. She walked away before I had time to say a word, leaving me as surprised as if I had witnessed a miracle and as troubled as if I had committed a crime.

'I did not return home for luncheon. I went to take a turn on the edge of the cliff, feeling that I would just as soon weep as laugh, looking on the adventure as both comic and deplorable and my position as ridiculous, believing her unhappy enough to go insane.

'I asked myself what I ought to do. It seemed best for me to leave the place, and I immediately resolved to do so.

'Somewhat sad and perplexed, I wandered about until dinner-time and entered the farmhouse just when the soup had been served.

'I sat down at the table as usual. Miss Harriet was there, eating away solemnly, without speaking to anyone, without even lifting her eyes. Her manner and expression were, however, the same as usual.

'I waited patiently till the meal had been finished, when, turning towards the landlady, I said: "Well, Madame Lecacheur, it will not be long now before I shall have to take my leave of you."

'The good woman, at once surprised and troubled, replied in her drawling voice: "My dear sir, what is it you say? You are going to leave us after I have become so accustomed to you?"

'I glanced at Miss Harriet out of the corner of my eye. Her countenance did not change in the least. But Céleste, the little servant, looked up at me. She was a fat girl, of about eighteen years of age, rosy, fresh, as strong as a horse, and possessing the rare attribute of cleanliness. I had kissed her at odd times in out-of-the way corners, after the manner of travellers – nothing more.

'Dinner being at length over, I went to smoke my pipe under the apple trees, walking up and down from one end of the enclosure to the other. All the reflections which I had made during the day, the strange discovery of the morning, that passionate and grotesque attachment for me, the recollections which that revelation had suddenly called up, recollections at once charming and perplexing, perhaps also that look which the little maid had cast on me at the announcement of my departure – all these things combined put me now in a reckless humour, gave me a tingling sensation of kisses on the lips and a feeling which urged me to commit some folly.

'Night was coming on, casting its dark shadows under the trees, when I descried Céleste, who had gone to lock up the poultry yard at the other end of the enclosure. I darted towards her, running so noiselessly that she heard nothing, and as she got up from shutting the small trapdoor by which the chickens got in and out, I clasped her in my arms and rained on her coarse, fat face a shower of kisses. She struggled, laughing all the time, as she was accustomed to do in such circumstances. Why did I suddenly loose my grip of her? Why did I abruptly check myself – What was it that I heard behind me?

'It was Miss Harriet, who had come upon us, who had seen us and who stood in front of us motionless as a spectre. Then she disappeared in the darkness.

'I was ashamed, embarrassed, more desperate at having been thus surprised by her than if she had caught me committing some criminal act.

'I slept badly that night. I was completely unnerved and haunted by sad thoughts. I seemed to hear loud weeping, but in this I was no doubt deceived. Moreover, I thought several times that I heard someone walking about the house and opening the hall door.

'Towards morning I was overcome by fatigue and fell asleep. I got up late and did not go downstairs until lunchtime, being still in a bewildered state, not knowing what line to take.

'No one had seen Miss Harriet. We waited for her at table, but she did not appear. At length Mother Lecacheur went to her room. The English woman was not there. She must have set out at break of day, as she was wont to do, in order to see the sun rise.

'Nobody seemed surprised at this, and we began to eat in silence.

'The weather was hot, very hot, one of those broiling, heavy days when not a leaf stirs. The table had been placed out of doors, under an apple tree, and from time to time Sapeur had gone to the cellar to draw a jug of cider; everybody was so thirsty. Céleste brought the dishes from the kitchen, a ragout of mutton with potatoes, a cold rabbit and a salad. Afterwards she placed before us a dish of cherries, the first of the season.

'As I wished to wash and freshen these, I begged the maid to go and draw me a bucket of cold water.

'In about five minutes she returned, declaring that the well was dry. She had lowered the rope to its full extent and the bucket had touched the bottom, and come up empty. Mother Lecacheur, anxious to examine the thing for herself, went and looked down the hole. She returned, announcing that one could see clearly something in the well, something altogether unusual. But this no doubt was bundles of straw, which a neighbour had thrown in out of spite.

'I wished to look down the well also, hoping I might be able to clear up the mystery, and I leaned over the edge and perceived indistinctly a white object. What could it be? I then conceived the idea of lowering a lantern at the end of a cord. When I did so the yellow flame danced on the layers of stone and gradually became clearer. All four of us were leaning over the opening, Sapeur and Céleste having now joined us. The lantern rested on a black-and-white indistinct mass, singular, incomprehensible. Sapeur exclaimed: "It is a horse. I see the hoofs. It must have got out of the meadow during the night and fallen in headlong."

'But suddenly a cold shiver froze me to the marrow. I first recognised a foot, then a leg sticking up; the whole body and the other leg were completely under water.

'I stammered out in a loud voice, trembling so violently that the lantern danced up and down above the shoe: "It is a woman who – who – is down there. It is Miss Harriet!"

'Sapeur alone did not manifest horror. He had seen many worse things in Africa.

'Mother Lecacheur and Céleste began to utter piercing screams and ran away.

'But it was necessary to recover the corpse of the dead woman. I attached the young man securely by the waist to the end of the pulley rope and lowered him very slowly, watching him disappear in the darkness. In one hand he held the lantern and a rope in the other. Soon

I recognised his voice, which seemed to come from the depths of the earth, saying: "Stop!"

'I then saw him fish something out of the water. It was the other leg. He then bound the two feet together and shouted anew: "Haul up!"

'I began to wind up, but I felt my arms crack, my muscles twitch, and I was in terror lest I should let the man fall to the bottom. When his head appeared at the brink, I asked: "Well?" as if I expected he had a message from the drowned woman.

'We both got on the stone slab at the edge of the well and from opposite sides we began to haul up the body.

'Mother Lecacheur and Céleste watched us from a distance, concealed from view behind the wall of the house. When they saw issuing from the hole the black shoes and white stockings of the drowned person they disappeared.

'Sapeur seized the ankles, and we drew up the body of the poor woman. The head was bruised and lacerated, and the long grey hair, out of curl for evermore, was hanging down tangled and disordered.

' "In the name of all that is holy! how thin she is," exclaimed Sapeur in a contemptuous tone.

'We carried her into the room, and as the women did not put in an appearance I, with the assistance of the stable-man, dressed the corpse for burial.

'I washed her disfigured face. Under the touch of my finger an eye was slightly opened and regarded me with that pale, cold look, that terrible look of a corpse which seems to come from the beyond. I braided as well as I could her dishevelled hair and with my clumsy hands arranged on her head a novel and singular coiffure. Then I took off her dripping garments, baring, not without a feeling of shame, as though I had been guilty of some profanation, her shoulders and her chest and her long arms, as slim as the twigs of a tree.

'Then I gathered some flowers, poppies, marguerites and fresh, sweet-smelling grass with which to strew her funeral couch.

'I next had to go through the usual formalities, as I was alone to attend to everything. A letter found in her pocket, written at the last moment, requested that her body be buried in the village in which she had passed the last days of her life. A sad suspicion weighed on my heart. Was it not on my account that she wished to be laid to rest in this place?

'Towards evening all the female gossips of the locality came to view the remains of the deceased, but I would not allow a single person to enter. I wanted to be alone, and I watched beside her all night.

'I looked at the corpse by the flickering light of the candles, at this unhappy woman, unknown to us all, who had died in such a lamentable manner and so far away from home. Had she left no friends, no relations behind her? What had her childhood been like? What had been her life? Whence had she come thither alone, a wanderer, lost like one driven from home? What secrets of sufferings and of despair were sealed up in that unprepossessing body, in that body whose outward appearance had driven from her all affection, all love?

'How many unhappy beings there are! I felt that there was laid upon that human creature the eternal injustice of implacable nature! It was all over with her, without her ever having experienced, perhaps, that which sustains the greatest outcasts – the hope of being loved once! Otherwise why should she thus have concealed herself, fled from the face of others? Why did she love everything so tenderly and so passionately, everything living that was not a man?

'I recognised the fact that she believed in God, and that she hoped to receive compensation from Him for all the miseries she had endured. She would now disintegrate and become, in turn, a plant. She would blossom in the sun, the cattle would browse on her leaves, the birds would bear away the seeds, and through these changes she would become again human flesh. But that which is called the soul had passed away at the bottom of the dark well. She suffered no longer. She had given her life for that of others yet to come.

'A pale light at length announced the dawn of a new day; then a red ray streamed in on the bed, making a bar of light across the coverlet and across her hands. This was the hour she had loved so much. The awakened birds began to sing in the trees.

'I opened the window to its fullest extent and drew back the curtains that the whole heavens might look in upon us, and, bending over the icy corpse, I took in my hands her head, and slowly, without terror or disgust, I imprinted upon those lips a kiss, a long kiss – the first they had ever received.'

Léon Chenal ceased speaking. The women wept. We heard on the box-seat the Comte d'Etraille blowing his nose from time to time. The coachman, unmoved, had gone to sleep. The horses, who no longer felt the touch of the whip, had slackened their pace and moved along slowly. The drag, hardly advancing at all, seemed suddenly to have lost the power of motion, as though heavily laden with sorrow.

The Necklace

She was one of those pretty and charming young girls who sometimes are born, as if by a slip of fate, into a family of clerks. She had no dowry, no expectations, no way of being known, understood, loved and wedded by any rich and distinguished man; so she let herself be married to a little clerk of the Ministry of Public Instruction.

She dressed plainly because she could not dress well, but she was as unhappy as if she had really fallen from a higher station; for with women there is neither caste nor rank, for beauty, grace and charm take the place of birth and breeding. Natural ingenuity, instinct for what is elegant and a supple mind are their sole hierarchy, and often make of women of the people the equals of the very greatest ladies.

Mathilde suffered ceaselessly, feeling herself born to enjoy all delicacies and all luxuries. She was distressed at the poverty of her dwelling, at the bareness of the walls, at the shabby chairs, the ugliness of the curtains. All those things, of which another woman of her rank would never even have been conscious, tortured her and made her angry. The sight of the little Breton peasant who did her humble housework aroused in her despairing regrets and bewildering dreams. She thought of silent antechambers hung with Oriental tapestry, illumined by tall bronze candelabra, and of two great footmen in knee breeches who sleep in the big armchairs, made drowsy by the oppressive heat of the stove. She thought of long reception halls hung with ancient silk, of the dainty cabinets containing priceless curiosities and of little coquettish perfumed reception rooms made for chatting at five o'clock with intimate friends, with men famous and sought after, whom all women envy and whose attention they all desire.

When she sat down to dinner, before the round table covered with a tablecloth in use three days, opposite her husband, who uncovered the soup tureen and declared with a delighted air, 'Ah, the good soup! I don't know anything better than that,' she thought of dainty dinners, of shining silverware, of tapestry that peopled the walls with ancient personages and with strange birds flying in the midst of a fairy forest; and she thought of delicious dishes served on marvellous plates and of the whispered gallantries to which you listen with a sphinx-like smile while you are eating the wings of a quail.

She had no gowns, no jewels, nothing. And she loved nothing but that. She felt made for that. She would have liked so much to please, to be envied, to be charming, to be sought after.

She had a friend, a former schoolmate at the convent, who was rich, and whom she did not like to go to see any more because she felt so sad when she came home.

But one evening her husband came home with a triumphant air and holding a large envelope in his hand.

'There,' said he, 'there is something for you.'

She tore the paper quickly and drew out a printed card which bore these words:

The Minister of Public Instruction and Madame Georges Ramponneau request the honour of M. and Madame Loisel's company at the palace of the Ministry on Monday evening, January 18th.

Instead of being delighted, as her husband had hoped, she threw the invitation on the table crossly, muttering: 'What do you wish me to do with that?'

'Why, my dear, I thought you would be glad. You never go out, and this is such a fine opportunity. I had great trouble to get it. Everyone wants to go; it is very select, and they are not giving many invitations to clerks. The whole official world will be there.'

She looked at him with an irritated glance and said impatiently: 'And what do you wish me to put on my back?'

He had not thought of that. He stammered: 'Why, the gown you go to the theatre in. It looks very well to me.'

He stopped, distracted, seeing that his wife was weeping. Two great tears ran slowly from the corners of her eyes towards the corners of her mouth.

'What's the matter? What's the matter?' he asked.

By a violent effort she conquered her grief and replied in a calm voice, while she wiped away her tears: 'Nothing. Only I have no gown, and, therefore, I can't go to this ball. Give your card to some colleague whose wife is better equipped than I am.'

He was in despair. He resumed: 'Come, let us see, Mathilde. How much would it cost, a suitable gown, which you could use on other occasions – something very simple?'

She reflected several seconds, making her calculations and wondering also what sum she could ask without drawing on herself an immediate refusal and a frightened exclamation from the economical clerk.

Finally she replied hesitatingly: 'I don't know exactly, but I think I could manage it with four hundred francs.'

He grew a little pale, because he was laying aside just that amount to buy a gun and treat himself to a little shooting next summer on the plain of Nanterre, with several friends who went to shoot larks there of a Sunday.

But he said: 'Very well. I will give you four hundred francs. But try to get a really pretty gown.'

The day of the ball drew near and Madame Loisel seemed sad, uneasy, anxious. Her frock was ready, however. Her husband said to her one evening: 'What is the matter? Come, you have seemed very queer these last three days.'

And she answered: 'It annoys me not to have a single piece of jewellery, not a single ornament, nothing to put on. I shall look poverty-stricken. I would almost rather not go at all.'

'You might wear natural flowers,' said her husband. 'They're quite fashionable at this time of year. For ten francs you can get two or three magnificent roses.'

She was not convinced.

'No; there's nothing more humiliating than looking poor among other women who are rich.'

'How stupid you are!' her husband cried. 'Go and look up your friend, Madame Forestier, and ask her to lend you some jewels. You're intimate enough with her to do that.'

She uttered a cry of joy: 'True! I never thought of it.'

The next day she went to her friend and told her of her distress.

Madame Forestier went to a wardrobe with a mirror, took out a large jewel box, brought it back, opened it and said to Madame Loisel: 'Choose, my dear.'

She saw first some bracelets, then a pearl necklace, then a Venetian gold cross set with precious stones, of admirable workmanship. She tried on the ornaments before the mirror, hesitated and could not make up her mind to part with them, to give them back. She kept asking: 'Haven't you any more?'

'Why, yes. Look further; I don't know what you like.'

Suddenly she discovered, in a black satin box, a superb diamond necklace, and her heart throbbed with an immoderate desire. Her hands trembled as she took it. She fastened it round her throat, and was lost in ecstasy at her reflection in the mirror.

Then she asked, hesitating, filled with anxious doubt: 'Will you lend me this, only this?'

'Why, yes, certainly.'

She threw her arms round her friend's neck, kissed her passionately, and then fled with her treasure.

The night of the ball arrived. Madame Loisel was a great success. She was prettier than any other woman present, elegant, graceful, smiling and filled with joy. All the men looked at her, asked her name, sought to be introduced. All the attachés of the Cabinet wished to waltz with her. She was remarked by the Minister himself.

She danced with rapture, with passion, intoxicated by pleasure, forgetting all in the triumph of her beauty, in the glory of her success, in a sort of cloud of happiness composed of all this homage and admiration, and of that sense of victory which is so sweet to woman's heart.

She left the ball about four o'clock in the morning. Her husband had been sleeping since midnight in a little deserted anteroom with three other gentlemen whose wives were enjoying the ball.

He threw over her shoulders the wraps he had brought, the modest wraps of common life, the poverty of which contrasted with the elegance of the ball dress. She felt this and wished to escape so as not to be remarked by the other women, who were enveloping themselves in costly furs.

Loisel held her back, saying: 'Wait a bit. You will catch cold outside. I will call a cab.'

But she did not listen to him and rapidly descended the stairs. When they reached the street they could not find a carriage and began to look for one, shouting after the cabmen passing at a distance.

They went towards the Seine in despair, shivering with cold. At last they found on the quay one of those ancient night cabs which, as though they were ashamed to show their shabbiness during the day, are never seen round Paris until after dark.

It took them to their dwelling in the Rue des Martyrs, and sadly they mounted the stairs to their flat. All was ended for her. As to him, he reflected that he must be at the ministry at ten o'clock that morning.

She removed her wraps before the glass so as to see herself once more in all her glory. But suddenly she uttered a cry. She no longer had the necklace round her neck!

'What is the matter with you?' demanded her husband, already half undressed.

She turned distractedly towards him.

'I have – I have – I've lost Madame Forestier's necklace,' she cried.

He stood up, bewildered.

'What! – how? Impossible!'

They looked among the folds of her skirt, of her cloak, in her pockets, everywhere, but did not find it.

'You're sure you had it on when you left the ball?' he asked.

'Yes, I felt it in the vestibule of the Minister's house.'

'But if you had lost it in the street we should have heard it fall. It must be in the cab.'

'Yes, probably. Did you take his number?'

'No. And you – didn't you notice it?'

'No.'

They looked, thunderstruck, at each other. At last Loisel put on his clothes.

'I shall go back on foot,' said he, 'over the whole route, to see whether I can find it.'

He went out. She sat waiting on a chair in her ball dress, without strength to go to bed, overwhelmed, without any fire, without a thought.

Her husband returned about seven o'clock. He had found nothing.

He went to police headquarters, to the newspaper offices to offer a reward; he went to the cab companies – everywhere, in fact, whither he was urged by the least spark of hope.

She waited all day, in the same condition of mad fear before this terrible calamity.

Loisel returned at night with a hollow, pale face. He had discovered nothing.

'You must write to your friend,' said he, 'that you have broken the clasp of her necklace and that you are having it mended. That will give us time to turn round.'

She wrote at his dictation.

At the end of a week they had lost all hope. Loisel, who had aged five years, declared: 'We must consider how to replace that ornament.'

The next day they took the box that had contained it and went to the jeweller whose name was found within. He consulted his books.

'It was not I, madame, who sold that necklace; I must simply have furnished the case.'

Then they went from jeweller to jeweller, searching for a necklace like the other, trying to recall it, both sick with chagrin and grief.

They found, in a shop at the Palais Royal, a string of diamonds that seemed to them exactly like the one they had lost. It was worth forty thousand francs. They could have it for thirty-six.

So they begged the jeweller not to sell it for three days yet. And they made a bargain that he should buy it back for thirty-four thousand francs, in case they should find the lost necklace before the end of February.

Loisel possessed eighteen thousand francs which his father had left him. He would borrow the rest.

He did borrow, asking a thousand francs of one, five hundred of another, five louis here, three louis there. He gave notes, took up ruinous obligations, dealt with usurers and all the race of lenders. He compromised all the rest of his life, risked signing a note without even knowing whether he could meet it; and, frightened by the trouble yet to come, by the black misery that was about to fall upon him, by the prospect of all the physical privations and moral tortures that he was to suffer, he went to get the new necklace, laying upon the jeweller's counter thirty-six thousand francs.

When Madame Loisel took back the necklace, Madame Forestier said to her with a chilly manner: 'You should have returned it sooner; I might have needed it .'

She did not open the case, as her friend had so much feared. If she had detected the substitution, what would she have thought, what would she have said? Would she not have taken Madame Loisel for a thief?

Thereafter Madame Loisel knew the horrible existence of the needy. She bore her part, however, with sudden heroism. That dreadful debt must be paid. She would pay it. They dismissed their servant; they changed their lodgings; they rented a garret under the roof.

She came to know what heavy housework meant and the odious cares of the kitchen. She washed the dishes, using her dainty fingers and rosy nails on greasy pots and pans. She washed the soiled linen, the shirts and the dishcloths, which she dried upon a line; she took the slops down to the street every morning and carried up the water, stopping for breath at every landing. And dressed like a woman of the people, she went to the fruiterer, the grocer, the butcher, a basket on her arm, bargaining, meeting with impertinence, eking out her miserable money, sou by sou.

Every month they had to meet some notes, renew others, obtain more time.

Her husband worked in the evenings, making up a tradesman's accounts, and late at night he often copied manuscript for five sous a page.

This life lasted ten years.

At the end of ten years they had paid everything, everything with the rates of usury and the accumulations of the compound interest.

Madame Loisel looked old now. She had become the woman of impoverished households – strong and hard and rough. With frowsy hair, skirts askew and red hands, she talked loud while washing the floor with great swishes of water. But sometimes, when her husband was at the office, she sat down near the window and thought of that gay evening of long ago, of that ball where she had looked so beautiful and been so much admired.

What would have happened if she had not lost that necklace? Who knows? who knows? How strange and changeful is life! How small a thing is needed to make or ruin us!

But one Sunday, having gone to take a walk in the Champs Elysées to refresh herself after the labours of the week, she suddenly saw a woman who was leading a child. It was Madame Forestier, still young, still beautiful, still charming.

Madame Loisel felt moved. Should she speak to her? Yes, certainly. And now that she had paid, she would tell her all about it. Why not?

She went up.

'Good day, Jeanne.'

The other, astonished to be familiarly addressed by this plain good-wife, did not recognise her at all and stammered: 'But – madame! – I do not know – You must be mistaken.'

'No. I am Mathilde Loisel.'

Her friend uttered a cry. 'Oh, my poor Mathilde! How you are changed!'

'Yes, I have had a very hard life, since I last saw you, and great poverty – and that because of you!'

'Of me! How so?'

'Do you remember that diamond necklace you lent me to wear at the ministerial ball?'

'Yes. Well?'

'Well, I lost it.'

'What do you mean? You brought it back.'

'I brought you back another exactly like it. And it has taken us ten years to pay for it. You can understand that it was not easy for us, for us who had nothing. At last it is ended, and I am very glad.'

Madame Forestier had stopped.

'You say that you bought a necklace of diamonds to replace mine?'

'Yes. You never noticed it, then! They were very similar.' And she smiled with a joy that was at once proud and ingenuous.

Madame Forestier, deeply moved, took her hands.

'Oh, my poor Mathilde! Why, my necklace was paste! It was worth at most only five hundred francs !'

Mademoiselle Pearl

What a strange idea it was for me to choose Mademoiselle Pearl for queen that evening!

Every year I celebrate Twelfth Night with my old friend Chantal. My father, who was his most intimate friend, used to take me round there when I was a child. I continued the custom, and doubtless shall continue it as long as I live and as long as there is a Chantal in this world.

The Chantals lead a peculiar existence; they live in Paris as though they were in Grasse, Yvetot or Pont-à-Mousson.

They have a house with a little garden near the Observatory. They live there as though they were in the country. Of Paris, the real Paris, they know nothing at all; they suspect nothing; they are so far, so far away! However, from time to time, they take a trip into it. Madame Chantal goes to lay in her provisions, as it is called in the family. This is how they go to purchase their provisions:

Mademoiselle Pearl, who has the keys to the kitchen closet (for the linen closets are administered by the mistress herself), gives warning that the supply of sugar is low, that the preserves are giving out, that there is not much left in the bottom of the coffee bag. Thus warned against famine, Madame Chantal passes everything in review, taking notes on a pad.

Then she puts down a lot of figures and goes through lengthy calculations and long discussions with Mademoiselle Pearl. At last they manage to agree, and they decide upon the quantity of each thing of which they will lay in a three months' provision: sugar, rice, prunes, coffee, preserves, cans of peas, beans, lobster, salt or smoked fish, etc. After which the day for the purchasing is determined on, and they go in a cab with a railing round the top and drive to a large grocery store on the other side of the river in the new section of the town.

Madame Chantal and Mademoiselle Pearl make this trip together, mysteriously, and only return at dinner time, tired out, although still excited, and shaken up by the cab, the roof of which is covered with bundles and bags, like an express wagon.

For the Chantals all that part of Paris situated on the other side of the Seine constitutes the new quarter, a section inhabited by a strange, noisy population, which cares little for honour, spends its days in dissipation, its nights in revelry, and throws money out of the windows. From time to time, however, the young girls are taken to the Opéra-Comique or the Théâtre Français, when the play is recommended by the paper which is read by Monsieur Chantal.

At present the young ladies are respectively nineteen and seventeen. They are two pretty girls, tall and fresh, very well brought up, in fact, too well brought up, so much so that they pass by unperceived like two pretty dolls. Never would the idea come to me to pay the slightest attention or to pay court to one of the young Chantal girls; they are so immaculate that one hardly dares speak to them; one almost feels indecent when bowing to them.

As for the father, he is a charming man, well educated, frank, cordial, but he likes calm and quiet above all else, and has thus contributed greatly to the mummifying of his family in order to live as he pleased in stagnant quiescence. He reads a lot, loves to talk and is easily moved. Lack of contact and of elbowing with the world has made his moral skin very tender and sensitive. The slightest thing affects him, excites him, and makes him suffer.

The Chantals have limited connections carefully chosen in the neighbourhood. They also exchange two or three yearly visits with relatives who live some distance from Paris.

As for me, I have dinner with them on the fifteenth of August and on Twelfth Night. That is as much one of my duties as Easter communion is for a Catholic.

On the fifteenth of August a few friends are invited, but on Twelfth Night I am the only guest.

Well, this year, as in former years, I went to the Chantals' for my Epiphany dinner.

According to my usual custom, I kissed Monsieur Chantal, Madame Chantal and Mademoiselle Pearl, and I made a deep bow to the Misses Louise and Pauline. I was questioned about a thousand and one things: about what had happened on the boulevards, about politics, about how matters stood in Tonkin, and about our representatives in Parliament. Madame Chantal, a fat lady, whose ideas always gave me the impression of being carved out square like building stones, was accustomed to exclaim at the end of every political discussion: 'All that is seed which does not promise much for the future!' Why have I always imagined that Madame Chantal's ideas are square? I don't know; but everything that she says takes that shape in my head: a big square, with four symmetrical angles. There are other people whose ideas always strike me as being round and rolling like a hoop. As soon as they begin a sentence on any subject it rolls on and on, coming out in ten, twenty, fifty round ideas, large and small, which I see rolling along, one behind the other, to the end of the horizon. Other people have pointed ideas – but enough of this.

We sat down as usual and finished our dinner without anything out of the ordinary being said. At dessert, the Twelfth Night cake was brought on. Now, Monsieur Chantal had been king every year. I don't know whether this was the result of continued chance or a family convention, but he unfailingly found the bean in his piece of cake, and he would proclaim Madame Chantal to be queen. Therefore, I was greatly surprised to find something very hard, which almost made me break a tooth, in a mouthful of cake. Gently I took this thing from my mouth and I saw that it was a little porcelain doll, no bigger than a bean. Surprise caused me to exclaim: 'Ah!' All looked at me, and Chantal clapped his hands and cried: 'It's Gaston! It's Gaston! Long live the king! Long live the king!'

All took up the chorus: 'Long live the king!' And I blushed to the tip of my ears, as one often does, without any reason at all, in situations which are a little foolish. I sat there looking at my plate, with this absurd little bit of pottery in my fingers, forcing myself to laugh and not knowing what to do or say, when Chantal once more cried out: 'Now, you must choose a queen!'

Then I was thunderstruck. In a second a thousand thoughts and suppositions flashed through my mind. Did they expect me to pick out one of the young Chantal ladies? Was that a trick to make me say which one I preferred? Was it a gentle, light, direct hint of the parents towards a possible marriage? The idea of marriage roams continually in houses with grown-up girls, and takes every shape and disguise, and employs every subterfuge. A dread of compromising myself took hold of me as well as an extreme timidity before the obstinately correct and reserved attitude of the Misses Louise and Pauline. To choose one of them in preference to the other seemed to me as difficult as choosing between two drops of water; and then the fear of launching myself into an affair which might, in spite of me, lead me gently into matrimonial ties, by means as wary and imperceptible and as calm as this insignificant royalty – the fear of all this haunted me.

Suddenly I had an inspiration, and I held out to Mademoiselle Pearl the symbolical emblem. At first everyone was surprised, then they doubtless appreciated my delicacy and discretion, for they applauded furiously. Everybody was crying: 'Long live the queen! Long live the queen!'

As for herself, poor old maid, she was so amazed that she completely lost control of herself; she was trembling and stammering: 'No – no – oh! no – not me – please – not me – I beg of you –'

Then for the first time in my life I looked at Mademoiselle Pearl and wondered what she was.

I was accustomed to seeing her in this house, just as one sees old upholstered armchairs on which one has been sitting since childhood without ever noticing them. One day, with no reason at all, because a ray of sunshine happens to strike the seat, you suddenly think: 'Why, that chair is very curious'; and then you discover that the wood has been worked by a real artist and that the material is remarkable. I had never thoughtfully observed Mademoiselle Pearl.

She was a part of the Chantal family, that was all. But how? By what right? She was a tall, thin person who tried to remain in the background, but who was by no means insignificant. She was treated in a friendly manner, better than a housekeeper, but not so well as a relative. I suddenly noticed several shades of distinction that I had never observed before. Madame Chantal said: 'Pearl,' the young ladies: 'Mademoiselle Pearl,' and Chantal only addressed her as 'Mademoiselle', with an air of greater respect, perhaps.

How old could she be? Forty? Yes, forty. She was not old; she made herself old. I was suddenly struck by this fact. She dressed in a ridiculous manner, but yet she was not in the least ridiculous; she had such simple, natural gracefulness, veiled and hidden. Truly, what a strange creature! How was it I had never observed her before? She dressed her hair in a grotesque manner with little old maid curls, most absurd; but beneath this, one could see a large, calm brow, cut by two deep lines, two wrinkles of long sadness, then two blue eyes, large and tender, so timid, so bashful, so humble, two beautiful eyes that had kept the expression of naïve wonder of a young girl, of youthful sensations, and also of sorrow, which had softened without spoiling them.

Her whole face was refined, a face the expression of which seemed to have gone out without being used up or faded by the fatigues and great emotions of life.

What a dainty mouth! and such pretty teeth! But one would have thought that she did not dare to smile.

Suddenly I compared her to Madame Chantal! Undoubtedly Mademoiselle Pearl was the better of the two, a hundred times better, daintier, prouder, more noble. I was surprised at my observation. They were pouring out champagne. I held my glass up to the queen and, with a well-turned compliment, I drank to her health. I could see that she felt inclined to hide her head in her napkin. Then, as she was dipping her lips in the clear wine, everybody cried: 'The queen drinks! the queen drinks!' She almost turned purple and choked. Everybody was laughing; but I could see that all loved her.

As soon as dinner was over Chantal took me by the arm. It was time for his cigar, a sacred hour. When alone, he would smoke it out in the street; when guests came to dinner he would take them to the billiard-room and smoke while playing. That evening they had lit a fire to celebrate Twelfth Night; my old friend took his cue, a very fine one, and chalked it with great care; then he said: 'You break, my boy!'

He called me 'my boy', although I was twenty-five, but he had known me as a young child.

I started the game and made a few cannons. I missed some others, but as the thought of Mademoiselle Pearl kept returning to my mind, I suddenly asked: 'By the way, Monsieur Chantal, is Mademoiselle Pearl a relative of yours?'

Greatly surprised, he stopped playing and looked at me: 'What! Don't you know? Haven't you heard about Mademoiselle Pearl?'

'No.'

'Didn't your father ever tell you?'

'No.'

'Well, well, that's strange! That certainly is strange! Why, it's a regular romance!'

He paused, and then continued: 'And if you only knew how odd it is that you should ask me that today, on Twelfth Night!'

'Why?'

'Why? Well, listen. Forty-one years ago today, the day of the Epiphany, we were living at Roüy-le-Tors, on the ramparts; but in order that you may understand, I must first explain the house. Roüy is built on a hill, or, rather, on a mound that overlooks a great plain. We had a house there with a beautiful hanging garden supported by the old battlemented wall; so that the house was in the town on the street, while the garden overlooked the plain. There was a door leading from the garden to the open country, at the bottom of a secret stair in the thick wall – the kind you read about in novels. A road passed in front of this door, which was provided with a big bell; for the peasants used to bring their provisions up this way.

'You now see the place, don't you? Well, this year, at Epiphany, it had been snowing for a week. One might have thought that the world was coming to an end. When we went to the ramparts to look over the plain, this immense white, frozen country, which shone like varnish, would chill our very souls. One might have thought that the Lord had packed the world in cottonwool to put it away in the store-room for old worlds.

'We were a very numerous family at that time: my father, my mother, my uncle and aunt, my two brothers and four cousins; they were pretty little girls; I married the youngest. Of all those, there are only three of us left: my wife, I, and my sister-in-law, who lives in Marseilles. Mon Dieu! how quickly a family like that dwindles away! I tremble when I think of it! I was fifteen years old then, now I am fifty-six.

'We were going to celebrate the Epiphany, and we were all happy, very happy! Everybody was in the parlour, awaiting dinner, and my oldest brother, Jacques, said: 'There has been a dog howling on the plain for about ten minutes; the poor beast must be lost.'

'He had hardly stopped talking when the garden bell began to ring. It had the deep sound of a church bell, which made one think of death. A shiver ran through everybody. My father called the servant and told him to go outside and look. We waited in complete silence; we were thinking of the snow which covered the ground. When the man returned he declared that he had seen nothing. The dog kept up its ceaseless howling, and always from the same spot.

'We sat down to dinner; but we were all uneasy, especially the young people. Everything went well up to the roast, then the bell began to ring again, three times in succession, three heavy, long strokes which stopped our conversation short. We sat there looking at each other, forks in the air, still listening, and shaken by fear of some of supernatural horror.

'At last my mother spoke: "It's surprising that they should have waited so long to come back. Do not go alone, Baptiste; one of these gentlemen will accompany you."

'My Uncle François arose. He was a kind of Hercules, very proud of his strength, and feared nothing in the world. My father said to him: "Take a gun. There is no telling what it might be."

'But my uncle only took a cane and went out with the servant.

'We others remained there trembling with fear and apprehension, without eating or speaking. My father tried to reassure us: "Just wait and see," he said; "it will be some beggar or some traveller lost in the snow. After ringing once, seeing that the door was not immediately opened, he attempted again to find his way, and being unable to, he has returned."

'My uncle seemed to stay away an hour. At last he came back, furious, swearing: "Nothing at all; it's some practical joker! There is nothing but that damned dog howling away at about a hundred yards from the walls. If I had taken a gun I would have killed him to keep him quiet."

'We sat down to dinner again, but everyone was overwrought; we felt that all was not over, that something was going to happen, that the bell would soon ring again.

'It rang just as the Twelfth Night cake was being cut. All the men jumped up together. My Uncle François, who had been drinking champagne, swore so furiously that he would murder it, whatever it might be, that my mother and my aunt threw themselves on him to prevent his going. My father, although very calm and a little helpless (he had limped ever since he had broken his leg when thrown by a horse), declared, in turn, that he wished to find out what was the matter and that he was going. My brothers, aged eighteen and twenty, ran to get their guns; and as no one was paying any attention to me I snatched up a little rifle that was used in the garden and got ready to accompany the expedition.

'It started out immediately. My father and uncle were walking ahead with Baptiste, who was carrying a lantern. My brothers, Jacques and Paul, followed, and I followed behind in spite of the prayers of my mother, who stood in front of the house with her sister and my cousins.

'It had been snowing again for the last hour, and the trees were weighed down. The pines were bending under this heavy, white garment, and looked like white pyramids or enormous sugar cones, and through the grey curtains of small hurrying flakes could be seen the lighter bushes that stood out pale in the shadow. The snow was falling so thick that we could hardly see ten feet ahead of us. But the lantern threw a bright light around us. When we began to go down the winding stairway in the wall I really grew frightened. I felt as though someone were walking behind me, were going to grab me by the shoulders and carry me away, and I had a strong desire to return; but, as I would have had to cross the garden all alone, I did not dare. I heard someone opening the door leading to the plain; my uncle began to swear again, exclaiming: "By God! He has gone again! If I can catch sight of even his shadow, I'll take care not to miss him, the swine!"

'It was a discouraging thing to see this great expanse of plain, or, rather, to feel it before us, for we could not see it; we could only see a thick, endless veil of snow, above, below, opposite us, to the right, to the left, everywhere. My uncle continued: "Listen! There is the dog howling again; I will show him how I can shoot. That will be something gained, anyhow."

'But my father, who was kind-hearted, told him: "It will be much better to go on and find the poor animal. The miserable fellow is barking for help; he is calling like a man in distress. Let us go to him."

'So we started out through this mist, through this thick, continuous fall of snow, which filled the air, which moved, floated, fell, and chilled the skin with a burning sensation like a sharp, rapid pain as each flake melted. We were sinking in up to our knees in this soft, cold mass, and we had to lift our feet very high in order to walk. As we advanced the dog's voice became clearer and stronger. My uncle cried: "Here he is!" We stopped to observe him as one does when one meets an enemy at night.

'I could see nothing, so I ran up to the others, and I caught sight of him; he was frightful and weird-looking; he was a big black shepherd's dog with long hair and a wolf's head, standing just within the gleam of light cast by our lantern on the snow. He did not move; he was silently watching us.

'My uncle said: "That's peculiar, he is neither advancing nor retreating. I feel like taking a shot at him."

'My father answered in a firm voice: "No, we must capture him."

'Then my brother Jacques observed: "But he is not alone. There is something behind him."

'There was indeed something behind him, something grey, impossible to distinguish. We started out again cautiously. When he saw us approaching the dog sat down. He did not look wicked. Instead, he seemed pleased at having been able to attract the attention of someone.

'My father went straight to him and petted him. The dog licked his hands. We saw that he was tied to the wheel of a little carriage, a sort of toy carriage entirely wrapped up in three or four woollen blankets. We carefully took off these coverings, and as Baptiste approached with his lantern to the front of this little vehicle, which looked like a rolling kennel, we saw in it a little baby sleeping peacefully.

'We were so astonished that we couldn't speak. My father was the first to collect his wits, and as he had a warm heart and a broad mind, he stretched his hand over the roof of the carriage and said: "Poor little waif, you shall be one of us!" And he ordered my brother Jacques to take the carriage with the foundling ahead of us. Thinking out loud, my father continued: "Some child of love whose poor mother rang at my door on this night of Epiphany in memory of the Child of God."

'He once more stopped and called at the top of his lungs through the night: "We have found it!" Then, putting his hand on his brother's shoulder, he murmured: "What if you had shot the dog, François?"

'My uncle did not answer, but in the darkness he crossed himself, for, notwithstanding his blustering manner, he was very religious.

'The dog, which had been untied, was following us.

'Ah! But you should have seen us when we got to the house! At first we had a lot of trouble in getting the carriage up through the winding stairway; but we succeeded and even rolled it into the vestibule.

'How funny mamma was! How happy and astonished! And my four little cousins (the youngest was only six), they looked like four chickens round a nest. At last we took the child from the carriage. It was still sleeping. It was a girl about six weeks old. In its clothes we found ten thousand francs in gold; yes, my boy, ten thousand francs! – which papa saved for her dowry. Therefore, it was not a child of poor people, but, perhaps, the child of some nobleman and a little bourgeoise of the town – or again – we made a thousand suppositions, but we never found out anything – never the slightest clue. The dog himself was recognised by no one. It was a stranger in the country. At any rate, the person who rang three times at our door must have known my parents well, to have chosen them thus.

'That is how, at the age of six weeks, Mademoiselle Pearl entered the Chantal household.

'It was not until later that she was called Mademoiselle Pearl. She was at first baptised "Marie Simonne Claire", Claire being intended for her family name.

'I can assure you that our return to the dining-room was amusing, with this baby now awake and looking round her at these people and these lights with her vague blue questioning eyes.

'We sat down to dinner again and the cake was cut. I was king, and for queen I took Mademoiselle Pearl, just as you did today. On that day she did not appreciate the honour that was being shown her.

'Well, the child was adopted and brought up in the family. She grew, and the years passed. She was so gentle and loving that everyone would have spoiled her abominably had not my mother prevented it.

'My mother was an orderly woman with a great respect for class distinctions. She consented to treat little Claire as she did her own sons, but, nevertheless, she wished the distance which separated us to be well marked, and our positions well established. Therefore, as soon as the child could understand, she acquainted her with her story and gently, even tenderly, impressed on the little one's mind that, for the Chantals, she was an adopted daughter, taken in, but, nevertheless, a stranger. Claire understood the situation with peculiar intelligence and with surprising instinct; she knew how to take the place which was allotted her, and to keep it with so much tact, gracefulness and gentleness that she often brought tears to my father's eyes. My mother herself was so often moved by the passionate gratitude and timid devotion of this dainty and loving little creature that she began calling her: "My daughter." At times, when the little one had done something kind and good, my mother would raise her spectacles on her forehead, a thing which always indicated emotion with her, and she would repeat: "This child is a pearl, a perfect pearl!" This name stuck to the little Claire, who became and remained for us Mademoiselle Pearl.'

Monsieur Chantal stopped. He was sitting on the edge of the billiard table, his feet hanging, and was playing with a ball with his left hand, while with his right he crumpled a rag which served to rub the chalk marks from the slate. A little red in the face, his voice thick, he was talking away to himself now, lost in his memories, gently drifting through the old scenes and events which awoke in his mind, just as we walk through old family gardens where we were brought up and where each tree, each walk, each hedge reminds us of some occurrence.

I stood opposite him, leaning against the wall, my hands resting on my idle cue.

After a slight pause he continued: 'By Jove! She was pretty at eighteen – and graceful – and perfect. Ah! She was so sweet – and good and true – and charming! She had such eyes – blue – transparent – clear – such eyes as I have never seen since!'

He was once more silent. I asked: 'Why did she never marry?'

He answered, not to me, but to the word 'marry' which had caught his ear: 'Why? why? She never would – she never would! She had a dowry of thirty thousand francs, and she received several offers – but she never would! She seemed sad at that time. That was when I married my cousin, little Charlotte, my wife, to whom I had been engaged for six years.'

I looked at Monsieur Chantal, and it seemed to me that I was looking into his very soul and was suddenly witnessing one of those humble tragedies of honest, straightforward, blameless hearts, one of those secret tragedies known to no one, not even to the silent and resigned victims. A rash intuition suddenly impelled me to exclaim: 'You should have married her, Monsieur Chantal!'

He started, looked at me, and said: 'I? Marry whom?'

'Mademoiselle Pearl.'

'Why?'

'Because you loved her more than your cousin.'

He stared at me with strange, round, bewildered eyes and stammered: 'I loved her – I? How? Who told you that?'

'Why, anyone can see that – and it's even on account of her that you delayed for so long your marriage to your cousin – who had been waiting for you for six years.'

He dropped the ball which he was holding in his left hand, and, seizing the chalk rag in both hands, he buried his face in it and began to sob. He was weeping in a heart-breaking yet ridiculous manner. He was coughing, spitting and blowing his nose in the chalk rag, wiping his eyes and sneezing; then the tears would again begin to flow down the wrinkles on his face and he would make a strange gurgling noise in his throat. I felt bewildered, ashamed; I wanted to run away, and I no longer knew what to say, do, or venture to do.

Suddenly Madame Chantal's voice sounded on the stairs. 'Haven't you men finished smoking your cigars?'

I opened the door and cried: 'Yes, madame, we are coming in a minute.'

Then I rushed to her husband, and, seizing him by the shoulders, I cried: 'Monsieur Chantal, my friend Chantal, listen to me; your wife is calling; pull yourself together; we must go downstairs.'

He stammered: 'Yes – yes – I am coming – poor girl! I am coming – tell her that I am coming.'

He began very carefully to wipe his face on the cloth which, for the last two or three years, had been used for cleaning off the chalk from his slate; as a result he was now half white and half red, his forehead, nose, cheeks and chin covered with chalk, and his eyes swollen, still full of tears.

I caught him by the hands and dragged him into his bedroom, muttering: 'I beg your pardon, I beg your pardon, Monsieur Chantal, for having caused you such sorrow – but – I did not know – you – you understand.'

He squeezed my hand, saying: 'Yes – yes – there are difficult moments.'

Then he plunged his face into a bowl of water. When he emerged from it he did not yet seem to me to be presentable; but I thought of a little stratagem. As he was growing worried, looking at himself in the mirror, I said to him: 'All you have to do is to say that a little dust flew into your eye and you can cry before everybody to your heart's content.'

He went downstairs rubbing his eyes with his handkerchief. All were worried; each one wished to look for the speck, which could not be found; and stories were told of similar cases where it had been necessary to call in a physician.

I went over to Mademoiselle Pearl and watched her, tormented by an ardent curiosity, which was turning to positive suffering. She must indeed have been pretty, with her gentle, calm eyes, so large that it looked as though she never closed them like other mortals. Her gown was a little ridiculous, a real old maid's gown, which was unbecoming but could not make her look graceless.

It seemed to me as though I were looking into her soul, just as I had into Monsieur Chantal's; that I was looking right from one end to the other of this humble life, so simple and devoted. I felt an irresistible longing to question her, to find out whether she, too, had loved him; whether she also had suffered, as he had, from this long, secret, poignant grief, which one cannot see, know, or guess, but which breaks forth at night in the loneliness of a dark room. I was watching her, and I could observe her heart beating. I wondered whether this sweet, candid face had wept on the soft pillow, her whole body shaken by the violence of her anguish.

I said to her in a low voice, like a child who is breaking a toy to see what is inside: 'If you could have seen Monsieur Chantal crying a while ago it would have moved you.'

She started, asking: 'What? He was weeping?'

'Ah, yes, he was indeed weeping!'

'Why?'

She seemed deeply moved. I answered: 'On your account.'

'On my account?'

'Yes. He was telling me how much he had loved you in the days gone by; and what a pang it had given him to marry his cousin instead of you.'

Her pale face seemed to grow a little longer; her calm eyes, which always remained open, suddenly closed so quickly that they seemed shut for ever. She slipped from her chair to the floor, and slowly, gently sank down as would a fallen garment.

I cried: 'Help! help! Mademoiselle Pearl is ill.'

Madame Chantal and her daughters rushed forward, and while they were looking for towels, water and vinegar, I ran out of the house.

I walked away with rapid strides, my heart heavy, my mind full of remorse and regret. And yet at the same time I felt pleased; I felt as though I had done a praiseworthy and necessary act. I asked myself again and again, 'Did I do wrong or right? They had their love for each other shut up in their hearts, just as some people carry a bullet in a closed wound. Will they not be happier now? It was too late for their torture to begin over again but not too late for them to remember it with tenderness.

And perhaps some evening, moved by a beam of moonlight falling through the branches at their feet, they will join and press their hands in memory of all this cruel and suppressed suffering; and, perhaps also, this hour will bring to those two dead souls more happiness in an instant than others can find during a whole lifetime!

The Piece of String

It was market-day, and from all the country round Goderville the peasants and their wives were coming towards the town. The men walked slowly, throwing the whole body forward at every step of their long, crooked legs. They were deformed from pushing the plough which makes the left shoulder higher, and bends their figures sideways; from reaping the grain, when they have to spread their legs so as to keep on their feet. Their starched blue blouses, glossy as though varnished, ornamented at collar and cuffs with a little embroidered design and blown out round their bony bodies, looked very much like balloons, whence issued two arms and two feet.

Some of these fellows dragged a cow or a calf at the end of a rope. And just behind the animal followed their wives beating it over the back with a leaf-covered branch to hasten its pace, and carrying large baskets out of which protruded the heads of chickens or ducks. These women walked more quickly and energetically than the men, with their erect, dried-up figures, adorned with scanty little shawls pinned over their flat bosoms, and their heads wrapped round with a white cloth, enclosing the hair and surmounted by a cap.

Now a wagonette passed by, jogging along behind a horse and shaking up strangely the two men on the seat, and the woman at the bottom of the cart who held fast to its sides to lessen the hard jolting.

In the marketplace at Goderville was a great crowd, a mingled multitude of men and beasts. The horns of cattle, the high, long-napped hats of wealthy peasants, the head-dresses of the women rose above the surface of the throng. And the sharp, shrill, barking voices made a continuous, wild din, while above it occasionally rose a huge burst of laughter from the sturdy lungs of a merry peasant or a prolonged bellow from a cow tied fast to the wall of a house.

Everywhere were the smells of the stable, of milk, of hay, of perspiration, and of that half-human, half-animal odour which is peculiar to country folks.

Maître Hauchecorne, of Bréauté, had just arrived at Goderville and was making his way towards the square when he perceived on the ground a little piece of string. Maître Hauchecorne, economical as are all true Normans, reflected that everything was worth picking up which could be of any use, and he stooped down, painfully, because he suffered from rheumatism. He took the bit of thin string from the ground and was carefully preparing to roll it up when he saw Maître Malandain, the harness-maker, on his doorstep staring at him. They had once had a quarrel about a halter, and they had borne each other malice ever since. Maître Hauchecorne was overcome with a sort of shame at being seen by his enemy picking up a bit of string on the road. He quickly hid it beneath his blouse and then slipped it into his breeches pocket, then pretended to be still looking for something in the dust which he did not discover and finally went off towards the marketplace, his head bent forward and his body almost doubled in two by rheumatic pains.

He was at once lost in the crowd, which kept moving about slowly and noisily as it bickered and bargained. The peasants examined the cows, went off, came back, always in doubt for fear of being cheated, never quite daring to decide, looking the seller square in the eye in the effort to discover the tricks of the man and the defect in the beast.

The women, having placed their great baskets at their feet, had taken out the poultry, which lay upon the ground, their legs tied together, with terrified eyes and scarlet combs.

They listened to propositions, maintaining their prices in a decided manner with an impassive face or perhaps deciding to accept the smaller price offered, suddenly calling out to the customer who was starting to go away: 'All right, I'll let you have them, Maît' Anthime.'

Then, little by little, the square became empty, and when the Angelus struck midday those who lived at a distance poured into the inns.

At Jourdain's the great room was filled with diners, just as the vast court was filled with vehicles of every sort – wagons, gigs, carts, tilburies, innumerable vehicles which have no name, yellow with mud, misshapen, pieced together, some raising their shafts to heaven like two arms, some with their noses on the ground and their tail in the air.

Just opposite to where the diners were at table the huge fireplace, with its cheerful blaze, gave out a burning heat on the backs of those who sat at the right. Three spits were turning, loaded with chickens, with pigeons and with joints of mutton, and a delectable odour of roast meat and of gravy flowing over crisp brown skin arose from the hearth, kindled merriment and caused mouths to water.

All the aristocracy of the plough were eating there at the board of Maît' Jourdain, innkeeper and horse-dealer, a sharp fellow who had made a great deal of money in his day.

The dishes were passed round and were emptied, as were the jugs of yellow cider. Everyone told of his affairs, of his purchases and his sales. They exchanged news about the crops. The weather was good for green stuff, but too wet for grain.

Suddenly the drum began to beat in the courtyard before the house; and they all, except some of the most indifferent, were on their feet at once and ran to the door, to the windows, their mouths full and napkins in their hands.

When the public crier had finished his tattoo he called forth in a jerky voice, pausing in the wrong places: 'Be it known to the inhabitants of Goderville and in general to all persons present at the market that there has been lost this morning on the Beuzeville road, between nine and ten o'clock, a black leather pocketbook containing five hundred francs and business papers. You are requested to return it to the mayor's office at once or to Maître Fortuné Houlbrèque, of Manneville. There will be twenty francs reward.'

Then the man went away. They heard once more at a distance the dull beating of the drum and the faint voice of the crier. Then they all began to talk of this incident, reckoning up the chances which Maître Houlbrèque had of finding or of not finding his pocketbook again.

The meal went on. They were finishing their coffee when the corporal of gendarmes appeared on the threshold.

He asked: 'Is Maître Hauchecorne, of Bréauté, here?'

Maître Hauchecorne, seated at the other end of the table, answered: 'Here I am, here I am.'

And he followed the corporal.

The mayor was waiting for him, seated in an armchair. He was the notary of the place, a tall, grave man of pompous speech.

'Maître Hauchecorne,' said he, 'this morning on the Beuzeville road you were seen to pick up the pocketbook lost by Maître Houlbrèque, of Manneville.'

The countryman looked at the mayor in amazement, frightened already at this suspicion which rested on him, he knew not why.

'I – I picked up that pocketbook?'

'Yes, you.'

'I swear I don't even know anything about it.'

'You were seen.'

'I was seen – I? Who saw me?'

'Monsieur Malandain, the harness-maker.'

Then the old man remembered, understood, and, reddening with anger, said: 'Ah! he saw me, did he, the rascal? He saw me picking up this string here, M'sieu le Maire.'

And fumbling at the bottom of his pocket, he pulled out of it the little end of string.

But the mayor incredulously shook his head: 'You will not make me believe, Maître Hauchecorne, that Monsieur Malandain, who is a man whose word can be relied on, has mistaken this string for a pocket-book.'

The peasant, furious, raised his hand and spat on the ground beside him as if to attest his good faith, repeating: 'For all that, it is God's truth, M'sieu le Maire. There! On my soul's salvation, I repeat it.'

The mayor continued: 'After you picked up the object in question, you even looked about for some time in the mud to see if a piece of money had not dropped out of it.'

The good man was choking with indignation and fear.

'How can they tell – how can they tell such lies as that to slander an honest man! How can they?'

His protestations were in vain; he was not believed.

He was confronted with Monsieur Malandain, who repeated and sustained his testimony. They railed at one another for an hour. At his own request Maître Hauchecorne was searched. Nothing was found on him.

At last the mayor, much perplexed, sent him away, warning him that he would inform the public prosecutor and ask for orders.

The news had spread. When he left the mayor's office the old man was surrounded, interrogated with a curiosity which was serious or mocking, as the case might be, but into which no indignation entered. And he began to tell the story of the string. They did not believe him. They laughed.

He passed on, buttonholed by everyone, himself buttonholing his acquaintances, beginning over and over again his tale and his protestations, showing his pockets turned inside out to prove that he had nothing in them.

They said to him: 'You old rogue!'

He grew more and more angry, feverish, in despair at not being believed, and kept on telling his story.

The night came. It was time to go home. He left with three of his neighbours, to whom he pointed out the place where he had picked up the string, and all the way he talked of his adventure.

That evening he made the round of the village of Bréauté for the purpose of telling everyone. He met only unbelievers.

He brooded over it all night long.

The next day, about one in the afternoon, Marius Paumelle, a farm hand of Maître Breton, the market gardener at Ymauville, returned the pocketbook and its contents to Maître Holbrèque, of Manneville.

This man said, indeed, that he had found it on the road, but not knowing how to read, he had carried it home and given it to his master.

The news spread to the environs. Maître Hauchecorne was informed. He started off at once and began to relate his story with the dénouement. He was triumphant.

'What grieved me,' said he, 'was not the thing itself, do you understand, but it was being accused of lying. Nothing does you so much harm as being in disgrace for lying.'

All day he talked of his adventure. He told it on the roads to the people who passed, at the cabaret to the people who drank, and next Sunday when they came out of church. He even stopped strangers to tell them about it. He was easy now, and yet something worried him without his knowing exactly what it was. People had a joking manner while they listened. They did not seem convinced. He seemed to feel their remarks behind his back.

On Tuesday of the following week he went to market at Goderville, prompted solely by the need of telling his story.

Malandain, standing on his doorstep, began to laugh as he saw him pass. Why?

He accosted a farmer of Criquetot, who did not let him finish, and giving him a punch in the pit of the stomach, cried in his face: 'Oh, you great rogue!' Then the farmer turned his heel upon him.

Maître Hauchecorne grew more and more uneasy. Why had they called him a 'great rogue'?

When seated at table in Jourdain's tavern he began again to explain the whole affair.

A horse dealer of Montivilliers shouted at him: 'Get out, get out, you old scamp! I know all about your piece of string.'

Hauchecorne stammered: 'But they have found it, the pocketbook!'

But the other continued: 'Hold your tongue; there's one who finds it and there's another who returns it. And no one's the wiser.'

The farmer was speechless. He understood at last. They accused him of having had the pocketbook brought back by an accomplice, by a confederate.

He tried to protest. The whole table began to laugh.

He could not finish his dinner, and went away amid a chorus of jeers.

He went home indignant, choking with rage, with confusion, the more cast down since with his Norman craftiness he was, perhaps, capable of having done what they accused him of and even of boasting of it as a good trick. He was dimly conscious that it was impossible to prove his innocence, his craftiness being so well known. He felt himself struck to the heart by the injustice of the suspicion.

He began anew to tell his tale, lengthening his recital every day, each day adding new proofs, more energetic declarations and more sacred oaths, which he thought of, which he prepared in his hours of solitude, for his mind was entirely occupied with the story of the string. The more he denied it, the more artful his arguments, the less he was believed.

'Those are a liar's proofs,' they said behind his back.

He felt this. It preyed upon him and he exhausted himself in useless efforts.

He was visibly wasting away.

Jokers would make him tell the story of 'the piece of string' to amuse them, just as you make a soldier who has been on a campaign tell his story of the battle. His mind kept growing weaker, and about the end of December he took to his bed.

He passed away early in January, and even in his death agony, he protested his innocence, repeating: 'A little piece of string – a little piece of string. See, here it is, M'sieu le Maire.'

Madame Husson's 'Rosier'

We had just left Gisors, where I was awakened by hearing the name of the town called out by the guard, and I was dozing off again when a terrific shock threw me forward on to the lap of a large lady who sat opposite me.

One of the wheels of the engine had broken, and the engine itself lay across the track. The tender and the baggage car were also derailed, and lay beside this mutilated engine, which rattled, groaned, hissed, puffed, sputtered, and resembled those horses that fall in the street with their flanks heaving, their breasts palpitating, their nostrils steaming and their whole bodies trembling, but incapable of the slightest effort to rise and start off again.

There were no dead or wounded; only a few with bruises, for the train was not going at full speed. And we looked with sorrow at the great crippled iron creature that could not draw us along any more, and that would be blocking the line perhaps for some time, for no doubt they would have to send to Paris for a special train to come to our aid.

It was then ten o'clock in the morning, and I at once decided to go back to Gisors for breakfast.

As I was walking along I said to myself: 'Gisors, Gisors – why, I know someone there! Who is it? Gisors? Let me see, I have a friend in this town.' A name suddenly came to my mind, 'Albert Marambot'. He was an old school friend whom I had not seen for at least twelve years, and who was practising medicine in Gisors. He had often written, inviting me to come and see him, and I had always promised to do so, without keeping my word. But at last I would take advantage of this opportunity.

I asked the first passer-by: 'Do you know where Dr Marambot lives?'

He replied, without hesitation, and with the drawling accent of the Normans: 'Rue Dauphine. There.'

I presently saw, on the door of the house he pointed out, a large brass plate on which was engraved the name of my old friend. I rang the bell, but the servant, a yellow-haired girl who moved slowly, said with a stupid air: 'He isn't here, he isn't here.'

I heard a sound of forks and of glasses and I cried: 'Hello, Marambot!'

A door opened and a large man, with whiskers and a cross look on his face, appeared, carrying a dinner napkin in his hand.

I certainly should not have recognised him. One would have said he was forty-five at least, and, in a second, all the provincial life which makes one grow heavy, dull and old came before me. In a single flash of thought, quicker than the act of extending my hand to him, I could see his life, his manner of existence, his line of thought and his theories of things in general. I guessed at the prolonged meals that had rounded out his stomach, his after-dinner naps from the torpor of a slow indigestion aided by cognac, and his vague glances cast on the patient while he thought of the chicken that was roasting before the fire. His conversations about cooking, about cider, brandy and wine, the way of preparing certain dishes and of blending certain sauces, were revealed to me at the sight of his puffy red cheeks, his heavy lips and his lustreless eyes.

'You do not recognise me. I am Raoul Aubertin,' I said.

He opened his arms and gave me such a hug that I thought he would choke me.

'You have not breakfasted, have you?'

'No.'

'How fortunate! I was just sitting down to table and I have an excellent trout.'

Five minutes later I was sitting opposite him at breakfast. I said: 'Are you a bachelor?'

'Yes, indeed.'

'And do you like it here?'

'Time does not hang heavy; I am busy. I have patients and friends. I eat well, have good health, enjoy laughing and shooting. I get along.'

'Is not life very monotonous in this little town?'

'No, my dear boy, not when one knows how to fill in the time. A little town, in fact, is like a large one. The incidents and amusements are less varied, but one makes more of them; one has fewer acquaintances, but one meets them more frequently. When you know all the windows in a street, each one of them interests you and puzzles you more than a whole street in Paris.

'A little town is very amusing, you know, very amusing, very amusing. Why, take Gisors. I know it at the tips of my fingers, from its beginning up to the present time. You have no idea what a queer history it has.'

'Do you belong to Gisors?'

'I? No. I come from Gournay, its neighbour and rival. Gournay is to Gisors what Lucullus was to Cicero. Here, everything is for glory; they say "the proud people of Gisors". At Gournay, everything is for the stomach; they say "the chewers of Gournay". Gisors despises Gournay, but Gournay laughs at Gisors. It is a very comical country, this.'

I perceived that I was eating something very delicious, hard-boiled eggs wrapped in a covering of meat jelly flavoured with herbs and put on ice for a few moments, and I said enthusiastically to Marambot: 'This *is* good.'

He smiled.

'Two things are necessary, good jelly, which is hard to get, and good eggs. Oh, how rare good eggs are, with the yolks slightly reddish, and with a good flavour! I have two poultry yards, one for eggs and the other for chickens. I feed my laying hens in a special manner. I have my own ideas on the subject. In an egg, as in the meat of a chicken, in beef, or in mutton, in milk, in everything, one perceives, and ought to taste, the juice, the quintessence of all the food on which the animal has been fed. How much better food we could have if more attention were paid to this!'

I laughed as I said: 'You are a gourmand?'

'*Parbleu.* It is only imbeciles who are not. One is a gourmand as one is an artist, as one is learned, as one is a poet. The sense of taste, my friend, is very delicate, capable of perfection, and quite as worthy of respect as the eye and the ear. A person who lacks this sense is deprived of an exquisite faculty, the faculty of discerning the quality of food, just as one may lack the faculty of discerning the beauties of a book or of a work of art; it means to be deprived of an essential organ, of something that belongs to higher humanity; it means to belong to one of those innumerable classes of the infirm, the unfortunate, and the fools of which our race is composed; it means to have the mouth of an animal, in a word, just like the mind of an animal. A man who cannot distinguish one kind of lobster from another; a herring – that admirable fish that has all the flavours, all the odours of the sea – from a mackerel or a whiting; and a Cresane from a Duchesse pear, may be compared to a man who should mistake Balzac for Eugène Sue; a symphony of Beethoven for a military march composed by the bandmaster of a regiment; and the Apollo Belvedere for the statue of General de Blaumont.

'Who is General de Blaumont?'

'Oh, that's true, you do not know. It is easy to tell that you do not belong to Gisors. I told you just now, my dear boy, that they called the inhabitants of this town "the proud people of Gisors", and never was an epithet better deserved. But let us finish breakfast first, and then I will tell you about our town and take you to see it.'

He stopped talking every now and then while he slowly drank a glass of wine which he gazed at affectionately as he replaced the glass on the table.

It was amusing to see him, with a napkin tied around his neck, his cheeks flushed, his eyes eager, and his whiskers spreading round his mouth as it kept working.

He made me eat until I was almost choking. Then, as I was about to return to the railway station, he seized me by the arm and took me through the streets. The town, of a pretty, provincial type, commanded by its citadel, the most curious monument of military architecture of the seventh century to be found in France, overlooks, in its turn, a long, green valley, where the large Norman cows graze and ruminate in the pastures.

The doctor quoted: ' "Gisors, a town of four thousand inhabitants in the department of Eure, mentioned in Caesar's *Commentaries*: Caesaris Ostium, then Caesartium, Caesortium, Gisortium, Gisors." I shall not take you to visit the old Roman encampment, the remains of which are still in existence.'

I laughed and replied: 'My dear friend, it seems to me that you are affected with a special malady that, as a doctor, you ought to study; it is called the spirit of provincialism.'

He stopped abruptly.

'The spirit of provincialism, my friend, is nothing but natural patriotism,' he said. 'I love my house, my town and my province because I discover there the customs of my own village; but if I love my country, if I become angry when a neighbour sets foot in it, it is because I feel that my home is in danger, because the frontier that I do not know is the high road to my province. For instance, I am a Norman, a true Norman; well, in spite of my hatred of the Germans and my desire for revenge, I do not detest them, I do not hate them by instinct as I hate the English, the real, hereditary natural enemy of the Normans; for the English traversed this soil inhabited by my ancestors, plundered and ravaged it twenty times, and my aversion from this perfidious people was transmitted to me at birth by my father. See, here is the statue of the general.'

'What general?'

'General de Blaumont! We had to have a statue. We are not "the proud people of Gisors" for nothing! So we discovered General de Blaumont. Look in this bookseller's window.'

He drew me towards the bookshop, where about fifteen red, yellow and blue volumes attracted the eye. As I read the titles, I began to laugh idiotically. They read: *Gisors, Its Origin, Its Future* by M. X—, member of several learned societies; *History of Gisors* by the Abbé A—; *Gisors, from the Time of Caesar to the Present Day* by M. B—, Landowner; *Gisors and Its Environs* by Doctor C. D—; *The Glories of Gisors* by a Discoverer.

'My friend,' resumed Marambot, 'not a year, not a single year, you understand, passes without a fresh history of Gisors being published here; we now have twenty-three.'

'And the glories of Gisors?' I asked.

'Oh, I will not mention them all, only the principal ones. We had first General de Blaumont, then Baron Davillier, the celebrated ceramist who explored Spain and the Balearic Isles, and brought to the notice of collectors the wonderful Hispano-Arabic china. In literature we have a very clever journalist, now dead, Charles Brainne, and among those who are living, the very eminent editor of the *Nouvelliste de Rouen*, Charles Lapierre . . . and many others, many others.'

We were traversing a long street with a gentle incline, with a June sun beating down on it and driving the residents into their houses.

Suddenly there appeared at the farther end of the street a drunken man who was staggering along, with his head forward, his arms and legs limp. He would walk forward rapidly three, six or ten steps and then stop. When these energetic movements landed him in the middle of the road he stopped short and swayed on his feet, hesitating between falling and a fresh start. Then he would dart off in any direction, sometimes falling against the wall of a house, against which he seemed to be fastened, as though he were trying to get in through the wall. Then he would suddenly turn round and look ahead of him, his mouth open and his eyes blinking in the sunlight, and getting away from the wall by a movement of the hips, he started off once more.

A little yellow dog, a half-starved cur, followed him, barking; stopping when he stopped, and starting off when he started.

'Hello', said Marambot, 'there is Madame Husson's "Rosier".'

'Madame Husson's "Rosier",' I exclaimed in astonishment. 'What do you mean?'

The doctor began to laugh.

'Oh, that is what we call drunkards round here. The name comes from an old story which has now become a legend, although it is true in all respects.'

'Is it an amusing story?'

'Very amusing.'

'Well, then, tell it to me.'

'Certainly I will. There lived formerly in this town a very upright old lady who was a great guardian of morals and was called Madame Husson. You know, I am telling you the real names and not imaginary ones. Madame Husson took a special interest in good works, in helping the poor and encouraging the deserving. She was a little woman with a quick walk, and wore a black wig. She was ceremonious, polite, on very good terms with the Almighty in the person of Abbé Malon, and had a profound horror, an inborn horror of vice, and, in particular, of the vice the Church calls lasciviousness. Any irregularity before marriage made her furious, exasperated her till she was beside herself.

'Now, this was the period when they presented a prize as a reward of virtue to any girl in the environs of Paris who was found to be chaste. She was called a "Rosière", and Madame Husson got the idea that she would institute a similar ceremony at Gisors. She spoke about it to Abbé Malon, who at once made out a list of candidates.

'However, Madame Husson had a servant, an old woman named Françoise, as upright as her mistress. As soon as the priest had left, Madame Husson called the servant and said: "Here, Françoise, here are the girls whose names Abbé Malon has submitted to me for the prize of virtue; try and find out what reputation they bear in the district."

'And Françoise set out. She collected all the scandal, all the stories, all the tittle-tattle, all the suspicions. That she might omit nothing, she wrote it all down together with her memoranda in her housekeeping book, and handed it each morning to Madame Husson, who, after adjusting her spectacles on her thin nose, read as follows:

> Bread – four sous
>
> Milk – two sous
>
> Butter – eight sous

Malvina Levesque got into trouble last year with Mathurin Poilu.

> Leg of mutton – twenty-five sous
>
> Salt – one sou

Rosalie Vatinel was seen in the Riboudet woods with Césaire Pienoir by Madame Onesime, the ironer, on July the 20th about dusk.

> Radishes – one sou
>
> Vinegar – two sous
>
> Oxalic acid – two sous

Josephine Durdent is not believed to have committed a fault, but she corresponds with young Oportun, who is in service in Rouen, and who sent her a present of a cap by diligence.

'Not one came out unscathed in this rigorous inquisition. Françoise enquired of everyone – neighbours, drapers, the principal, the teaching sisters at school – and gathered the slightest details.

'As there is not a girl in the world about whom gossips have not found something to say, there was not found in all the countryside one young girl whose name was free from some scandal.

'But Madame Husson, desired that the "Rosière" of Gisors, like

Caesar's wife, should be above suspicion, and she was horrified, saddened and in despair at the record in her servant's housekeeping account-book.

'They then extended their circle of enquiries to the neighbouring villages; but with no satisfaction.

'They consulted the mayor. His candidates failed. Those of Dr Barbesol were equally unlucky, in spite of the exactness of his professional guarantees.

'But one morning Françoise, on returning from one of her expeditions, said to her mistress: "You see, madame, that if you wish to give a prize to anyone, there is only Isidore in all the country round."

'Madame Husson remained thoughtful. She knew him well, this Isidore, the son of Virginie the greengrocer. His proverbial virtue had been the delight of Gisors for several years, and served as an entertaining theme of conversation in the town, and of amusement to the young girls who loved to tease him. He was past twenty-one, was tall, awkward, slow and timid; helped his mother in the business, and spent his days picking over fruit and vegetables, seated on a chair outside the door.

'He had an abnormal dread of a petticoat and cast down his eyes whenever a female customer looked at him smilingly, and this well-known timidity made him the butt of all the wags in the country.

Bold words, coarse expressions, indecent allusions, brought the colour to his cheeks so quickly that Dr Barbesol had nicknamed him 'the thermometer of modesty'. Was he as innocent as he looked? ill-natured people asked themselves. Was it the mere presentiment of unknown and shameful mysteries or else indignation at the relations ordained as the concomitant of love that so strongly affected the son of Virginie the greengrocer? The urchins of the neighbourhood as they ran past the shop would fling disgusting remarks at him just to see him cast down his eyes. The girls amused themselves by walking up and down before him, cracking jokes that made him go into the store. The boldest among them teased him to his face just to have a laugh, and to amuse themselves, made appointments with him and proposed all sorts of things.

'So Madame Husson had become thoughtful.

'Certainly, Isidore was an exceptional case of notorious, unassailable virtue. No one, among the most sceptical, most incredulous, would have been able, would have dared, to suspect Isidore of the slightest infraction of any law of morality. He had never been seen in a café, never been seen at night on the street. He went to bed at eight o'clock and rose at four. He was a paragon, a pearl.

'But Madame Husson still hesitated. The idea of substituting a boy for a girl, a "Rosier" for a "Rosière", troubled her, worried her a little, and she resolved to consult Abbé Malon.

'The abbé responded: "What do you desire to reward, madame? It is virtue, is it not, and nothing but virtue? What does it matter to you, therefore, if it is masculine or feminine? Virtue is eternal; it has neither gender nor country; it is 'Virtue'."

'Thus encouraged, Madame Husson went to see the mayor.

'He approved heartily. "We will have a fine ceremony," he said. "And another year if we can find a girl as worthy as Isidore we will give the reward to her. It will even be a good example that we shall set to Nanterre. Let us not be exclusive; let us welcome all merit."

'Isidore, who had been told about this, blushed deeply and seemed pleased.

'The ceremony was fixed for the 15th of August, the festival of the Virgin Mary and of the Emperor Napoleon. The municipality had decided to make an imposing ceremony and had built the platform on the *couronneaux*, a delightful extension of the ramparts of the old citadel where I will take you presently.

'With the natural upsurge of public feeling, the virtue of Isidore, ridiculed hitherto, had suddenly become respected and envied, as it would bring him in five hundred francs besides a savings-bank book, a mountain of consideration, and glory enough and to spare. The girls now regretted their frivolity, their ridicule, their bold manners; and Isidore, although still modest and timid, had now a little contented air that bespoke his internal satisfaction.

'The evening before the 15th of August the entire Rue Dauphine was decorated with flags. They had scattered flowers all along the road as they do for processions at the Fête-Dieu, and the National Guard was present, acting on the orders of their chief, Commandant Desbarres, an old soldier of the Grand Army, who pointed with pride to the beard of a Cossack he had cut with a single sword stroke from the chin of its owner during the retreat from Russia, which hung beside the frame containing the cross of the Legion of Honour presented to him by the emperor himself.

'The regiment that he commanded was, besides, a picked regiment celebrated all through the province, and the company of grenadiers of Gisors was called on to attend all important ceremonies for a distance of fifteen to twenty leagues. The story goes that Louis Philippe, while reviewing the militia of Eure, stopped in astonishment before the company from Gisors, exclaiming: "Oh, who are those splendid grenadiers?"

' "The grenadiers of Gisors," replied the general.

' "I might have known it," murmured the king.

'So Commandant Desbarres came at the head of his men, preceded by the band, to get Isidore from his mother's shop.

'After a little air had been played by the band beneath the windows, the "Rosier" himself appeared on the threshold. He was dressed in white duck from head to foot and wore a straw hat with a little bunch of orange blossoms as a cockade.

'The question of his clothes had bothered Madame Husson a good deal, and she hesitated some time between the black coat of those who make their first communion and an entire white suit. But Françoise, her counsellor, induced her to decide on the white suit, pointing out that the "Rosier" would look like a swan.

'Behind him came his guardian, his godmother, Madame Husson, in triumph. She took his arm to go out of the shop, and the mayor placed himself on the other side of the "Rosier". The drums beat. Commandant Desbarres gave the order "Present arms!" The procession resumed its march towards the church amid an immense crowd of people who had gathered from the neighbouring districts.

'After a short mass and an affecting discourse by Abbé Malon, they continued on their way to the *couronneaux*, where the banquet was served in a tent.

'Before they took their seats at table, the mayor gave an address. This is it, word for word. I learned it by heart: "Young man, a woman of means, beloved by the poor and respected by the rich, Madame Husson, whom the whole country is thanking here, through me, had the idea, the happy and benevolent idea, of founding in this town a prize for virtue, which should serve as a valuable encouragement to the inhabitants of this beautiful country.

' "You, young man, are the first to be rewarded in this dynasty of goodness and chastity. Your name will remain at the head of this list of the most deserving, and your life, understand me, your whole life, must correspond to this happy beginning. Today, in presence of this noble woman, of these soldier-citizens who have taken up their arms in your honour, in presence of these sympathetic people assembled to applaud you, or, rather, to applaud virtue, in your person, you make a solemn contract with the town, with all of us, to continue until your death the excellent example of your youth.

' "Do not forget, young man, that you are the first seed cast into this field of hope; give us the fruits that we expect of you."

'The mayor advanced three steps, opened his arms and pressed Isidore to his heart.

'The "Rosier" was sobbing without knowing why, from a confused emotion, from pride and a vague and happy feeling of tenderness.

'Then the mayor placed in one hand a silk purse in which gold jingled – five hundred francs in gold! – and in his other hand a savings-bank book. And he said in a solemn tone: "Homage, glory and riches to virtue."

'Commandant Desbarres shouted, "Bravo!" the grenadiers vociferated, and the crowd applauded.

'Madame Husson wiped her eyes, in her turn. Then they all sat down at the table where the banquet was served.

'The repast was magnificent and seemed interminable. One course followed another; yellow cider and red wine in fraternal contact blended in the stomach of the guests. The rattle of plates, the sound of voices, and of music softly played, made an incessant deep hum, and was dispersed abroad in the clear sky where the swallows were flying. Madame Husson occasionally readjusted her black wig, which would slip over on one side, and chatted with Abbé Malon. The mayor, who was excited, talked politics with Commandant Desbarres, and Isidore ate and drank as if he had never eaten or drunk before. He helped himself repeatedly to all the dishes, becoming aware for the first time of the pleasure of having one's stomach full of good things which tickle the palate from the first taste. He had let out a reef in his belt and, without speaking, and although he was a little uneasy at a wine stain on his white waistcoat, he ceased eating in order to take up his glass and hold it to his mouth as long as possible, to enjoy the taste slowly.

'It was time for the toasts. They were many and loudly applauded. Evening was approaching and they had been at the table since noon. Fine, milky vapours were already floating in the air in the valley, the light night-robe of streams and meadows; the sun neared the horizon; the cows were lowing in the distance amid the mists of the pasture. The feast was over. They returned to Gisors. The procession, now disbanded, walked in detachments. Madame Husson had taken Isidore's arm and was giving him a quantity of urgent, excellent advice.

'They stopped at the door of the fruit shop, and the "Rosier" was left at his mother's house. She had not come home yet. Having been invited by her family to celebrate her son's triumph, she had taken luncheon with her sister after having followed the procession as far as the banqueting tent.

'So Isidore remained alone in the shop, which was growing dark. He sat down on a chair, excited by the wine and by pride, and looked about him. Carrots, cabbages and onions gave out their strong odour in the closed room, that coarse smell of the garden blended with the sweet, penetrating odour of strawberries and the delicate, slight, evanescent fragrance of a basket of peaches.

'The "Rosier" took one of these and ate it, although he was as full as an egg. Then, all at once, intoxicated with joy, he began to dance about the shop, and something rattled in his waistcoat.

'He was surprised, and put his hand in his pocket and brought out the purse containing the five hundred francs, which he had forgotten in all the excitement. Five hundred francs! What a fortune! He poured the gold pieces on to the counter and spread them out with his big hand with a slow, caressing touch so as to see them all at the same time. There were twenty-five, twenty-five round gold pieces, all gold! They glistened on the wood in the dim light and he counted them over and over, one by one. Then he put them back in the purse, which he replaced in his pocket.

'Who will ever know or who can tell what a terrible conflict took place in the soul of the "Rosier"between good and evil, the tumultuous attack of Satan, his artifices, the temptations which he offered to this timid virgin heart? What suggestions, what imaginations, what desires were not invented by the evil one to excite and destroy this chosen one? He seized his hat, Madame Husson's saint, his hat which still bore the little bunch of orange blossoms, and going out through the alley at the back of the house, he disappeared in the darkness.

'Virginie, the fruiterer, on learning that her son had returned, went home at once, and found the house empty. She waited, without thinking anything about it at first; but at the end of a quarter of an hour she made enquiries. The neighbours had seen Isidore come home and had not seen him go out again. They began to look for him, but could not find him. His mother, in alarm, went to the mayor. The mayor knew nothing, except that he had left him at the door of his home. Madame Husson had just retired when they informed her that her protégé had disappeared. She immediately put on her wig, dressed herself and went to Virginie's house. Virginie, whose plebeian soul was readily moved, was weeping copiously amid her cabbages, carrots and onions.

'They feared some accident had befallen him. What could it be? Commandant Desbarres notified the police, who made a circuit of the town, and on the high road to Pontoise they found the little bunch of orange blossoms. It was taken back and placed on the table around which the authorities gathered to deliberate. The "Rosier" must have been the victim of some stratagem, some trick, some jealousy; but in what way? What means had been employed to kidnap this innocent creature, and with what object?

'Weary of looking for him without any result, Virginie, alone, remained watching and weeping.

'The following evening, when the coach passed on its return from Paris, Gisors learned with astonishment that its "Rosier" had stopped the vehicle at a distance of about two hundred metres from the town, had climbed up on it and paid his fare, handing over a gold piece and receiving the change, and that he had quietly alighted in the centre of the busy city.

'There was great excitement all through the countryside. Letters passed between the mayor and the chief of police in Paris, but brought no result.

'The days followed one another; a week passed.

'Then, one morning, Dr Barbesol, who had gone out early, perceived, sitting on a doorstep, a man dressed in a grimy linen suit, who was sleeping with his head leaning against the wall. He approached him and recognised Isidore. He tried to rouse him, but did not succeed in doing so. The ex-"Rosier" was in that profound, invincible sleep that is alarming, and the doctor, in surprise, went to seek help to carry the young man to Boncheval's drugstore. When they lifted him up they found an empty bottle under him, and when the doctor sniffed at it, he declared that it had contained brandy. That gave a suggestion as to what treatment he would require. They succeeded in rousing him.

'Isidore was drunk – drunk and degraded by a week of guzzling – drunk and so disgusting that a ragman would not have touched him. His beautiful white duck suit was a grey rag, greasy, muddy, torn and revolting, and he smelt of the gutter and of vice.

'He was washed, sermonised, shut up, and did not leave the house for four days. He seemed ashamed and repentant. They could not find on him either his purse, containing the five hundred francs, or the bankbook, or even his silver watch, a sacred heirloom left by his father, the fruiterer.

'On the fifth day he ventured into the Rue Dauphine. Curious glances followed him and he walked along with a furtive expression in his eyes and his head bent down. As he got outside the town towards the valley they lost sight of him; but two hours later he returned laughing and rolling against the walls. He was drunk, absolutely drunk.

'Nothing could cure him.

'Driven from home by his mother, he became a wagon-driver, and drove the charcoal wagons for the Pougrisel firm, which is still in existence.

'His reputation as a drunkard became so well known and spread so far that even at Evreux they talked of Madame Husson's "Rosier", and the sots of the countryside have been given that nickname.

'A good deed is never lost.'

Dr Marambot rubbed his hands as he finished his story.

I asked: 'Did you know the "Rosier"?'

'Yes. I closed his eyes.'

'What did he die of?'

'An attack of delirium tremens, of course.'

We had arrived at the old citadel, a pile of ruined walls dominated by the enormous tower of St Thomas of Canterbury and the one called the Prisoner's Tower.

Marambot told me the story of this prisoner, who, with the aid of a nail, covered the walls of his dungeon with carvings, tracing the reflections of the sun as it glanced through the narrow slit of a loophole.

I also learned that Clothaire II had given the patrimony of Gisors to his cousin, St Romain, Bishop of Rouen; that Gisors ceased to be the capital of the whole of Vexin after the treaty of St-Clair-sur-Epte; that the town is the chief strategic centre of all that portion of France, and that in consequence of this advantage it was taken and retaken over and over again. At the command of William Rufus, the eminent engineer, Robert de Bellesme, constructed there a powerful fortress that was attacked later by Louis le Gros, then by the Norman barons, was defended by Robert de Candos, was finally ceded to Louis le Gros by Geoffrey Plantagenet, was retaken by the English in consequence of the treachery of the Knights-Templars, was contested by Philippe-Augustus and Richard the Lionheart, was set on fire by Edward III of England, who could not take the castle, was again taken by the English in 1419, restored later to Charles VIII by Richard de Marbury, was taken by the Duke of Calabria, occupied by the League, inhabited by Henry IV, and so on and so forth.

And Marambot, eager and almost eloquent, continued: 'What beggars, those English! And what sots, my boy; they are all "Rosiers", those hypocrites!'

Then, after a silence, stretching out his arm towards the tiny river that glistened in the meadows, he said: 'Did you know that Henry Monnier was one of the most untiring fishermen on the banks of the Epte?'

'No, I did not know it.'

'And Bouffe, my boy, Bouffe was a painter on glass.'

'You are joking!'

'No, indeed. How is it you do not know these things?'

That Pig of a Morin

I

'There, my friend,' I said to Labarbe, 'you have just repeated those five words, "that pig of a Morin". Why on earth do I never hear Morin's name mentioned without his being called a pig?'

Labarbe, who is a deputy, looked at me with his owl-like eyes and said: 'Do you mean to say that you do not know Morin's story and you come from La Rochelle?'

I was obliged to declare that I did not know Morin's story, so Labarbe began his recital.

'You knew Morin, did you not, and you remember his large linen-draper's shop on the Quai de La Rochelle?'

'Yes, perfectly.'

'Well, then. You must know that some years ago Morin went to spend a fortnight in Paris for pleasure, or for his pleasures, but under the pretext of renewing his stock, and you also know what a fortnight in Paris means to a country shopkeeper; it fires his blood. The theatre every evening, women's dresses rustling up against you and continual excitement; one goes almost mad with it. One sees nothing but dancers in tights, actresses in very low dresses, round legs, bare shoulders, all nearly within reach of one's hands, without daring, or being able, to touch them. When one leaves the city one's heart is still all in a flutter and one's mind still exhilarated by a sort of longing for kisses.

'Morin was in that condition when he took his ticket for La Rochelle by the eight-forty night express. As he was walking up and down outside the waiting-room at the station he stopped suddenly in front of a young lady who was kissing an old one. She had her veil up, and Morin murmured with delight: "By Jove, what a pretty woman!"

'When she had said goodbye to the old lady she went into the waiting-room, and Morin followed her; then she went on the platform and Morin still followed her; then she got into an empty carriage, and he again followed her. There were very few travellers on the express. The engine whistled and the train started. They were alone. Morin devoured her with his eyes. She appeared to be about nineteen or twenty and was fair, tall, with a bold look. She wrapped a rug round her and stretched herself on the seat to sleep.

'Morin asked himself: "I wonder who she is?" And a thousand conjectures, a thousand projects went through his head. He said to himself: "So many adventures are told as happening on railway journeys that this may be one that is going to present itself to me. Who knows? A piece of good luck like that happens very suddenly, and perhaps I need only be a little venturesome. Was it not Danton who said: 'Audacity, more audacity and always audacity'? If it was not Danton it was Mirabeau, but that does not matter. But then I have no audacity, and that is the difficulty. Oh! If one only knew, if one could only read people's minds! I will bet that every day one passes by magnificent opportunities without knowing it, though a gesture would be enough to let me know her mind."

'Then he imagined to himself combinations which conducted him to triumph. He pictured some chivalrous deed or merely some slight service which he rendered her, a lively, gallant conversation which ended in a declaration.

'But he could find no opening, had no pretext, and he waited for some fortunate circumstance, with his heart beating and his mind topsy-turvy. The night passed and the pretty girl still slept, while Morin was meditating his own fall. The day broke and soon the first ray of sunlight appeared in the sky, a long, clear ray which shone on the face of the sleeping girl and woke her. She sat up, looked at the country, then at Morin and smiled. She smiled like a happy woman, with an engaging and bright look, and Morin trembled. Certainly that smile was intended for him; it was a discreet invitation, the signal which he was waiting for. That smile meant to say: "How stupid, what a dolt you are, to have sat there on your seat like a post all night! Just look at me, am I not charming? And you have sat like that for the whole night, when you have been alone with a pretty woman, you great simpleton!"

'She was still smiling as she looked at him; she even began to laugh; and he lost his head trying to find something suitable to say, no matter what. But he could think of nothing, nothing, and then, seized with a coward's courage, he said to himself: "So much the worse, I will risk everything," and suddenly, without the slightest warning, he went towards her, his arms extended, his lips protruding, and, seizing her in his arms, tried to kiss her.

'She sprang up immediately with a bound, crying: "Help! help!" and screaming with terror; and then she opened the carriage door and waved her arms, mad with terror and trying to jump out, while Morin, who was almost distracted, held her by the skirt and stammered: "Oh, madame! Oh, madame!"

'The train slackened speed and then stopped. Two guards rushed up at the young woman's frantic signals. She threw herself into their arms, stammering: "That man wanted – wanted to – to – " And then she fainted.

'They were at Mauzé station, and the gendarme on duty arrested Morin. When the victim of his indiscreet admiration had regained her consciousness, she made her charge against him, and the police drew it up. The poor linen-draper did not reach home till night; and there was a prosecution hanging over him for an outrage to morals in a public place.'

II

'At that time I was editor of the *Fanal des Charentes*, and I used to meet Morin every day at the Café du Commerce; and the day after his adventure he came to see me, as he did not know what to do. I did not hide my opinion from him, but said to him: "You are no better than a pig. No decent man behaves like that."

'He cried. His wife had given him a beating, and he foresaw his trade ruined, his name dragged through the mire and dishonoured, his friends scandalised and taking no notice of him. In the end he excited my pity, and I sent for my colleague, Rivet, a jocular but very sensible little man, to give us his advice.

'He advised me to see the public prosecutor, who was a friend of mine, and so I sent Morin home and went to call on the magistrate. He told me that the young lady who had been insulted was a Mademoiselle Henriette Bonnel, who had just received her certificate as governess in Paris and was spending her holidays with her uncle and aunt, who were very respectable tradespeople in Mauzé. What made Morin's case all the more serious was that the uncle had lodged a complaint, but the public official had consented to let the matter drop if this complaint were withdrawn; so we must try and get him to do this.

'I went back to Morin's and found him in bed, ill with agitation and distress. His wife, a tall raw-boned woman with a beard, was abusing him continually, and she showed me into the room, shouting at me: "So you have come to see that pig of a Morin. Well, there he is!" And she planted herself in front of the bed, with her hands on her hips. I told him how matters stood, and he begged me to go and see the girl's uncle and aunt. It was a delicate mission, but I undertook it, and the poor devil never ceased repeating: "I assure you I did not even kiss her; no, not even that. I swear to it!"

'I replied: "It is all the same; you are nothing but a pig." And I took a thousand francs which he gave me to employ as I thought best, but as I did not care to venture to her uncle's house alone, I begged Rivet to go with me, which he agreed to do on condition that we went immediately, for he had some urgent business at La Rochelle that afternoon. So two hours later we rang at the door of a pretty country house. An attractive girl came and opened the door to us, assuredly the young lady in question, and I said to Rivet in a low voice: "Confound it! I begin to understand Morin!"

'The uncle, Monsieur Tonnelet, subscribed to the *Fanal*, and was a fervent political co-religionist of ours. He received us with open arms and congratulated us and wished us joy; he was delighted at having the two editors in his house, and Rivet whispered to me: "I think we shall be able to arrange the matter of that pig of a Morin for him."

'The niece had left the room and I introduced the delicate subject. I waved the spectre of scandal before his eyes; I accentuated the inevitable depreciation which the young lady would suffer if such an affair became known, for nobody would believe in a simple kiss, and the good man seemed undecided, but he could not make up his mind about anything without his wife, who would not be in until late that evening. But suddenly he uttered an exclamation of triumph: "Look here, I have an excellent idea; I will keep you here to dine and sleep, and when my wife comes home I hope we shall be able to arrange matters."

'Rivet resisted at first, but the wish to extricate Morin decided him, and we accepted the invitation, and the uncle got up radiant, called his niece and proposed that we should take a stroll in his grounds, saying: "We will leave serious matters until the morning." Rivet and he began to talk politics, while I soon found myself lagging a little behind with the girl who was really charming, and with the greatest precaution I began to speak to her about her adventure and try to make her my ally. She did not, however, appear in the least confused, and listened to me like a person who was enjoying the whole thing very much.

'I said to her: "Just think, mademoiselle, how unpleasant it will be for you. You will have to appear in court, to encounter malicious looks, to speak before everybody and to recount that unfortunate occurrence in the railway carriage in public. Do you not think, between ourselves, that it would have been much better for you to have put that dirty scoundrel back in his place without calling for assistance?" She began to laugh and replied: "What you say is quite true, but what could I do? I was frightened, and when one is frightened one does not stop to reason with oneself. As soon as I realised the situation I was very sorry that I had called out, but then it was too late. You must also remember that the idiot threw himself upon me like a madman, without saying a word and looking like a lunatic. I did not even know what he wanted of me."

'She looked me full in the face without being nervous, and I said to myself: "She is a queer sort of girl: I can quite see how Morin came to make a mistake," and I went on jokingly: "Come, mademoiselle, confess that it was excusable, for, after all, a man cannot find himself opposite such a pretty girl as you are without feeling a natural desire to kiss her."

'She laughed more than ever and showed her teeth and said: "Between the desire and the act, monsieur, there is room for respect." It was an odd expression to use, although it was not very clear, and I asked abruptly: "Well, now, suppose I were to kiss you, what would you do?" She stopped to look at me from head to foot and then said calmly: "Oh, you? That is quite another matter."

'I knew perfectly well that it was not the same thing at all, as everybody in the neighbourhood called me "Handsome Labarbe" – I was thirty years old in those days – but I asked her: "And why, pray?" She shrugged her shoulders and replied: "Well! because you are not so stupid as he is." And then she added, looking at me slyly: "Nor so ugly, either." And before she could make a movement to avoid me I had implanted a hearty kiss on her cheek. She sprang aside, but it was too late, and then she said: "Well, you are not very bashful, either! But don't do that sort of thing again."

'I put on a humble look and said in a low voice: "Oh, mademoiselle! as for me, if I long for one thing more than another it is to be summoned before a magistrate for the same reason as Morin."

' "Why?" she asked. And, looking steadily at her, I replied: "Because you are one of the most beautiful creatures living; because it would be an honour and a glory for me to have wished to offer you violence, and because people would have said, after seeing you: "Well, Labarbe has richly deserved what he has got, but he is a lucky fellow, all the same."

'She began to laugh heartily again and said: "How funny you are!" And she had not finished the word "funny" before I had her in my arms and was kissing her ardently wherever I could find a place, on her forehead, on her eyes, on her lips occasionally, on her cheeks, all over her head, some part of which she was obliged to leave exposed, in spite of herself, to defend the others; but at last she managed to release herself, blushing and angry. "You are very unmannerly, monsieur," she said, "and I am sorry I listened to you."

'I took her hand in some confusion and stammered out: "I beg your pardon. I beg your pardon, mademoiselle. I have offended you; I have acted like a brute! Do not be angry with me for what I have done. If you knew – " I vainly sought for some excuse, and in a few moments she said: "There is nothing for me to know, monsieur." But I had found something to say, and I cried: "Mademoiselle, I love you!"

'She was really surprised and raised her eyes to look at me, and I went on: "Yes, mademoiselle, and pray listen to me. I do not know Morin, and I do not care anything about him. It does not matter to me in the least if he is committed for trial and locked up meanwhile. I saw you here last year, and I was so taken with you that the thought of you has never left me since, and it does not matter to me whether you believe me or not. I thought you adorable, and the remembrance of you took such a hold on me that I longed to see you again, and so I made use of that fool Morin as a pretext, and here I am. Circumstances have made me exceed the due limits of respect, and I can only ask you to pardon me."

'She looked at me to see if I was in earnest and was ready to smile again. Then she murmured: "You humbug!" But I raised my hand and said in a sincere voice (and I really believe that I was sincere): "I swear to you that I am speaking the truth," and she replied quite simply: "Don't talk nonsense!"

'We were alone, quite alone, as Rivet and her uncle had disappeared down a path, and I made her a real declaration of love, while I squeezed and kissed her hands, and she listened to it as to something new and agreeable, without exactly knowing how much of it she was to believe, while in the end I felt agitated, and at last really myself believed what I said. I was pale, anxious and trembling, and I gently put my arm round her waist and spoke to her softly, whispering into the little curls over her ear. She seemed in a trance, so absorbed in thought was she.

'Then her hand touched mine, and she pressed it, and I gently squeezed her waist with a trembling, and gradually firmer, grasp. She did not move now, and I touched her cheek with my lips and suddenly without seeking them my lips met hers. It was a long, long kiss, and it would have lasted longer still if I had not heard a *Hm! Hm!* just behind me, at which she made her escape through the bushes, and turning round I saw Rivet coming towards me, and, standing in the middle of the path, he said without even smiling: "So that is the way you settle the affair of that pig of a Morin." And I replied conceitedly: "One does what one can, my dear fellow. But what about the uncle? How have you got on with him? I will answer for the niece."

' "I have not been so fortunate with him," he replied.

'Whereupon I took his arm and we went indoors.'

'Dinner made me lose my head altogether. I sat beside her, and my hand continually met hers under the tablecloth; my foot touched hers and our glances met.

'After dinner we took a walk by moonlight, and I whispered all the tender things I could think of to her. I held her close to me, kissed her every moment, while her uncle and Rivet were arguing as they walked in front of us. They went in, and soon a messenger brought a telegram from her aunt, saying that she would not return until the next morning at seven o'clock by the first train.

' "Very well, Henriette," her uncle said, "go and show the gentlemen their rooms." She showed Rivet his first, and he whispered to me: "There was no danger of her taking us into yours first." Then she took me to my room, and as soon as she was alone with me I took her in my arms again and tried to arouse her emotion; but when she saw the danger she escaped out of the room, and I retired, very much put out and excited and feeling rather foolish, for I knew that I should not sleep much, and I was wondering how I could have committed such a mistake, when there was a gentle knock at my door, and on my asking who was there a low voice replied: "I."

'I dressed myself quickly and opened the door, and she came in. "I forgot to ask you what you take in the morning," she said; "chocolate, tea or coffee?" I put my arms round her impetuously and said, devouring her with kisses: "I will take – I will take – "

'But she freed herself from my arms, blew out my candle and disappeared and left me alone in the dark, furious, trying to find some matches, and not able to do so. At last I got some and I went into the passage, feeling half mad, with my candlestick in my hand.

'What was I about to do? I did not stop to reason. I only wanted to find her, and I would. I went a few steps without reflecting, but then I suddenly thought: "Suppose I should walk into the uncle's room, what should I say?" And I stood still, with my head a void and my heart beating. But in a few moments I thought of an answer: "Of course, I shall say that I was looking for Rivet's room to speak to him about an important matter." Then I began to inspect all the doors, trying to find hers, and at last I took hold of a handle at a venture, turned it and went in. There was Henriette, sitting on her bed and looking at me in tears. So I gently turned the key, and going up to her on tiptoe, I said: "I forgot to ask you for something to read, mademoiselle." '

*   *   *

'I was stealthily returning to my room when a rough hand seized me and a voice – it was Rivet's – whispered in my ear: "So you have not yet quite settled that affair of Morin's?"

'At seven o'clock the next morning Henriette herself brought me a cup of chocolate. I never have drunk anything like it, soft, velvety, perfumed, delicious. I could hardly take away my lips from the cup, and she had hardly left the room when Rivet came in. He seemed nervous and irritable, like a man who had not slept, and he said to me crossly: "If you go on like this you will end by spoiling that affair of Morin's!"

'At eight o'clock the aunt arrived. Our discussion was very short; they withdrew their complaint, and I left five hundred francs for the poor of the town. They wanted to keep us for the day, and they arranged an excursion to go and see some ruins. Henriette made signs to me to stay, behind their back, and I accepted, but Rivet was determined to go, and though I took him aside and begged and prayed him to do this for me, he appeared quite exasperated and kept saying to me: "I have had quite enough of Morin's affair, do you hear?"

'Of course I was obliged to leave also, and it was one of the hardest moments of my life. I could have gone on arranging that business as long as I lived, and when we were in the railway carriage, after shaking hands with her in silence, I said to Rivet: "You are a brute!" And he replied: "My dear fellow, you were beginning to annoy me."

'On getting to the *Fanal* office, I saw a crowd waiting for us, and as soon as they saw us they all exclaimed: "Well, have you settled the affair of that pig of a Morin?" All La Rochelle was excited about it, and Rivet, who had got over his ill humour on the journey, had great difficulty in keeping himself from laughing as he said: "Yes, we have managed it, thanks to Labarbe." And we went to Morin's.

'He was sitting in an easy chair with mustard plasters on his legs and cold bandages on his head, nearly dead with misery. He was coughing with the short cough of a dying man, without anyone knowing how he had caught it, and his wife looked at him like a tigress ready to eat him. As soon as he saw us he trembled so violently that his hands and knees shook, so I said to him at once: "It is all settled, you dirty scamp, but don't do such a thing again."

'He got up, choking, took my hands and kissed them as if they had belonged to a prince, cried, nearly fainted, embraced Rivet and even kissed Madame Morin, who gave him such a push as to send him staggering back into his chair; but he never got over the blow; his mind had been too much upset. In all the country round, moreover, he was called nothing but "that pig of a Morin", and the epithet went through him like a sword thrust every time he heard it. When a street boy called after him, "Pig!" he turned his head instinctively. His friends also overwhelmed him with horrible jokes and used to ask him, whenever they were eating ham, "Is it a bit of yourself?" He died two years later.

'As for myself, when I was a candidate, twelve years afterwards, for the Chamber of Deputies, I called on the new notary at Tous-serre, Monsieur Belloncle, to solicit his vote, and a tall, beautiful and buxom lady received me. "You do not know me again?" she said. And I stammered out: "Why – no, madame." "Henriette Bonnel." "Ah!" And I felt myself turning pale, while she seemed perfectly at her ease and looked at me with a smile. As soon as she had left me alone with her husband he took both my hands, and, squeezing them as if he meant to crush them, he said: "I have been intending to go and see you for a long time, my dear sir, for my wife has very often talked to me about you. I know, yes, I know in what painful circumstances you made her acquaintance, and I know also how perfectly you behaved, how full of delicacy, tact and devotion you showed yourself in the affair – " he hesitated and then spoke in a lower tone, as if he had been saying something coarse, "in the affair of that pig of a Morin."'

Useless Beauty

I

About half-past five one afternoon at the end of June when the sun was shining warm and bright into the large courtyard, an elegant victoria with two beautiful black horses drew up in front of the mansion.

The Comtesse de Mascaret came down the steps just as her husband, who was coming home, appeared in the carriage entrance. He stopped for a few moments to look at his wife and turned rather pale. The countess was very beautiful, graceful and distinguished looking, with her long oval face, her complexion like yellow ivory, her large grey eyes and her black hair; and she got into her carriage without looking at him, without even seeming to have noticed him, with such a particularly high-bred air that the furious jealousy by which he had been devoured for so long again gnawed at his heart. He went up to her and said: 'You are going for a drive?'

She merely replied disdainfully: 'You see I am!'

'In the Bois de Boulogne?'

'Most probably.'

'May I come with you?'

'The carriage belongs to you.'

Without being surprised at the tone in which she answered him, he got in and sat down by his wife's side and said: 'Bois de Boulogne.' The footman jumped up beside the coachman, and the horses as usual pranced and tossed their heads until they were in the street. Husband and wife sat side by side without speaking. He was thinking how to begin a conversation, but she maintained such an obstinately hard look that he did not venture to make the attempt. At last, however, he cunningly, accidentally as it were, touched the countess's gloved hand with his own, but she drew her arm away with a movement which was so expressive of disgust that he remained thoughtful, in spite of his usual authoritative and despotic character, and he said: 'Gabrielle!'

'What do you want?'

'I think you are looking adorable.'

She did not reply, but remained lying back in the carriage, looking like an irritated queen. By that time they were driving up the Champs Elysées, towards the Arc de Triomphe. That immense monument, at the end of the long avenue, raised its colossal arch against the red sky and the sun seemed to be descending on it,[showering fiery dust on it from the sky.]The stream of carriages, with dashes of sunlight reflected in the silver trappings of the harness and the glass of the lamps, flowed on in a double current towards the town and towards the Bois, and the Comte de Mascaret continued: 'My dear Gabrielle!'

Unable to control herself any longer, she replied in an exasperated voice: 'Oh! do leave me in peace, pray! I am not even allowed to have my carriage to myself now.'

He pretended not to hear her and continued: 'You never have looked so pretty as you do today.'

Her patience had come to an end, and she replied with irrepressible anger: 'You are wrong to notice it, for I swear to you that I will never have anything to do with you in that way again.'

The count was decidedly stupefied and upset, and, his violent nature gaining the upper hand, he exclaimed: 'What do you mean by that?' in a tone that betrayed rather the brutal master than the lover.

She replied in a low voice, so that the servants might not hear amid the deafening noise of the wheels: 'Ah! What do I mean by that? What do I mean by that? Now I recognise you again! Do you want me to tell everything?'

'Yes.'

'Everything that has weighed on my heart since I have been the victim of your terrible selfishness?'

He had grown red with surprise and anger and he growled between his closed teeth: 'Yes, tell me everything.'

[He was a tall, broad-shouldered man, with a big red beard, a handsome man, a man of the world, who passed as a perfect husband and an excellent father, and now, for the first time since they had started, she turned towards him and looked him full in the face.]

'Ah! You will hear some disagreeable things, but you must know that I am prepared for everything, that I fear nothing, and you less than anyone today.'

He also was looking into her eyes and was already shaking with rage as he said in a low voice: 'You are mad.'

'No, but I will no longer be the victim of the hateful penalty of maternity which you have inflicted on me for eleven years! I wish to take my place in society as I have the right to do, as all women have the right to do.'

He suddenly grew pale again and stammered: 'I do not understand you.'

'Oh! yes; you understand me well enough. It is now three months since I had my last child, and as I am still very beautiful, and as, in spite of all your efforts, you cannot spoil my figure, as you just now perceived when you saw me on the doorstep, you think it is time that I should think of having another child.'

'But you are talking nonsense!'

'No, I am not, I am thirty, and I have had seven children, and we have been married eleven years, and you hope that this will go on for ten years longer, after which you will leave off being jealous.'

He seized her arm and squeezed it, saying: 'I will not allow you to talk to me like that much longer.'

'And I shall talk to you till the end, until I have finished all I have to say to you, and if you try to prevent me, I shall raise my voice so that the two servants, who are on the box, may hear. I only allowed you to come with me for that object, for I have these witnesses who will oblige you to listen to me and to contain yourself, so now pay attention to what I say. I have always felt an antipathy to you, and I have always let you see it, for I have never lied, monsieur. You married me in spite of myself; you forced my parents, who were in embarrassed circumstances, to give me to you, because you were rich, and they made me marry you in spite of my tears.

'So you bought me, and as soon as I was in your power, as soon as I had become your companion, ready to attach myself to you, to forget your coercive and threatening proceedings in order that I might only remember that I ought to be a devoted wife and to love you as much as it might be possible for me to love you, you became jealous, jealous as no man has ever been before, with the base, ignoble jealousy of a spy, which was as degrading to you as it was to me. I had not been married eight months when you suspected me of every perfidiousness, and you even told me so. What a disgrace! And as you could not prevent me from being beautiful and from pleasing people, from being called in drawing-rooms and also in the newspapers one of the most beautiful women in Paris, you tried everything you could think of to keep admirers from me, and you hit upon the abominable idea of making me spend my life in a constant state of motherhood, until the time should come when I should disgust every man. Oh, do not deny it. I did not understand it for some time, but then I guessed it. You even boasted about it to your sister, who told me of it, for she is fond of me and was disgusted at your boorish coarseness.

'Ah! Remember how you have behaved in the past! How for eleven years you have compelled me to give up all society and simply be a mother to your children. And when during each pregnancy you grew disgusted with me, I was sent into the country, the family château, among fields and meadows. And when I reappeared, fresh, pretty and unspoiled, still seductive and constantly surrounded by admirers, hoping that at last I should live a little more like a rich young society woman, you were seized with jealousy again, and you began once more to persecute me with that infamous and hateful desire from which you are suffering at this moment by my side. And it is not the desire of possessing me, for I should never have refused myself to you, but it is the wish to make me unsightly.

'And then that abominable and mysterious thing occurred which I was a long time in understanding (but I grew sharp by dint of watching your thoughts and actions): you attached yourself to your children with all the security which they gave you while I bore them. You felt affection for them, with all your aversion to me, and in spite of your ignoble fears, which were momentarily allayed by your pleasure in seeing me lose my symmetry.

'Oh! how often have I noticed that joy in you! I have seen it in your eyes and guessed it. You loved your children as victories, and not because they were of your own blood. They were victories over me, over my youth, over my beauty, over my charms, over the compliments which were paid me and over those that were whispered around me without being paid to me personally. And you are proud of them, you make a parade of them, you take them out for drives in the Bois de Boulogne and you give them donkey rides at Montmorency. You take them to theatrical matinées so that you may be seen in the midst of them, so that the people may say: "What a kind father," and that it may be repeated –'

He had seized her wrist with savage brutality, and he squeezed it so violently that she was quiet and nearly cried out with the pain and he said to her in a whisper: 'I love my children, do you hear? What you have just told me is disgraceful in a mother. But you belong to me; I am master – your master – I can exact from you what I like and when I like – and I have the law on my side.'

He was trying to crush her fingers in the strong grip of his large, muscular hand, and she, livid with pain, tried in vain to free them from that vice which was crushing them. The agony made her breathe hard, and the tears came into her eyes.

'You see that I am the master and the stronger,' he said.

When he somewhat loosened his grip, she asked him: 'Do you think that I am a religious woman?'

He was surprised and stammered, 'Yes.'

'Do you think that I could lie if I swore to the truth of anything to you before an altar on which Christ's body is?'

'No.'

'Will you go with me to some church?'

'What for?'

'You shall see. Will you?'

'If you absolutely wish it, yes.'

She raised her voice and said: 'Philippe!' And the coachman, bending down a little, without taking his eyes from his horses, seemed to turn his ear alone towards his mistress, who continued: 'Drive to St Philippe-du-Roule.' And the victoria, which had reached the entrance of the Bois de Boulogne, returned to Paris.

Husband and wife did not exchange a word further during the drive, and when the carriage stopped before the church Madame de Mascaret jumped out and entered it, followed by the count, a few yards distant. She went, without stopping, as far as the choir-screen, and falling on her knees at a chair, she buried her face in her hands. She prayed for a long time, and he, standing behind her, could see that she was crying. She wept noiselessly, as women weep when they are in great, poignant grief. There was a kind of undulation in her body, which ended in a little sob, which was hidden and stifled by her fingers. But the Comte de Mascaret thought that the situation was lasting too long, and he touched her on the shoulder. That contact recalled her to herself, as if she had been burned, and getting up, she looked straight into his eyes. 'This is what I have to say to you. I am afraid of nothing, whatever you may do to me. You may kill me if you like. One of the children is not yours, and one only; that I swear to you before God, who hears my words. That was the only revenge that was possible for me in return for all your abominable masculine tyrannies, in return for the servitude of child-bearing to which you have condemned me. Who was my lover? That you never will know! You may suspect everyone, but you will never find out. I gave myself to him, without love and without pleasure, only for the sake of betraying you, and he also made me a mother. Which is the child? That also you never will know. I have seven; try to find out! I intended to tell you this later, for one has not avenged oneself on a man by deceiving him unless he knows it. You have driven me to confess it today. I have now finished.'

She hurried through the church towards the open door, expecting to hear behind her the quick steps of her husband whom she had defied, and to be knocked to the ground by a blow of his fist, but she heard nothing and reached her carriage. She jumped into it at a bound, overwhelmed with anguish and breathless with fear, and called out to the coachman: 'Home!' and the horses set off at a quick trot.

II

The Comtesse de Mascaret was waiting in her room for dinner-time as a condemned man awaits the hour of his execution. What was her husband going to do? Had he come home? Despotic, passionate, ready for any violence as he was, what was he meditating, what had he made up his mind to do? There was no sound in the house, and every moment she looked at the clock. Her maid had come and dressed her for the evening and had then left the room again. Eight o'clock struck and almost at the same moment there were two knocks at the door, and the butler came in and announced dinner.

'Has the count come in?'

'Yes, Madame la Comtesse. He is in the dining-room.'

For a few seconds she felt inclined to arm herself with a small revolver which she had bought some time before, foreseeing the tragedy which was being rehearsed in her heart. But she remembered that all the children would be there, and she took nothing except a bottle of smelling salts. He rose somewhat ceremoniously from his chair. They exchanged a slight bow and sat down. The three boys with their tutor, Abbé Martin, were on her right and the three girls, with Miss Smith, their English governess, were on her left. The youngest child, who was only three months old, remained upstairs with his nurse.

The abbé said grace as usual when there was no company, for the children did not come down to dinner when guests were present. Then they began dinner. The countess, suffering from emotion, which she had not calculated upon, remained with her eyes cast down, while the count scrutinised now the three boys and now the three girls with an uncertain, unhappy expression, which travelled from one to the other. Suddenly he pushed his glass from him and it broke, and the wine was spilt on the tablecloth, and at the slight noise caused by this little accident the countess started up from her chair, and for the first time they looked at each other. Then, in spite of themselves, in spite of the irritation of their nerves caused by every glance, they continued to exchange looks, rapid as pistol shots.

The abbé, who felt that there was some cause for embarrassment which he could not divine, attempted to begin a conversation and tried various subjects, but his useless efforts elicited no response. The countess, with feminine tact and obeying the instincts of a woman of breeding, attempted to answer him two or three times, but in vain. She could not find words in the perplexity of her mind, and her own voice almost frightened her in the silence of the large room, where nothing was heard except the slight sound of plates and knives and forks. Suddenly her husband said to her, bending forward: 'Here, amid your children, will you swear to me that what you told me just now is true?'

The hatred which was fermenting in her veins suddenly roused her, and replying to that question with the same firmness with which she had replied to his looks, she raised both her hands, the right pointing towards the boys and the left towards the girls, and said in a strong, resolute voice and without any hesitation: 'On the heads of my children, I swear that I have told you the truth.'

He got up and throwing his table napkin on the table with a movement of exasperation, he turned round and flung his chair against the wall, and then went out without another word, while she, uttering a deep sigh, as if after a first victory, went on in a calm voice: 'You must not pay any attention to your father's behaviour, my darlings; he was very much upset a short time ago, but he will be all right again in a few days.'

Then she talked with the abbé and Miss Smith and had tender, pretty words for all her children, those sweet, tender mother's ways which unfold little hearts. When dinner was over she went into the drawing-room, all her children following her. She made the elder ones chatter and told stories to the younger ones and when their bedtime came she kissed them for a long time and then went alone into her room. She waited, for she had no doubt that the count would come, and she made up her mind then, as her children were not with her, to protect herself, and in the pocket of her dress she put the little loaded revolver which she had bought a few days previously. The hours went by, the hours struck, and every sound was hushed in the house. The cabs continued to rumble through the streets, but their noise was only heard vaguely through the shuttered and curtained windows. She waited, full of nervous energy, without any fear of him now, ready for anything, and almost triumphant, for she had found means of torturing him continually during every moment of his life. But the first gleam of dawn came in through the fringe at the bottom of her curtain without his having entered her room, and then she awoke to the fact, with much amazement, that he was not coming. Having locked and bolted her door, for greater security, she went to bed at last and remained there, with her eyes open, thinking and barely understanding it all, without being able to guess what he was going to do. When her maid brought her tea she at the same time handed her a letter from her husband. He told her that he was going to undertake a long journey and in a postscript added that his lawyer would provide her with any sums of money she might require for all her expenses.

III

It was at the Opera, between two acts of *Robert the Devil*. In the stalls the men were standing up, with their hats on, their waistcoats cut very low so as to show a large amount of white shirt-front in which gold and jewelled studs glistened. They were looking at the boxes full of ladies in low dresses covered with diamonds and pearls, who were expanding like flowers in that illuminated hothouse, where the beauty of their faces and the whiteness of their shoulders seemed to bloom in order to be gazed at, amid the sound of the music and of human voices.

Two friends, with their backs to the orchestra, were scanning those rows of elegance, that exhibition of real or false charms, of jewels, of luxury and of pretension which displayed itself in all parts of the house. Roger de Salnis said to his companion, Bernard Grandin: 'Just look how beautiful the Comtesse de Mascaret is still.'

The older man in turn looked through his opera glasses at a tall lady in a box opposite. She appeared to be still very young, and her striking beauty seemed to attract all eyes in every corner of the house. Her pale complexion, of an ivory tint, gave her the appearance of a statue, while a small diamond coronet glistened on her black hair like a streak of light. When he had looked at her for some time, Bernard Grandin replied with a jocular accent of sincere conviction: 'You may well call her beautiful!'

'How old do you think she is?'

'Wait a moment. I can tell you exactly, for I have known her since she was a child and I saw her make her début into society when she was quite a girl. She is – she is thirty . . . thirty-six.'

'Impossible!'

'I am sure of it.'

'She looks twenty-five.'

'She has had seven children.'

'It is incredible.'

'And what is more, they are all seven alive, as she is a very good mother. I occasionally go to the house, which is a very quiet and pleasant one, where one may see the phenomenon of the family in the midst of society.'

'How very strange! And have there never been any reports about her?'

'Never.'

'But what about her husband? He is peculiar, is he not?'

'Yes and no. Very likely there has been a little drama between them, one of those domestic dramas which one suspects, never finds out exactly, but guesses at pretty closely.'

'What is it?'

'I do not know anything about it. Mascaret leads a very fast life now, after being a model husband. As long as he remained a good spouse he had a shocking temper, was crabbed and easily took offence, but since he has been leading his present wild life he has become quite different. But one might surmise that he has some trouble, a worm gnawing somewhere, for he has aged very much.'

Thereupon the two friends talked philosophically for some minutes about the secret, unknowable troubles which differences of character or perhaps physical antipathies, which are not perceived at first, give rise to in families, and then Roger de Salnis, who was still looking at Madame de Mascaret through his opera glasses, said: 'It is almost incredible that that woman can have had seven children!'

'Yes, in eleven years; after which, when she was thirty, she refused to have any more, in order to take her place in society, which she seems likely to do for many years.'

'Poor women!'

'Why do you pity them?'

'Why? Ah! my dear fellow, just consider! Eleven years in a condition of motherhood for such a woman! What a hell! All her youth, all her beauty, every hope of success, every poetical ideal of a brilliant life sacrificed to that abominable law of reproduction which turns the normal woman into a mere machine for bringing children into the world.

'Does anyone know why and how her husband, having such a companion by his side, and especially after having been boorish enough to make her a mother seven times, suddenly left her, to run after bad women?'

Grandin replied: 'Oh, my dear fellow, it was probably because he found that an increasing family was becoming too expensive.'

Just then the curtain rose for the third act, and they turned round, took off their hats and sat down.

IV

The Comte and Comtesse de Mascaret were sitting side by side, without speaking, in the carriage which was taking them home from the Opera, when suddenly the husband said to his wife: 'Gabrielle! don't you think this has lasted long enough?'

'What?'

'The horrible punishment to which you have condemned me for the last six years?'

'What do you want? I can't help it.'

'Then tell me which of them it is.'

'Never.'

'Think that I can no longer see my children or feel them round me, without having my heart burdened with this doubt. Tell me which of them it is, and I swear that I will forgive you and treat it like the others.'

'I have not the right to do so.'

'Do you not see that I can no longer endure this life, this thought which is wearing me out, or this question which I am constantly asking myself, this question which tortures me each time I look at them? It is driving me mad.'

'Then you have suffered a great deal?' she said.

'Terribly. Should I, without that, have accepted the horror of living by your side, and the still greater horror of feeling and knowing that there is one among them whom I cannot recognise and who prevents me from loving the others?'

'Then you have really suffered very much?' she repeated.

And he replied in a constrained and sorrowful voice: 'Yes, for do I not tell you every day that it is intolerable torture to me? Should I have remained in that house, near you and them, if I did not love them? Oh! You have behaved abominably towards me. All the affection of my heart I have bestowed upon my children, and that you know. I am for them a father of a past generation, as I was for you a husband of the old school. I am a man who acts on his instincts, a man of former days. Yes, I will confess it, you have made me terribly jealous, because you are a woman of another race, of another soul, with other requirements. Oh! I shall never forget the things you said to me, but from that day I troubled myself no more about you. I did not kill you, because then I should have had no means on earth of ever discovering which of our – of your children is not mine. I have waited, but I have suffered more than you would believe, for I can no longer venture to love them, except, perhaps, the two eldest; I no longer venture to look at them, to call them to me, to kiss them; I cannot take them on my knee without asking myself, "Can it be this one?" I have been correct in my behaviour towards you for six years, and even complaisant. Tell me the truth, and I swear that I will do nothing unkind.'

He thought, in spite of the darkness of the carriage, that he could perceive she was moved, and feeling certain that she was going to speak at last, he said: 'I beg you, I beseech you to tell me – '

'I have been more guilty than you think perhaps,' she replied, 'but as I could no longer endure that life of continual motherhood, I had only one means of driving you from me. I lied before God, and I lied, with my hand raised above the heads of my children, for I have never, never been faithless to you.'

He seized her arm in the darkness, and squeezing it as he had done on that terrible day of their drive in the Bois de Boulogne, he stammered: 'Is that true?'

'It is true.'

But, wild with grief, he said with a groan: 'I shall have fresh doubts that will never end! When did you lie, the last time or now? How am I to believe you at present? How can one believe a woman after that? I shall never again know what I am to think. I would rather you had said to me, "It is Jacques," or, "It is Jeanne." '

The carriage drove into the courtyard of the house and when it had drawn up in front of the steps the count alighted first, as usual, and offered his wife his arm to mount the stairs. As soon as they reached the first floor he said: 'May I speak to you for a few moments longer?' And she replied, 'Certainly.'

They went into a small drawing-room and a footman, in some surprise, lighted the wax candles. As soon as he had left the room and they were alone the count continued: 'How am I to know the truth? I have begged you a thousand times to speak, but you have remained dumb, impenetrable, inflexible, inexorable, and now today you tell me that you have been lying. For six years you have actually allowed me to believe such a thing! No, you are lying now, I do not know why, but out of pity for me, perhaps?'

She replied in a sincere and convincing manner: 'If I had not done so, I should have had four more children in the last six years!'

'Can a mother speak like that?'

'Oh!' she replied, 'I do not feel that I am the mother of children who have never been born; it is enough for me to be the mother of those that I have and to love them with all my heart. I am a woman of the civilised world – we all are – and we are no longer, and we refuse to be, mere females to restock the earth.'

She got up, but he seized her hands. 'Only one word, Gabrielle. Tell me the truth!'

'I have just told you. I have never been unfaithful to you.'

He looked her full in the face, observing how beautiful she was, with her eyes grey as a frosty sky. In her night-black hair the diamond coronet scintillated like a milky way. He suddenly felt, by a kind of intuition, that this splendid creature was not merely a being destined to perpetuate the race, but the strange and mysterious product of all our complicated desires which have been accumulating in us for aeons, but which have been turned aside from their primitive and divine object and have wandered after a mystic, imperfectly perceived and intangible beauty.

There are such women to be found, who bloom only in our dreams, adorned with all that civilisation has to give of poetry, of luxury, of coquetry, and of inherent feminine aesthetic charm – living statues who waken, as though in some voluptuous dream, desires vague and mysterious and unnameable.

Her husband remained standing before her, stupefied at his tardy and obscure discovery, confusedly hitting on the cause of his former jealousy and understanding it all very imperfectly. At last he said: 'I believe you, for I feel at this moment that you are not lying, and before I really thought that you were.'

She held out her hand to him: 'We are friends then?'

He took her hand and kissed it and replied: 'We are friends. Thank you, Gabrielle.'

Then he went out, continuing to look at her, surprised that she was still so beautiful and feeling a strange emotion arising in him, more formidable, perhaps, than the old love in its primitive and simple form.

The Olive Orchard

I

When the loafers of the little Provençal harbour of Garandou, on the Bay of Pisca, between Marseilles and Toulon, caught sight of the Abbé Vilbois's boat coming in from fishing, they went down to the beach to help him land.

The abbé was alone, and he was rowing like a real sailor, with uncommon energy in spite of his fifty-eight years. With sleeves rolled up over his muscular arms, his cassock pulled up between his knees and unbuttoned across his chest, his shovel-hat beside him and a pith helmet covered with white cloth on his head, he seemed like a sturdy, rather odd-looking priest from the tropics, more ready for exciting deeds than for saying Mass.

Occasionally he looked over his shoulder to find the exact landing-place, then pulled rhythmically and hard, to show, and not for the first time, those poor sailors of the south how men from the north can row. The boat sped forward lightly over the sand, as if it were going to climb to the very top of the beach, then stopped dead, burying its keel in the shingle, and the five men who had been watching came to its side, pleasant fellows all, cheery, and on the best of terms with their curé.

'Well, monsieur le curé,' said one of them, with a strong Provençal accent, 'had good luck?'

The Abbé Vilbois shipped his oars, exchanged his pith helmet for his priest's hat, rolled down his sleeves, buttoned up his cassock, and, once more in garb and bearing the curé of the village, replied proudly: 'Yes, indeed, very good: three catfish, two congers and some flounders.'

The five fishermen examined the catch as experts – the fat catfish, the flat-headed congers, ugly sea-serpents, and the flounders with their violet zigzag stripes and orange bands.

One of them said: 'I will carry them up to the house, monsieur le curé.'

'Thanks, my good man.'

Shaking hands all round, the priest started off, followed by one of the men and leaving the others to see to his boat. Strong, and with the dignity of his high position, he walked slowly but steadily on. Still warm after his vigorous row, he took off his hat as he passed under the olive trees to expose to the night air, with its warmth tempered by a sea breeze, his big head, covered with white hair cut straight and short, more the head of an officer than of a priest. The village was on a little hill in the middle of a broad valley which ran down to the sea.

It was an evening in July. The dazzling sun, which was just touching the jagged peaks of distant hills, made longer and yet longer the shadow of the priest on the road in its shroud of dust, while his enormous hat, making a broad, dark blot upon the field beside him, seemed, as it were, to climb quickly up the olives, only to fall as quickly to earth and to creep among the trunks of the trees.

There rose from under the Abbé Vilbois' feet a cloud of fine dust, that thin flour with which roads in Provence are covered in summer, and it curled, like grey smoke, round his cassock, the bottom of which it covered as with a veil. Cooler now, with his hands in his pockets he went steadily forward, like a mountaineer making a stiff ascent. With calm eyes he looked towards the village, that village in which he had been curé for twenty years, the village which he had chosen and which had been given to him as a great favour, and in which he hoped to die. The church, his church, raised itself high above the mass of houses in a cluster round its walls, with its two uneven square towers of brown stone, whose outlines had been seen for years untold in this beautiful southern valley, more like the strong towers of a castle than the steeples of a church.

The abbé was feeling pleased with himself, for he had caught three catfish, two congers and some flounders. He would have yet another little victory in the eyes of his parishioners, he whom they respected, most of all, perhaps, because, in spite of his age, he was the strongest man in the district. Such innocent little vanities were his chief pleasure. He was such a good shot with a pistol that he could pick off the stalk of a flower; he sometimes fenced with his neighbour, the tobacconist, once the fencing-master of a regiment; and he rowed better than anyone on that coast.

In years gone by, the Baron Vilbois had been well known in the fashionable world, turning priest after an unfortunate love affair.

Scion of an old family of Picardy, which was royalist and pious, and which for centuries had given its sons to the Army, the Law or the Church, he had at one time the intention of becoming a priest, on the advice of his mother, but, his father objecting, he decided to go to Paris, study law, and then look out for some good post in the courts. As he was finishing his studies, his father died of pneumonia, caught while shooting on the marshes, and his mother, overwhelmed with grief, died shortly afterwards. So, having thus come into a considerable fortune, he gave up his idea of following a profession and was content to live the life of a man of means.

Handsome, intelligent, though his outlook on life was prejudiced by the beliefs, the traditions and the principles which, as well as his native strength, he inherited, he was a favourite everywhere, popular in the more intellectual circles of society, and enjoying life as a wealthy, austere and well-liked young man generally does.

After some meetings at a friend's house, he fell in love with a young actress, a young student of the Conservatoire, who made a brilliant début at the Odéon.

He fell in love with all the violence, all the passion of a man born to believe in absolutism. He fell in love with her as he saw her in the romantic part in which she won great success on her first appearance in public.

She was pretty, by nature perverse, with the look of an unspoilt child which he used to call her angel-look. She was clever enough to conquer him completely, turning him into one of those love-stricken fools whom a woman's look or petticoat burns on the pyre of deadly passions. So he took her for his mistress, made her leave the stage, and loved her for four years with ever-increasing intensity. Indeed, in spite of his name and the great traditions of his family, he would have married her, had he not discovered one day that she was deceiving him with the friend who had introduced her to him. The horror of the shock was the greater because she was pregnant, and he was awaiting the birth of the child to decide on marrying her.

When he obtained all the proofs of her infidelity, letters which he came across in a drawer, he raged at her for her treachery and low deceit with all the ferocity of the half-savage that he was.

But she, the guttersnipe, impudent and shameless, sure of the other man as she was of him, bold, too, as the women who stand atop the barricades out of pure devilry, defied and insulted him, and, as he raised his hand, pointed to her condition.

He stopped and turned pale, imagining that a child of his was in that defiled flesh, in that vile body, in that unclean beast – a child of his! Then he threw himself upon her to crush them both, to annihilate the double shame. She was frightened, giving herself up for lost, and as she recoiled from his fist and saw his foot ready to destroy herself and the child unborn, she cried out: 'Don't kill me: it is not yours, it is his!'

He started back, dumbfounded and bewildered, and stammered: 'What are you saying?'

She, suddenly mad with fear of the death which she saw in this man's eyes and gestures, repeated: 'It is not yours; it is his.'

He, completely prostrated, murmured through his teeth: 'The child?'

'Yes.'

'You lie!'

And again he made to crush her, while she, on her knees, and trying to get away from him, went on babbling: 'But I tell you it is his: if it were yours, would not I have had it long ago?'

This argument convinced him. In one of those flashes of thought, when all arguments are seen with brilliant clearness, concise, un-answerable, conclusive, irresistible, he was convinced. He was absolutely sure that he was not the father of that wretched unborn child, and, relieved, freed, of a sudden almost pacified, he gave up the idea of killing its detestable mother.

He said, more gently: 'Get up, go away, never let me see you again.'

She obeyed, crushed, and went away.

He never saw her again.

He, too, went away down south, to the sun, and halted at a village in the middle of a valley on the Mediterranean. He took a room in an inn looking out on the sea, and remained there for eighteen months of grief and despair, away from everybody.

Ever before him were the memories of the woman who had betrayed him, her charm, her surroundings, her inexpressible witchery, and his longing for her presence and her kisses.

He wandered through the valleys of Provence, seeking to forget his sorrow in the sun which was softened by the grey leaves of the olive trees.

Here, in this solitude of pain, the old piety, the more reasonable fervour of his early faith came back to him gently and mercifully. The religion which had formerly seemed to him a refuge from the unknown world, now seemed a haven of rest from the world of treachery and torture. He had never lost the habit of prayer. To prayer, then, he devoted himself in his trouble, often going at dusk to kneel in the darkened church, where a solitary light, holy guardian of the sanctuary and symbol of the Divine Presence, was shining.

He laid his sorrows before this God, his God, craving for advice, pity, help, protection, consolation, and every day his prayers became more and more fervent. His bleeding heart, consumed by love of a woman, was bare and throbbing, eager for tenderness. Little by little, through prayer and the solitary life, with ever-increasing piety, and by giving himself up entirely to that secret communion of the devout with the

Saviour who consoles and draws the unhappy unto Him, he found the Divine Love and drove the other from him.

Then he went back to the plans of his youth and decided to offer to the Church a broken life which should have been hers in its early vigour.

He became a priest. Through family influence he was appointed curé of the Provençal village to which chance had directed him, and having handed over a large part of his fortune to charity, only keeping sufficient to enable him to be of use and of help to the poor, he retired from the world to a life of piety and of devotion to his fellow creatures.

He was a priest of strict views, but kindly, a sort of religious guide with the temperament of a soldier, a guide who led, with forcibleness, into the path of righteousness poor humanity, blind, straying, lost in this forest of life, in which all our instincts, our tastes, our desires, are as a maze of paths. But much of the man of old days remained alive within him. He was still fond of vigorous exercise, of sport, of fencing, and he hated women, all of them, with the fear of a child before some mysterious danger.

II

The sailor who was following the priest had a desire, natural enough in one of the south, for a talk, but he hardly dared take the risk, for the abbé was a somewhat stern shepherd to his flock. At last he ventured: 'You are comfortable in your shack, monsieur le curé?'

This shack was one of those tiny retreats in which the Provençals of the towns and villages rest and enjoy fresh air in summer. The abbé had taken this cottage in the middle of an olive orchard, five minutes' walk from his stuffy presbytery, which adjoined the church and was in the very middle of his parish. Even in summer, however, he did not actually live in the shack but only went there for a few days occasionally to be in the open and practise with his pistol.

'Yes, my friend,' replied the priest, 'I am very happy there.'

They saw the low dwelling among the trees before them. Painted pink, with the swaying branches and leaves of the olive trees giving effects of stripes and spots, it had the appearance of some gigantic Provençal mushroom.

They saw, too, a tall woman walking backwards and forwards, getting the little dinner-table set, putting down, in her own slow way, one after the other, a fork and spoon, a plate, a napkin, a piece of bread, a glass.

She wore the little bonnet of the people of Arles, a pointed cone of black silk or velvet with a white mushroom as ornament.

When the abbé was within calling distance, he hailed her: 'Marguerite!'

She stopped to look round, and, recognising her master, replied: 'Ah, it's you, monsieur le curé!'

'Yes, and I am bringing you a good catch. Grill me a catfish with butter, nothing but butter, you understand?'

The servant, coming to meet them, examined with the eye of an expert the fish which the sailor was carrying.

'We have already got a fowl cooked with rice,' she said.

'That can't be helped. Tomorrow's fish is not so good as one just out of the sea. For once in a way I am going to indulge myself in a really fine feed: the sin is not great.'

The servant chose the fish and, as she was taking it away, turned to say: 'Ah! a man has come three times to see you, monsieur le curé.'

He asked, quite unconcernedly: 'A man? What sort of man?'

'The sort of man whom one doesn't want to see.'

'What! A beggar?'

'Perhaps, perhaps not. I should rather think he was a *maoufatan*.'

The abbé burst out laughing at that Provençal word, which means scallywag, or tramp, for he knew how nervous Marguerite was, and that she was always imagining, especially at night, that they would both be murdered in the cottage.

He gave the sailor a few coppers and sent him off. Then, as he still kept his old habit of cleanliness and neatness, he said: 'I am going to wash my hands and face.'

Marguerite called out to him from the kitchen where she was scraping the fish, whose scales were coming off like tiny pieces of silver: 'Why! There he is!'

The abbé looked out on the road and saw a man, who, at that distance, seemed very badly dressed, and who was coming slowly towards the house. He awaited him, still smiling at his servant's fright, and thinking: 'Upon my word, I believe she is right. He certainly has the look of a *maoufatan*.'

Without hurrying, his hands in his pockets, his eyes on the priest, the unknown fellow drew near. He was young, with a fair, curly beard, and bunches of his curly hair escaped from under his soft felt hat, a hat which was so dirty and so battered that nobody could ever have guessed its original colour and shape. He had on a long, faded brown greatcoat, a ragged pair of trousers, and straw shoes, which gave him a soft, silent, disquieting walk – the walk of a tramp.

A few yards from the priest, he took off his ragged hat with a theatrical flourish, baring a blotched and dirty but well-formed head, bald on the top, a sure sign of hardship or youthful excess, for he certainly was not more than twenty-five.

The priest immediately took off his hat, too, guessing and feeling that this was no ordinary vagabond, no out-of-work labourer or habitual criminal who hardly knows any language but the mysterious talk of prisons.

'Good-day, monsieur le curé,' said the man.

The priest replied, simply: 'Good-day,' not wishing to call this suspicious-looking, ragged wayfarer 'sir'.

They looked hard at each other, and under the gaze of this tramp the abbé felt uneasy, troubled as if he were facing an unknown enemy, beset by one of those curious sensations which make the body shiver and the blood run cold.

At last the vagabond said: 'Well, do you recognise me?'

Very much astonished, the priest replied: 'I? Not at all. I don't know you.'

'Ah! You don't know me. Look at me again.'

'I have had a good look at you. I have never seen you before.'

'That's true enough,' replied the fellow sarcastically, 'but I am now going to show you somebody whom you know better.'

He put on his hat and unbuttoned his coat, showing his bare chest underneath it. A red belt round his thin stomach held up his trousers.

From his pocket he took an envelope, one of those impossible envelopes which every sort of stain has marked, one of those envelopes in which wandering, broken men keep hidden away in the lining of their clothes the odd papers, legitimate or forged, stolen or their own lawful property, which are their trusty safeguard against casual police officers. From the envelope he took a photograph, the cabinet size of those days, all yellow and faded after its many wanderings, and stained by the heat of his body.

Holding it up next to his face, he asked: 'Do you know this one, then?'

The priest stammered: 'Yes!'

'Who is it?'

'Myself.'

'You are sure?'

'Yes.'

'Well, look at us both, now, your portrait and me.'

The wretched old man had already seen that the two, the man of the photograph and the one laughing beside it were as alike as two brothers, but he did not yet understand, and he stammered: 'What do you want from me, then?'

In a nasty tone, the ruffian replied: 'What do I want? Well, first of all, I want you to recognise me.'

'Who are you?'

'What am I? Ask anyone on the road, ask your maid, go and ask the mayor of the district if you want to, while showing him this, and he'll have a good laugh, I'm telling you. Ah! Don't you want to recognise that I am your son, father curé?'

Then the old man, raising his arms with a biblical and despairing gesture, groaned: 'That is not true.'

The young man came closer to him.

'Ah! it is not true. Abbé, you must stop telling lies, do you hear?'

His looks were threatening and his fists were clenched, and he spoke with such rough conviction that the priest, moving back a few steps, began to ask himself which of them was wrong.

Once more, however, he insisted: 'I have never had a child.'

The other retorted: 'And no mistress, perhaps?'

The old man uttered firmly only one word, a proud assent: 'Yes.'

'And was not this mistress with child when you drove her out of your house?'

Suddenly the old wrath, stifled twenty-five years ago – not stifled, but walled up deep down in the heart of the lover – broke through the walls of pious devotion and self-renunciation which he had raised round it, and in wild fury he shouted: 'I drove her out because she was false to me and because she was with child by another. But for that, I would have killed her and you, sir, too!'

The young man hesitated, surprised in his turn by the sincerity of the curé's fury, and replied in a more gentle tone: 'Who told you that the child was another's?'

'She, herself, as she faced me.'

Then the vagabond, without arguing this statement, said, as casually as a guttersnipe pronouncing judgement: 'Well, all that need be said is that mamma was wrong when she defied you.'

Master of himself once more, after his outburst, the abbé asked: 'Who told you that you were my son?'

'She did, on her deathbed, monsieur le curé, and then this!' And he held up the little photograph.

The old man took it, and slowly and quietly, his heart full of sorrow, compared this unknown passer-by with the old picture of himself, and he no longer doubted that this outcast was his son.

Distress, unutterable emotion, appalling pain, like remorse for some bygone crime, filled his heart. He understood a little, he guessed the rest; he recalled the brutal scene of their parting. It was to save her life, threatened by him whom she had wronged, that the woman, the deceitful, faithless creature, had hurled that lie at him. And the lie had been successful. A son of his had been born, had grown up, had become this dirty tramp, stinking of vice as some filthy goat.

He whispered: 'Will you come for a little walk, to talk matters over?'

The other chuckled unpleasantly: 'Of course; that is what I have come for.'

They went off together, side by side, through the olive orchard. The sun had gone down, and the cool of a southern twilight spread its invisible cloak over the countryside. The abbé shivered, and raising his eyes in the usual priest-like manner, he saw all around him, shaking against the sky, the little greyish leaves of the holy tree which had sheltered under its slight shade the greatest pain of all – the one and only weakness of Christ.

A short and despairing prayer rose to his lips, a prayer made by that inner voice which does not utter it, the prayer of the believer calling on his Saviour: 'O God, help me!'

Then, turning to his son: 'So your mother is dead?'

A fresh grief passed through him and tore his heart, as he said the words, 'Your mother is dead.' It was a strange torment of the flesh of the man unable to forget, a cruel echo of the torture he had suffered. But even more bitter, perhaps, because she was dead, was the thrill of the memory of that delirious and brief happiness of his youth, of which nothing now remained but a scar.

The young man replied: 'Yes, monsieur le curé, my mother is dead.'

'Long ago?'

'Three years ago.'

A fresh doubt crossed the priest's mind.

'Why, then, did you not come sooner to find me?'

The other hesitated before replying: 'I could not. There were obstacles. For the moment, excuse me if I ask you to let me stop this confidential talk, which can be resumed by and by, when I will give you as many details as you please, for I must tell you I have had nothing to eat since yesterday morning.'

A wave of pity swept over the old man, and, quickly holding out his hands, he said: 'Oh! my poor child!'

The other took the two big hands which closed over his thinner, clammy and feverish fingers. Then he replied with his usual humbugging air: 'Well, well, I am beginning to believe that we shall understand each other after all.'

The curé started walking again.

'Let us go in to dinner,' he said.

Suddenly, with a little feeling of natural joy, curious and not unmixed, perhaps, he thought of the fine fish, which, with the chicken and rice, would make a good meal that day for this wretched creature.

The Arlesian servant, uneasy and already inclined to grumble, was waiting for them.

'Marguerite,' cried the abbé, 'carry the table inside, and as quickly as you can, and set it for two. Hurry up, I tell you!'

The servant stood still, amazed that her master was going to dine with this villainous-looking fellow.

Then the abbé himself set to work to carry the things set out for him into the only room on the ground floor.

Five minutes later he was seated opposite the vagabond before a tureen of cabbage soup which sent up between their faces a little cloud of steam.

III

When the plates were filled, the tramp hastened to swallow his soup greedily.

The abbé was no longer hungry, and only drank the soup slowly, leaving the bread at the bottom of his plate. Then suddenly he asked: 'What is your name?'

The fellow laughed, pleased to be satisfying his hunger.

'Unknown father, no other surname but my mother's, which probably you have not forgotten yet. On the other hand, I have two Christian names which certainly don't suit me: Philippe Auguste.'

The abbé grew pale and in a half-choked voice asked: 'Why did they give you those names?'

The vagabond shrugged his shoulders.

'You ought to be able to guess. After leaving you, mamma wanted to make your rival believe that I was his son, and he did believe it till I was nearly fifteen, when I began to grow too like you. Then he repudiated me, the skunk. They had given me his two Christian names, Philippe Auguste, and if I had had the luck to be like nobody in particular, or to be merely the son of some third bad-lot, I should be calling myself today the Vicomte Philippe Auguste da Pravallon, tardily recognised son of the count of the same name, senator. As it is, I christened myself 'No luck!'

'How do you know all that?'

'Because there were scenes and explanations in my presence – and jolly rough ones, I can tell you! Ah! that's what life teaches you!'

The priest was oppressed by a feeling even more painful and torturing than he had suffered in the last half-hour. He felt a sort of strangling, which was beginning, which would increase and which would finish by killing him. This feeling was the result, not so much of what he was hearing, as of the way in which it was being said, and the vile face of the blackguard who was emphasising it all. Between this man and himself, between his son and himself, he was beginning just now to see that open sewer of moral filth which for certain minds is deadly poison. That was his son? He could not yet believe it. He wanted all the proofs, every bit of them. He wanted to learn all, understand all, hear all, suffer all. He thought once more of the olive trees surrounding his little house, and for the second time he murmured: 'O God, help me!'

Philippe Auguste had finished his soup. He asked: 'Nothing more to eat, abbé?'

As the kitchen was in an annex outside the house, and Marguerite could not hear the curé when he called to her, he used to do so by striking a Chinese gong hung behind him near the wall.

He took up the leather gong-stick and struck the round metal plaque several times. A faint sound, which grew and grew, vibrating, sharp, piercing, horrible, came from it, the lament of beaten copper.

The servant came in. Her face was drawn with anger and she looked furiously at the *maoufatan*, as if, with her instinct of a faithful dog, she had a foreboding of the tragedy hanging over her master. She was carrying the grilled catfish, from which there arose the savoury smell of melted butter.

The abbé split the fish with a spoon, and as he gave the choicest portion to the child of his youth, said with a remnant of pride despite his misery: 'I myself caught him a little while ago!'

Marguerite remained in the room.

The priest turned to her.

'Bring some wine, good wine, the white wine of Cape Corsica.'

She looked as if she would almost refuse, and he had to repeat, a little sternly: 'Come along! Two bottles.' For when he had the rare pleasure of offering wine to anybody, he used to have a bottle, too.

Philippe Auguste, delighted, muttered: 'Capital! A fine idea! I haven't had such a good feed for a long time.'

The servant returned in a couple of minutes. The abbé considered them as long as two eternities, for a desire to know all was scorching his blood and devouring him with fires as of hell.

The corks of the bottles were drawn, but the servant remained in the room, staring at the young man.

'Leave us,' said the curé.

She pretended not to hear.

He repeated, almost roughly: 'I have told you to leave us alone.'

Then she went out.

Philippe Auguste was eating the fish, quickly and greedily, and his father was looking at him, more and more surprised and distressed at the evil which he saw in a face so like his own. The little pieces that the abbé put in his mouth remained in it, his choking throat refusing to let them pass, and he went on chewing them, seeking in his mind the question to which, among them all, he most desired the reply.

At last he said: 'What did she die of?'

'Lungs.'

'Was she ill long?'

'About eighteen months.'

'How did it begin?'

'No one knows.'

They stopped talking. The abbé went on thinking. So many things which he wanted to know were troubling him, for since their rupture, since the day he nearly killed her, he had heard nothing of her. True, he had had no desire to hear; for he had buried her in oblivion, her and his period of happiness. Now, however, that she was dead, he began to feel growing within him a desire to get news of her, an envious desire, almost the desire of a lover.

He went on: 'She was not alone, was she?'

'No. She was always living with him.'

The old man shuddered.

'With him! With Pravallon?'

'Of course.'

The man who had been betrayed in days gone by calculated that this very woman who had deceived him had lived for more than thirty years with his rival. Almost in spite of himself, he stammered: 'Were they happy together?'

The young man replied with a sneer: 'Certainly – with ups and downs. But for me, it would have been all right. I spoilt everything – in the end.'

'How, and why?' asked the priest.

'I have already told you. Because, until I was about fifteen, he always believed I was his son. But the old chap was no fool, and he found out the likeness all on his own, and then there were scenes. I was listening outside the door. He accused mamma of taking him in. Mamma retorted: "Is it my fault? You knew quite well when you took me on that I was the other man's mistress." The other man was you.'

'So they talked of me sometimes?'

'Yes, but never in front of me till the end, the very end, in those last days when mamma felt her death approaching. They did not trust me.'

'And you? Did you soon gather that your mother was not straight?'

'Of course. I am not a fool, you know, and I never have been. One gets a notion of such things as soon as one knows something of life.'

Philippe Auguste began to pour out glass after glass for himself. His eyes sparkled, his long fast hurrying on his intoxication.

The priest saw it. He nearly stopped him, but it struck him that intoxication made men foolish and talkative, so he filled up the young fellow's glass again.

Marguerite brought in the chicken with rice. Having put it on the table, she again stared at the tramp. Then she said, somewhat shocked: 'Look how drunk he is, monsieur le curé.'

'Leave us alone and go away,' answered the priest.

She went out, slamming the door.

He asked: 'What used your mother to say about me?'

'Why, the usual things a woman says about the man she has left: you were not easy to get on with, tiresome for a woman to live with, and with your fine ideas you would have made things difficult.'

'Did she say that often?'

'Yes; sometimes in a roundabout way, so that I should not understand. But I could always guess her meaning.'

'And how did they treat you in your home?'

'Me? Very well at first, and then very badly. When mamma saw that I was spoiling her game, she chucked me out.'

'How?'

'How? Why, when I was about sixteen I kicked over the traces, and then the idiots sent me to a reformatory, to get rid of me.'

He put his elbows on the table, his cheeks between his hands, and quite drunk, his mind fuddled by the wine, he was suddenly seized by one of those irresistible desires to talk about himself, which make drunkards in their cups drivel and romance. He smiled pleasantly with woman-like grace, that perverse grace which the priest recognised. And not only did he recognise it, but once more he felt that grace, so detestable and yet so caressing, which had conquered and destroyed him in bygone days. At that moment the young man was most like his mother, not in face, but in the ensnaring and treacherous look, and especially in the seduction of that tricky smile, which seemed to reveal all the baseness within.

Philippe Auguste told his story: 'Ha, ha! I have had a deuce of a life, I have, since I left the reformatory, a queer life for which a great novelist would pay well. Certainly, old Dumas, with his *Monte Cristo*, never invented queerer adventures than mine.'

He stopped for a moment, turning things over in his mind with the philosophical seriousness of one who is drunk, and then went on: 'When you want a boy to turn out well, you should never send him to a reformatory, whatever he may have done, because of the acquaintances he will make there. I played a practical joke that turned out badly. One evening as I was fooling around with three pals, all of us a little drunk – it was about nine o'clock – on the high road near the ford over the Folac, I came on a carriage in which everybody was asleep, the driver and his family, folk from Martinon who had been out to dinner. I caught hold of the horse by the bridle, got it and the trap on to the ferryboat, and shoved off the whole thing into midstream. That made some noise, and the chap who was driving woke up, and, not seeing anything, whipped up his horse. The horse gave a start and jumped into the river, dragging the trap after it. They were all drowned! My pals gave me away, though they had laughed all right when they saw me playing the fool. True, we never thought our fun would end so badly. We were only hoping to give the people a bath, which would have been funny enough.

'Since then, I have done nastier things, out of revenge for that little one, which, upon my soul, did not deserve punishment. But I won't bother you by telling you of them. I am only going to tell you the last, because I am sure it will please you. I have avenged you, papa.'

The abbé, who was eating nothing, looked at his son, terrified.

Philippe Auguste was going to talk again.

'No,' said the priest, 'by and by, not now.'

Turning round, he struck the strident Chinese gong.

Marguerite came in at once, and her master said, so roughly that she hung her head, frightened and obedient: 'Bring in the lamp and anything you have still to put on the table. After that, don't come back until you hear the gong.'

She went out and returned to place on the table a white china lamp with a green shade, a good piece of cheese and some fruit. Then she left the room.

'Now,' said the abbé firmly, 'I am listening.'

Philippe Auguste quietly filled his plate with dessert and his glass with wine; the second bottle was almost empty though the curé had not touched it.

The young man, stammering, his tongue clogged with too much food and drink, continued his story: 'Now I am going to tell you the last of my escapades, and rather a brutal one it is. I had got home again, and I was staying there in spite of their objections, for they were afraid of me – would you believe it? – of me. Oh! you must not annoy me. Oh no! I am ready to do anything when I am annoyed. You know, they were living together, and yet not together. He had two separate establishments, one the senator's, the other the lover's. But he was living with mamma more often than alone, for he couldn't do without her very long. Ah! mamma was jolly clever and strong of will; she knew how to keep a man, she did! She had got him, body and soul, and she kept him till the end. What idiots men are! Well, I had come back, and I was terrorising them. I am an artful dodger, I am, when I have to be, and I can beat anybody if it comes to spite or cuteness or a row. Then mamma fell ill and he settled her in a fine house near Meulan, in the middle of a park as big as a forest. That, as I have already told you, went on for about eighteen months. Then we felt the end approaching; he came from Paris every day and was really very much distressed.

'Well, one morning they had been jawing together for nearly an hour, and I was beginning to ask myself what it was all about, when they called me into the room, and mamma said: "I am near death, and there is something I want to disclose to you, in spite of the count's opinion." She always called him "the count" when she spoke of him. "It is the name of your father, who is still alive."

'I had asked her for it more than a hundred times . . . more than a hundred times . . . my father's name . . . more than a hundred times . . . and she had always refused to tell it me. I even think that one day I knocked her about, to get it out of her, but it was no use. Then, to get rid of me, she told me you were dead without a sixpence, that you never had been of any use, a mistake of her youth, a girl's slip, and so forth and so on. She told the yarn so well that I swallowed it whole, your death included. Now she said: "I am going to tell you your father's name." The other, who was seated in an armchair, said three times, just like this: "You are making a mistake, Rosette, you are making a mistake, you are making a mistake."

'Mamma raised herself in her bed. I see her still with her red cheeks and shining eyes, for, in spite of everything, she loved me. She said to him: "Then do something for him, Philippe!" When talking to him, she used to call him "Philippe" and me "Auguste".

'He started shouting like a madman: "For that blackguard, never, for that scamp, for that convict, for that – " and he called me names as if he had been doing nothing else but think them up all his life.

'I was beginning to lose my temper, but mamma told me to hold my tongue, and said to him: "You want him to die of hunger, then, as I have no money?" He answered quite unconcernedly: "Rosette, for thirty years I have given you thirty-five thousand francs a year; that comes to more than a million francs. Thanks to me, you have had the life of a woman who is rich, loved, and, if I may say so, happy. I owe nothing to this blackguard who has spoiled our last years, and he will get nothing from me. There is no point in insisting. Tell him the name of the other man, if you like. I am sorry, but I wash my hands of the affair."

'Then mamma turned to me. I said to myself: "Good. I am going to get my own father back. If he has any money, I am saved!"

'She went on: "Your father, the Baron de Vilbois, is known nowadays as the Abbé Vilbois; he is curé of Garandou, near Toulon. He was my lover when I left him for this man."

'Then she told me everything, except how she humbugged you about her pregnancy. But, you know, women never tell the truth.'

He grinned unconcernedly, showing freely all his beastliness. He went on drinking, and, still laughing, continued: 'Mamma died two days later. We followed her coffin to the grave, he and I – rather funny, eh? He and I – and three servants; that was all. He cried like a baby. We were side by side, and we might have been put down as papa and papa's son. Then we went back to the house – only we two. I said to myself: "He'll throw me out without a halfpenny" – I had just fifty francs. What could I do to get even with the fellow? He touched my arm, saying, "I have something to talk to you about." I followed him into his study. He sat down at his table, and then, weeping dismally, he told me he would not be as nasty to me as he had told mamma he would. He begged me not to worry you – but that's our affair, yours and mine. He offered me a thousand-franc note – a thousand, what on earth could I do with a thousand francs – me, a chap like me! I saw he had lots more in the drawer, a great heap of them. The sight of all those notes made me want to go for him. I held out my hand to take the note he was offering me, but, instead of taking his charity, I sprang upon him, threw him down, and squeezed his throat until his eyes bulged out. Then, when I saw he was nearly dead, I gagged him, tied him up, undressed him, turned him over, and then, ha, ha! I avenged you in the funniest way.'

Philippe Auguste coughed, choking with delight, and, once more, on those lips, smiling but savage, the abbé saw the old smile of the woman who had made him lose his head.

'Then?' he said.

'Then, ha, ha! There was a big fire in the grate, it was December; mamma died from the cold. There was a big coal fire. I took up the poker, made it red hot, and then I made crosses on his back, eight or ten, I don't know how many, and then I turned him over and made as many on his belly. He wriggled like an eel, but I had gagged him well, so he couldn't squeal. Then I took the notes, a dozen of them, with my own that made thirteen – that didn't bring me luck – and I bolted after telling the servants not to disturb the count till dinner-time, as he was asleep.

'I thought he would keep the thing quiet, for fear of a scandal, considering that he was a senator, but I was wrong; days after, I was arrested in a restaurant in Paris, and I got three years. That's why I could not come to look you up sooner.'

He still went on drinking, and gabbling so that he could hardly speak clearly.

'Now, papa – papa curé – how funny it is to have a curé for a papa! Ha, ha! Papa must be very, very nice to his little boy, because his little boy is not an ordinary one, and he did score off the old chap rather well, didn't he?'

The same rage which once had maddened the abbé in the presence of the mistress who had betrayed him, now filled him in the face of this horrible fellow. He, who in the name of God had so often forgiven inexpressible horrors whispered in the secrecy of the confessional, felt without pity, without mercy, as an individual, and he did not call out to his loving and merciful God for help, for he knew that no divine or earthly intervention can save those on whom such misfortunes fall.

All the fire of his passionate heart and impetuous nature, kept in check by his priestly office, awoke in an irresistible outburst against this wretch who was his son, against this likeness to himself, and against the mother, the worthless mother, who had conceived him in her own likeness, and against the fate which had riveted this blackguard to his foot like the chains of a galley-slave.

He saw, he foresaw everything with sudden clearness, awakened, as he was, by this shock from his twenty-five years of peace and piety.

Convinced at once that he had to take a strong line in order to frighten this scoundrel and to get in the first blow, he said, his teeth clenched in his fury, and with no further thought of the fellow's drunkenness: 'Now that you have told me everything, listen. You will go away tomorrow morning. You will live in a district which I will name to you, and which you will never leave without my permission. I will make you an allowance there, which will be enough for you to live on, but it will only be a small one, for I have no money. If you disobey me one single time, the arrangement will cease, and you will come up against me.'

Although fuddled by the wine, Philippe Auguste understood the threat, and the criminal in him suddenly rose. Hiccoughing, he spat out: 'Oh, papa, don't try that on with me. You're a curé, and I've got you, and you'll go quietly like the others.'

The abbé bristled, and felt an irresistible longing to seize this monster in his brawny arms, bend him like a cane, and show him that he had met his match. Shaking the table and pushing it against him, he shouted: 'Take care, take care! I am afraid of nobody!'

The drunkard, losing his balance, reeled in his chair. Feeling that he was about to fall and that he was in the priest's power, he stretched out his hand with the glare of a murderer to one of the knives on the table. The abbé saw the act and gave the table such a push that his son fell backwards and lay prone upon the floor. The lamp rolled off the table and went out.

For a few seconds there was a little jingling of broken glass in the darkness. There followed a sound, as it were, of a soft body crawling over the stone floor. After that, nothing.

With the lamp broken, darkness came down upon them so suddenly and unexpectedly that they were horrified by it as by some fearful thing. The drunkard, cowering by the wall, did not move again. The priest remained in his chair, his anger quenched by the darkness. That black veil, holding back his rage, disarmed, too, the impetuous fury in his soul, into which other ideas, black and sorrowful as the darkness itself, entered.

There was a silence, a silence as profound as that of a tomb, in which nothing seemed to breathe or live any longer. No sound was heard from without, of a carriage in the distance, or the barking of a dog, or even the whispering of the wind among the leaves up against the house.

The silence lasted a long time, a very long time, perhaps an hour. Then, suddenly, the gong rang out. Struck by a single hard and strong blow, it rang, and there followed a queer noise of a fall and of an overturned chair.

Marguerite, on the watch, rushed in, but as soon as she opened the door she recoiled, frightened by the impenetrable darkness. Trembling, her heart beating violently, she called out with bated breath: 'Monsieur le curé, monsieur le curé!'

No one answered. Nothing stirred.

'My God, my God,' she said to herself, 'what have they done? What has happened?' She dared not go in; she dared not return with a light. A mad desire to run away, to scream, seized her, although she felt her legs trembling so much that she nearly collapsed. She repeated: 'Monsieur le curé, monsieur le curé, it's me, Marguerite.'

Suddenly, in spite of her fear, an instinctive desire to help her master, and one of those fits of bravery which, on occasion, make heroines of women, filled her soul with terrified daring, and running to the kitchen she fetched her lamp.

She stopped on the threshold of the room. She saw, first of all, the vagabond, who was lying along the wall, asleep or apparently asleep, then the broken lamp, then, under the table, the two black-shod feet and black-stockinged legs of the abbé, who must have fallen over on his back, striking the gong with his head as he fell.

Shaking with fright, her hands trembling, she repeated: 'My God, my God, what has happened?'

As she stepped forward slowly, with little steps, she slipped on something greasy and nearly fell. Bending down, she saw on the red-tiled floor a red liquid trickling round her feet in the direction of the door. She knew it was blood.

Wild with terror, she ran out of the room, extinguishing her lamp so as not to see more. She rushed towards the village, knocking against the trees as she ran, her eyes fixed on the lights in the distance, screaming continuously. Her shrill voice was borne on the night like the fateful scream of the owl as she cried repeatedly: 'The *maoufatan*, the *maoufatan*, the *maoufatan*!'

When she came to the first of the houses, scared men rushed out and surrounded her, but she struggled with them, without answering their questions, for she had completely lost her head. At last they understood that an accident had happened at the curé's house, and some of them picked up weapons and went off to help him.

The little rose-coloured house in the middle of the olive orchard was now invisible in the black of the deep, silent night. Ever since the only light in its window had gone out, as an eye that closes, it had remained drowned in the shadows, lost in the darkness, undiscoverable by any who did not know the district.

Soon lights approached quickly through the trees. They threw long yellow rays on the burnt grass, and under their wandering beams the twisted trunks of the olive trees seemed like hideous monsters, hellish serpents, all twisting and entangled together. The beams thrown forward suddenly made something pale and indefinable rise out of the darkness. Then the low, square wall of the little house turned pink in the light of the lanterns. Some peasants were carrying them, escorting two gendarmes with revolvers, the village policeman, the mayor, and Marguerite, whom some of them were supporting, as she had nearly collapsed.

They hesitated before the dreaded door, still standing open and rather awesome. Then the chief gendarme seized a light and went in, followed by the others.

The servant had not lied. Blood, now congealed, covered the floor as with a carpet. It had trickled as far as the vagabond, soaking one of his legs and one of his hands.

Father and son were sleeping, the one, his throat cut, the eternal sleep, the other the sleep of the drunkard. The gendarmes threw themselves upon him, and, before he was awake, had him handcuffed. He rubbed his eyes, stupefied, fuddled by the wine, and when he saw the dead body of the priest, he seemed terrified and unable to understand the meaning of it all.

'Why didn't he make a run for it?' said the mayor.

'Too drunk,' answered the officer.

And everybody agreed, for it never occurred to them that, perhaps, the Abbé Vilbois might himself have put an end to his life.

A Deal

The accused, Césaire-Isidore Brument and Prosper-Napoléon Cornu, appeared before the Court of Assizes of the Seine-Inférieure on a charge of the attempted murder, by drowning, of Madame Brument, lawful wife of the first named. The two prisoners sat side by side on the bench for the accused. They were peasants.

The first was small and stout, with short arms, short legs and a round head with a red pimply face planted direct upon the trunk, which was also round and short, and with apparently no neck. He was a breeder of pigs and lived at Cacheville-la-Goupil, in the district of Criquetot.

Cornu (Prosper-Napoléon) was thin, of medium height, with enormously long arms. His head was askew, his jaw awry, and he squinted. A blue blouse, as long as a shirt, reached to his knees, and his yellow hair, which was scanty and plastered down on his head, gave his face a worn-out, dirty look that was frightful. He had been nicknamed 'the curé' because he could imitate to perfection the chanting in church, and even the sound of the serpent [a musical instrument used in churches]. This talent attracted to his bar – for he was an innkeeper at Criquetot – a great many customers who preferred the 'mass à la Cornu' to the mass in church.

Madame Brument, seated on the witness bench, was a thin peasant woman who seemed to be always asleep. She sat there motionless, her hands crossed on her knees, and gazed fixedly before her with a stupid expression.

The judge continued his interrogation.

'Well, then, Madame Brument, they came into your house and threw you into a barrel full of water. Tell us the details. Stand up.'

She rose. She looked as tall as a flagpole with her white cap on the top of her head. She stated in a drawling tone: 'I was shelling beans. Just then they came in. I said to myself, "What's the matter with them? They don't seem natural, they seem up to some mischief." They watched me sideways, like this, especially Cornu, because he squints. I don't like seeing them together, for they are two good-for-nothings and egg each other on. I said: "What do you want with me?" They did not answer. I was a little frightened –'

The prisoner Brument interrupted the witness hastily, saying: 'I was tipsy.'

Then Cornu, turning towards his accomplice, said in the deep tones of an organ: 'Say that we were both tipsy, and you will be telling no lie.'

The judge (severely): 'You mean by that that you were both drunk?'

Brument: 'There can be no question about it.'

Cornu: 'That might happen to anyone.'

The judge to the victim: 'Continue your evidence, Madame Brument.'

'Well, Brument said to me, "Do you wish to earn a hundred sous?" "Yes," I replied, seeing that a hundred sous are not picked up every day. Then he said: "Open your eyes and do as I tell you," and he went to fetch the large empty barrel, which is under the rain pipe in the corner, turned it over and brought it into my kitchen, stuck it down in the middle of the floor, and then said to me: "Go and fetch water and keep on pouring it in until the barrel is full."

'So I went to the pond with two pails and carried water, and still more water, for an hour, seeing that the barrel was as large as a vat, saving your presence, m'sieur le président.

'All this time Brument and Cornu were drinking one glass after another. They were finishing their drinks when I said to them: "You are full, fuller than this barrel." And Brument answered me: "Don't worry, go on with your work, your turn will come; each one has his share." I paid no attention to what he said because of the state he was in.

'When the barrel was filled to the brim, I said: "There, that's done."

'And then Cornu gave me a hundred sous, not Brument, Cornu; it was Cornu gave them to me. And Brument said: "Do you wish to earn a hundred sous more?"

"Yes," I said, for I am not accustomed to presents like that.

Then he said: "Take off your clothes."

"Take off my clothes?"

"Yes," he said.

"How much shall I take off?"

"If it worries you at all, keep on your chemise; that won't bother us."

'A hundred sous is a hundred sous, and so I undressed; but I did not fancy doing so before those two good-for-nothings. I took off my cap, then my jacket, then my skirt, and then my shoes. Brument said, "Keep on your stockings, also; we are good fellows."

'And Cornu said, too, "We are good fellows."

'So there was I, almost like Mother Eve. And they got up from their chairs, but could not stand straight; they were so tipsy, saving your presence, m'sieur le président.

'I said to myself: "What are they up to?"

'And Brument said: "Are you ready?"

'And Cornu replied: "I'm ready!"

'And then they took me, Brument by my head, and Cornu by my feet, as one might take a sheet that has been washed. Then I began to scream.

'And Brument said: "Keep still, you wretched creature!"

'And they lifted me up in the air and put me into the barrel of water, so that I was chilled to my very bones.

'And Brument said: "Is that all?"

'Cornu said: "That's all."

'Brument said: "The head is not in; that will make a difference to the measure."

'Cornu said: "In with her head."

'And then Brument pushed down my head as if to drown me, so that the water ran into my nose, and I could already see the pearly gates. And he pushed me down, and I disappeared.

'And then he must have been frightened, for he pulled me out and said: "Go and get dry, you scarecrow."

'As for me, I took to my heels and ran as far as m'sieur le curé's. He lent me a skirt belonging to his servant, for I was almost stark naked, and he went to fetch Maître Chicot, the country watchman, who set out for Criquetot to bring the police who came to my house with me.

'Then we found Brument and Cornu fighting each other like two rams.

'Brument was shouting: "It isn't true; I tell you that there is at least a cubic metre in it. It is the method that was no good."

'Cornu bawled: "Four pails, that is almost half a cubic metre. You need not reply, that's what it is."

'The police officer put them both under arrest. I have no more to tell.'

She sat down. The people in the courtroom laughed. The jurors looked at one another in astonishment. The judge said: 'Prisoner Cornu, you seem to have been the instigator of this infamous plot. What have you to say?'

And Cornu rose in his turn.

'Monsieur le président,' he replied, 'I was drunk.'

The judge answered gravely: 'I know it. Proceed.'

'I will. Well, Brument came to my place about nine o'clock, and ordered two drinks, and said: "There's one for you, Cornu." I sat down opposite him and drank, and out of politeness, I stood him a drink also. Then he returned the compliment and so did I, and so it went on from glass to glass until noon, when we were both drunk.

'Then Brument began to cry. That touched me. I asked him what was

the matter. He replied: "I must have a thousand francs by Thursday."
That cooled me off a little, as you can understand. Then he said to me all
at once: "I will sell you my wife."

'I was drunk, and I am a widower. You understand, that stirred me up.
I did not know his wife, but she was a woman, wasn't she? I asked him:
"How much would you sell her for?"

'He reflected, or pretended to reflect. When one is drunk one is not
very clear-headed, and he replied: "I will sell her by the cubic metre."

'That did not surprise me, for I was as drunk as he was, but I knew
what a cubic metre is in my business. It is a thousand litres; that suited
me.

'But the price remained to be settled. All depends on the quality. I
said: "How much do you want a cubic metre?"

'He answered: "Two thousand francs."

'I gave a bound like a rabbit, and then it struck me that a woman ought
not to measure more than four hundred litres. But all the same I said:
"That's too dear."

'He answered: "I cannot do it for less. I should lose by it."

'You understand, he is not a dealer in pigs for nothing. He knows his
business. But if he is smart, the seller of bacon, I am smarter, seeing that
I sell it also. Ha, ha, ha! So I said to him: "If she were new, I wouldn't say
anything, but she has been married to you for some time, so she is not so
fresh as she was. I will give you fifteen hundred francs a cubic metre, not
a sou more. Will that suit you?"

'He answered: "That will do. That's a bargain!"

'I agreed, and we started out, arm in arm. We must help each other in
this world.

'But a fear came to me: "How can you measure her unless you put her
into liquid?"

'Then he explained his idea, not without difficulty, for he was drunk.
He said to me: "I take a barrel, and fill it with water to the brim. I put her
in it. All the water that comes out we will measure; that's the way to do it."

'I said: "I see, I understand. But this water that overflows will run
away; how are you going to gather it up?"

'Then he began laughing at me and explained that all we should have
to do would be to refill the barrel with the water his wife had displaced as
soon as she was out of it. All the water we should pour in would be the
measure. I supposed about ten pails would be a cubic metre. He isn't a
fool even when he is drunk, that old rascal.

'To be brief, we reached his house and I took a look at its mistress. A
beautiful woman she certainly was not. Anyone can see her, for there she

is. I said to myself: "I am disappointed, but never mind, she will be of some use; handsome or ugly, it is all the same, is it not, monsieur le président?"

Then I saw that she was as thin as a rail, and I said to myself: "She will not measure four hundred litres." I understand the matter, being in the liquor trade.

'She has told you about the proceeding. I even let her keep on her chemise and stockings, to my own disadvantage.

'When that was done she ran away. I said: "Look out, Brument! She is escaping."

'He replied: "Don't be afraid. I'll catch her all right. She will have to come back to sleep. I will measure the deficit."

'We measured. Not four pailfuls. Ha, ha, ha!'

The witness began to laugh so persistently that a gendarme was obliged to punch him in the back.

Having quieted down, he resumed: 'In short, Brument exclaimed: "The bargain's off, that is not enough." I bawled and bawled, and bawled again; he punched me and I hit back. That might have kept on till the Day of Judgement, seeing we were both drunk.

'Then came the gendarmes! They swore at us; they took us off to prison. I ask for damages.'

He sat down.

Brument confirmed in every particular the statements of his accomplice. The jury, aghast, retired to deliberate.

At the end of an hour they returned a verdict of acquittal for the defendants, with some severe strictures on the dignity of marriage, and laying down the precise limits of business transactions.

Brument went home accompanied by his wife.

Cornu went back to his business.

Love

(being pages from a sportsman's notebook)

I have just been reading in a newspaper the story of a love-tragedy. He killed her: then he killed himself: therefore, he loved her. What do He or She signify to me? Alone, it is only their love that matters. And it does not interest me in the least because it touches me, or because it amazes me, or because it moves me, or because it makes me think, but only because it brings back to my mind a memory of the days of my youth, a curious sporting experience, when love shone out before me as crosses in the sky shone out before early Christians.

I have by nature within me all the instincts and feelings of primitive man, tempered by the humaner understanding of a civilised being. I am passionately devoted to sport, but the bleeding victim, the blood on the feathers of a bird, harrow my feelings and almost make me faint with horror.

About the end of the autumn of the year I have in my mind the cold weather suddenly set in, and I was invited by one of my cousins, Karl de Rauville, to shoot duck with him at daybreak over the marshes.

My cousin, a jolly, red-headed and big-bearded, immensely powerful fellow of forty, a lively and likeable sort of beast, who had within him just that pinch of Attic salt which makes mediocrity tolerable, lived the life of a country gentleman in a house which was half-farm, half-mansion, in a broad valley through which a river flowed. Woods covered the hills on either side – ancient ancestral woods, with magnificent trees, in which were to be found more rare examples of game-birds than in any other district close by. Sometimes eagles were shot, and birds flying south, which hardly ever come near our over-populated parts of the country, almost invariably used to break their journey when they came to these centuries-old trees, as if they knew and saw once more a little corner of a very old forest, which still existed to give them shelter during their short night's rest.

The valley was covered with huge pastures, irrigated by ditches and divided by hedges. The river, narrow at first, spread out at some little distance away into an immense marsh. This marsh, the best bit of shooting I have ever known, was my cousin's very special care, and he looked after it as he would a park. Narrow avenues had been cut through the great masses of reeds which covered it, and whose rustling and swaying seemed to make it alive, and along these passages flat-bottomed boats, propelled and steered with poles, silently passed over the still water, grazing the rushes, while fishes darted through the weeds, and wildfowl, with their black and pointed heads, dived and vanished in a flash.

I love water passionately and whole-heartedly: the sea, although it is too vast, too turbulent, impossible to call one's own; rivers, which are so pretty, but which hurry by and vanish for ever; but, above all, the water of marshes, in which there throbs all the unknown life of birds, beasts and fishes. A marsh is a world of its own upon this earth of ours, a different world, with its own habits, its fixed population, and its people who come and go, its voices, its sounds, and, essentially, its mystery. There is at times nothing more disturbing, more disquieting, more terrifying, than bog-land. Whence comes this fear which hovers over low-lying tracts of land covered with water? Is it in the whispering of the reeds, the weird will-o'-the-wisps, the deep silence in which they are wrapped on still nights, or the fantastic mists which cover the rushes as with a shroud, or the barely-noticeable noises, so light, so gentle, yet, at times, more terrifying than the thunder of man or of the gods? Do these give marshes the appearance of some dreamland, of some dread country, which hides some secret, harmful and not to be known by mortal man?

No! something else stands forth clearly. Another and deeper and more solemn mystery is floating in those dense mists, perhaps, even, the mystery of creation! For did not the first germ of life stir, and become restless, and come into being in stagnant and muddy water, in the heavy damp of lands steaming under the burning sun?

I arrived at my cousin's house in the evening. It was freezing hard enough to split stones.

During dinner, in the great hall whose sideboards, walls and ceiling were all covered with stuffed birds, with outstretched wings or perched upon branches – hawks, herons, owls, nightjars, buzzards, vultures, falcons – my cousin, himself like some strange animal of the Arctic regions, in his sealskin jacket, put before me all the plans he had made for this very night.

We were to leave at half-past three in the morning, so as to arrive about half-past four at the place chosen for our shooting expedition. At this place a hut had been constructed out of blocks of ice to shelter us a little from the terrible wind which rises just before dawn [that wind laden with an iciness which tears one's flesh as with a saw] cuts it as with the blade of a sword, pricks it as with poisoned goads, twists it as with red-hot pincers and scorches it as with fire.]

My cousin, rubbing his hands, said: 'I have never known such a frost. At six this evening it was already twelve degrees below zero!'

Immediately after dinner I threw myself on my bed, and went off to sleep by the light of a great fire blazing in the grate.

As three o'clock struck I was awakened. I put on a sheepskin and found my cousin Karl clothed in a bearskin. After two cups of hot coffee and a couple of glasses of cognac, we set out with our gamekeeper and our dogs, Plongeon and Pierrot.

The moment I got outside, I felt frozen to the bones. It was one of those nights when the earth seems to be frozen to death. The icy air rises before one as a veritable wall which one can feel horribly and painfully: no breath of wind moves it; there it is, solid and immovable; it bites, pierces, withers, kills trees, plants, insects, even little birds, which fall from the branches on to the hard ground, and themselves become hard in the embrace of the cold.

[The moon, in its last quarter, all pale, appeared to be dying in the midst of space, so weak that it could not move and was standing still up there, paralysed, in the clutch of the bitter sky.]It shed a thin and melancholy light upon the world below, the pale and dying beam which it casts every month as it wanes.

personi-fication

With bent backs, hands in pockets and guns under our arms, Karl and I strode along. Our boots, wrapped round with wool to prevent us slipping on the frozen brooks, made no noise. I noticed how our dogs' breath turned to steam in the cold air.

We soon reached the edge of the marsh, and we entered one of the avenues of dry reeds leading through the low forest.

A soft sound came from the long ribbon-like leaves as we brushed them aside, and I was suddenly seized, for the first time, by the powerful and strange sensation which bog-lands produce in me. This one was dead, frozen to death, for we were tramping over it, through its forest of dried-up rushes.

Suddenly, at the bend of one of the avenues, I saw the hut made of ice which had been set up as a shelter for us. I went in, and, as we had still an hour to pass before the birds awakened, I rolled myself up in my sheepskin to try to get warm. Lying on my back, I began to watch the misshapen moon shining mistily through the transparent walls of that icy house. But the cold of the frozen marshland, of those walls, of earth and sky without, soon went through me so horribly that I began to cough.

My cousin Karl was alarmed. 'It will be a great nuisance if we don't shoot something today,' he said. 'I don't want you to catch cold, so we must have a fire.'

He then ordered the gamekeeper to cut some reeds. They made a pile in the centre of our hut, with its top knocked off to let the smoke escape, and as the red flame licked the crystal-like walls, they began to melt, quietly, almost imperceptibly, [just as if the ice-bricks were sweating.]

Karl, who had remained outside, called to me: 'Come and look!'

I went out, and stood for a moment completely lost in amazement. [Our cone-shaped hut seemed like some enormous diamond with a heart of fire, thrust suddenly on to the frozen marsh.] Within were seen two fantastical shapes – our dogs warming themselves.

Then a strange, frightened, wandering cry was heard over our heads. Our fire was awakening the wildfowl.

To me there is nothing more affecting than this first cry of some absolutely invisible living thing, hurrying through the dark air, so swiftly and so far away, just before there appears on the horizon the earliest light of a winter's day. At that freezing hour of dawn I can imagine that the faint cry borne on the wings of a bird is a sigh escaping from the soul of the world.

Karl said: 'Put out the fire: dawn is breaking.'

Certainly the sky began to grow pale, and across it flocks of ducks made long, black, quickly disappearing streaks.

A flash of light blazed through the darkness. Karl had just fired, and the dogs sped forward. Then no minute went by without one of us quickly taking aim, as soon as the outline of some flying mass appeared above the reeds; and Pierrot and Plongeon, out of breath and happy, brought us bleeding creatures, whose eyes sometimes still looked at us.

Day broke, clear with a blue sky. The sun came up over the bottom of the valley, and we were thinking of going home when two birds, with necks and wings outstretched, suddenly glided over our heads. I fired, and one of them, a teal with a silver breast, fell almost at my feet. Then, high above me, the cry of the survivor of the two was heard – a little, heart-rending wail, which it uttered again and again. And the little creature began to circle round in the blue sky above us, watching its dead companion which I was holding.

Karl, on one knee, his gun at his shoulder, was watching it keenly, waiting till it came within range.

'You have killed the hen,' he said, 'the cock won't go away.'

Indeed, it did not go away, but continued to circle and to cry piteously over our heads. Never has the groan of one in pain harrowed my heart so much as that call of distress, as that wail of reproach from the poor creature high up in the sky.

Once or twice it fled as it saw the threat of the gun which followed its flight, and it seemed prepared to continue its journey across the sky, all alone. Then, as if unable to make up its mind, it would instead return to look for its companion.

'Put the other one down, and it will return by and by,' said Karl.

In truth, it came back, indifferent to danger, maddened by its wild love for the creature I had killed.

Karl fired. It was as if the cord which was holding the bird above us had been cut. I saw a black thing come down. I heard the noise of its fall in the reeds. And Pierrot brought it to me.

I put the two, already cold, into the same game-bag . . . and I went back to Paris that very day.

Two Little Soldiers

Every Sunday, as soon as they were free, the little soldiers would go for a walk. They turned to the right on leaving the barracks, crossed Courbevoie with rapid strides, as though on a forced march, and then, as the houses grew scarcer, they slowed down and followed the dusty road that leads to Bezons.

They were small and thin, lost in their ill-fitting capes, too large and too long, whose sleeves covered their hands; their ample red trousers fell in folds around their ankles. Under the high, stiff shakos one could just barely perceive two thin, hollow-cheeked Breton faces, with their calm, naïve blue eyes. They never spoke during their journey, going straight before them, the same idea in each one's mind taking the place of conversation. For at the entrance of the little forest of Champioux they had found a spot which reminded them of home, and they did not feel happy anywhere else.

At the crossing of the Colombes and Chatou roads, when they arrived under the trees, they would take off their heavy, oppressive headgear and wipe their foreheads.

They always stopped for a while on the bridge at Bezons, and looked at the Seine. They stood there several minutes, bending over the railing, watching the white sails, which perhaps reminded them of their home and of the fishing smacks leaving for the open sea.

As soon as they had crossed the Seine, they would purchase provisions at the baker's and the wine merchant's. Two pennyworth of bread and a quart of wine made up the luncheon which they carried away, wrapped up in their handkerchiefs. But as soon as they were out of the village their gait would slacken and they would begin to talk.

Before them was a plain with a few clumps of trees, which led to the woods, a little forest which seemed to remind them of that other forest at Kermarivan. The wheat and oat fields bordered on the narrow path, and Jean Kerderen said each time to Luc Le Ganidec: 'It's just like home, just like Plounivon.'

'Yes, it's just like home.'

And they went on, side by side, their minds full of dim memories of home. They saw the fields, the hedges, the forests and the beaches.

Each time they stopped near a large stone on the edge of the private estate, because it reminded them of the dolmen of Locneuven.

As soon as they reached the first clump of trees, Luc Le Ganidec would cut off a small stick, and, whittling it slowly, would walk on, thinking of his people at home.

Jean Kerderen carried the provisions.

From time to time Luc would mention a name, or allude to some boyish prank which would give them food for plenty of thought. And the home country, so dear and so distant, would little by little gain possession of their minds, sending them back through space to the well-known forms and noises, to the familiar scenery, with the fragrance of its green fields and sea air. They no longer noticed the smells of the city. And in their dreams they saw their friends leaving, perhaps for ever, for the dangerous fishing grounds.

They were walking slowly, Luc Le Ganidec and Jean Kerderen, contented and sad, haunted by a sweet sorrow, the slow and penetrating sorrow of a captive animal which remembers the days of its freedom.

And when Luc had finished whittling his stick, they came to a little nook, where every Sunday they took their meal. They found the two bricks, which they had hidden in a hedge, and they made a little fire of dry branches and roasted their sausages on the end of their knives.

When their last crumb of bread had been eaten and the last drop of wine had been drunk, they stretched themselves out on the grass side by side, without speaking, their half-closed eyes looking away in the distance, their hands clasped as in prayer, their red-trousered legs mingling with the bright colours of the wild flowers.

Towards noon they glanced, from time to time, towards the village of Bezons, for the dairymaid would soon be coming. Every Sunday she would pass in front of them on the way to milk her cow, the only cow in the neighbourhood which was sent out to pasture.

Soon they would see the girl coming through the fields, and it pleased them to watch the sparkling sunbeams reflected from her shining pail. They never spoke to her. They were just glad to see her, without understanding why.

She was a tall, strapping girl, freckled and tanned by the open air – a girl typical of the Parisian suburbs.

Once, on noticing that they were always sitting in the same place, she said to them: 'Do you always come here?'

Luc Le Ganidec, more daring than his friend, stammered: 'Yes, we come here for our rest.'

That was all. But the following Sunday, on seeing them, she smiled with the kindly smile of a woman who understood their shyness, and she asked: 'What are you doing here? Are you watching the grass grow?'

Luc, cheered up, smiled: 'P'raps.'

She continued: 'It's not growing fast, is it?'

He answered, still laughing: 'Not exactly.'

She went on. But when she came back with her pail full of milk, she stopped before them and said: 'Want some? It will remind you of home.'

She had, perhaps instinctively, guessed and touched the right spot.

Both were moved. Then, not without difficulty, she poured some milk into the bottle in which they had brought their wine. Luc started to drink, carefully watching lest he should take more than his share. Then he passed the bottle to Jean. She stood before them, her hands on her hips, her pail at her feet, enjoying the pleasure she was giving them. Then she went on, saying: 'Well, goodbye until next Sunday!'

For a long time they watched her tall form as it receded in the distance, blending with the background, and finally disappeared.

The following week as they left the barracks, Jean said to Luc: 'Don't you think we ought to buy her something good?'

They were sorely perplexed by the problem of choosing something to bring to the dairymaid. Luc was in favour of bringing her some chitterlings; but Jean, who had a sweet tooth, thought that some sweets would be the best thing. He won, and so they went to a grocery to buy two sous' worth of red and white sweets.

This time they ate more quickly than usual, excited by anticipation.

Jean was the first one to notice her. 'There she is,' he said; and Luc answered: 'Yes, there she is.'

She smiled when she saw them and cried: 'Well, how are you today?'

They both answered together, 'All right! How's everything with you?'

Then she started to talk of simple things which might interest them: of the weather, of the crops, of her masters.

They didn't dare to offer their sweets, which were slowly melting in Jean's pocket. Finally Luc, growing bolder, murmured: 'We have brought you something.'

She asked: 'Let's see it.'

Then Jean, blushing to the tips of his ears, reached in his pocket, and drawing out the little paper bag, handed it to her.

She began to eat the sweets. The two soldiers sat in front of her, moved and delighted.

At last she went to do her milking, and when she came back she again gave them some milk.

They thought of her all through the week and often spoke of her. The following Sunday she sat beside them for a longer time.

The three of them sat there, side by side, their eyes looking far away in the distance, their hands clasped over their knees, and they told each other little incidents and little details of the villages where they were born, while the cow, waiting to be milked, stretched her heavy head towards the girl and mooed.

Soon the girl consented to eat with them, and to take a sip of wine. Often she brought them plums in her pocket, for plums were now ripe. Her presence enlivened the little Breton soldiers, who chattered away like two birds.

One Tuesday something unusual happened to Luc Le Ganidec; he asked for leave and did not return until ten o'clock at night.

Jean worried and racked his brain to account for his friend having obtained leave.

The following Friday, Luc borrowed ten sous from one of his friends, and once more asked and obtained leave for several hours.

When he started out with Jean on Sunday he seemed queer, disturbed and somehow changed. Kerderen did not understand; he vaguely suspected something, but he could not guess what it might be.

They went straight to the usual place, and lunched slowly. Neither was hungry.

Soon the girl appeared. They watched her approach as they always did. When she was near, Luc arose and went towards her. She placed her pail on the ground and kissed him. She kissed him passionately, throwing her arms around his neck, without paying attention to Jean, without even noticing that he was there.

Poor Jean was dazed, so dazed that he could not understand. His mind was upset and his heart broken, without his even realising why.

Then the girl sat down beside Luc, and they started to chat.

Jean was not looking at them. He understood now why his friend had gone out twice during the week. He felt the pain and the sting which treachery and deceit leave in their wake.

Luc and the girl went together to attend to the cow.

Jean followed them with his eyes. He saw them disappear side by side, the red trousers of his friend making a scarlet spot against the white road. It was Luc who sank the stake to which the cow was tethered. The girl stooped down to milk the cow, while he absent-mindedly stroked the animal's glossy neck. Then they left the pail in the grass and disappeared in the woods.

Jean could no longer see anything but the wall of leaves through which they had passed. He was unmanned so that he did not have strength to stand. He stayed there, motionless, bewildered and grieving – filled with simple, passionate grief. He wanted to weep, to run away, to hide somewhere, never to see anyone again.

Then he saw them coming back again. They were walking slowly, hand in hand, as village lovers do. Luc was carrying the pail.

After kissing him again, the girl went on, nodding carelessly to Jean. She did not offer him any milk that day.

The two little soldiers sat side by side, motionless as always, silent and quiet, their calm faces in no way betraying the trouble in their hearts. The sun shone down on them. From time to time they could hear the plaintive lowing of the cow. At the usual time they arose to return.

Luc was whittling a stick. Jean carried the empty bottle. He left it at the wine merchant's in Bezons. Then they stopped on the bridge, as they did every Sunday, and watched the water flowing by.

Jean leaned over the railing, farther and farther, as though he had seen something in the stream that hypnotised him. Luc said to him: 'What's the matter? Do you want a drink?'

He had hardly said the last word when Jean's head carried away the rest of his body, and the little blue and red soldier fell like a stone and disappeared in the water.

Luc, paralysed with horror, tried vainly to shout for help. In the distance he saw something under the surface; then his friend's head bobbed up out of the water only to disappear again.

Farther down he again noticed a hand, just one hand, which appeared and again went out of sight. That was all.

The boatmen who had rushed to the scene found no body that day.

Luc ran back to the barracks, crazed, and with eyes and voice full of tears, he related the accident: 'He leaned – he – he was leaning – so far over – that his head carried him away – and – he – fell – he – fell – '

Emotion choked him so that he could say no more. If only he had known!

Happiness

It was teatime, before the lamps were brought in. The villa looked down on the sea; the sundown had left the sky all rosy and golden, and the Mediterranean, without a wrinkle on its surface, without a tremor, smooth, and still shimmering as the day departed, seemed like a huge sheet of polished metal.

In the distance, away to the right, the jagged peaks of the mountains stood out black against the faint purple of the western sky.

They were talking about love, that old subject, and they were saying things that had already been said very often. The gentle melancholy of the twilight brought a feeling of tenderness into the discussion, and this word 'love', which was constantly being uttered, now in the deep voice of a man, now in the higher tones of a woman, seemed to fill the little room, to flutter round it as a bird, to hover over it as a spirit.

'Can one go on loving for several years in succession?'

'Yes,' said some.

'No,' asserted others.

They recognised distinctions of degree, set down limits and brought forward examples. And all of them, men and women, filled with recollections, which rose up within them and disturbed their souls, which came to their lips and which they could not quote, spoke of that something, commonplace and all-powerful, the tender and mysterious agreement between two human beings, with profound emotion and devouring interest.

Suddenly, someone who was looking out over the sea shouted: 'Look down there. What is it?'

Away out to sea could be seen just above the horizon a great grey mass rising, indistinct, from the water.

The women had got up and were looking, uncomprehendingly, at that strange thing which they had never seen before.

Somebody said: 'It is Corsica. It can be seen like this two or three times a year in certain exceptional atmospherical conditions, when the air is perfectly clear and it is no longer hidden by those sea-mists which always veil the distance.'

They could just see the mountains and thought they could distinguish the snow on their tops. They all stood surprised, disturbed, almost frightened, by this sudden apparition of an unknown world, this phantom rising from the sea. Perhaps those who, like Columbus, set forth across unexplored oceans had the same strange visions.

Then, an old gentleman, who had not yet spoken, said: 'I have known on this island, which is now rising before us as if itself to answer the question we have been discussing and to recall to me a curious memory, an admirable example of constant love, of love which was quite marvellously happy. Let me tell you about it.

'Five years ago I took a trip to Corsica. The wilds of that island are less known to us and farther away from us than America, though we sometimes see it from the coast of France, as we can just now.

'Picture to yourselves a world still in a state of chaos, a confused mass of mountains divided by narrow ravines through which torrents rush. There is not a plain – nothing but immense masses of granite and great stretches of rolling country covered with scrub or chestnut and pine forests. It is a virgin, uncultivated, barren country, though from time to time one comes across a village, perched, like a heap of rocks, on the top of a mountain. There is no culture, no industry, no art. One never comes across a single piece of carved wood or sculptured stone or anything to remind one of the feeling, be it primitive or refined, of the ancestors of these people for what is charming and beautiful. What indeed, impresses one most in that magnificent but rough country is the age-long indifference of the people to that seeking for charm in expression which we know as art.

'Italy, where every palace, full of masterpieces, is itself a masterpiece; where marble, wood, bronze, iron, metals and stone, all bear witness to man's genius; where the smallest objects scattered about in old houses reveal the heaven-born instinct for charm; Italy is for us the divine country, which we love because there we see the greatness, the power, the unwearying striving and the triumph of the creative intelligence of man.

'And opposite it, Corsica has remained as barbaric as it was in the beginning. There man lives in his rude house, indifferent to everything that does not concern himself or his family feuds. And there he has existed through all the years, with all the defects and all the good points of half-civilised races, easily moved to anger, malicious, thoughtlessly cruel, yet hospitable, generous, loyal, simple-minded, opening his door to the passer-by, and giving his faithful friendship in exchange for the smallest mark of sympathy.

'For a month I wandered through this magnificent island, with the feeling that I was at the end of the world. No inns, no taverns, no roads.

You reach by mule-paths those little villages, which seem to be hooked on to the sides of mountains and which look down on winding abysses, from which you hear, at night, the everlasting, melancholy, long-drawn-out roar of the mountain torrent. You knock at a door and ask for shelter and food till next morning. You sit down at their poor table, and you sleep under their poor roof, and in the morning you shake the hand of your host as he leaves you at the end of the village.

'Well, one evening after a ten hours' tramp I reached a little lonely house at the bottom of a narrow valley which opened out to the sea a league farther on. The two steep slopes of the mountain, covered with brushwood, loose rocks and big trees, shut in this inexpressibly melancholy valley as with two dark walls.

'Round the cottage were to be seen a few vines, a small garden and, at a little distance, some big chestnut trees, something to live on, anyhow, and a fortune in this poor land.

'The woman who opened the door was old, stern and exceptionally clean. The man, sitting in a rush chair, rose to greet me, and then sat down again without saying a word. His companion said: "Excuse him, he is deaf now; he is eighty-two."

'She spoke perfect French, to my surprise.

'I asked: "You are not Corsicans?"

'She replied: "No. We come from the mainland, but we have been here for fifty years."

'I had a feeling of sorrow and of fear as I thought of those fifty years spent in this dark hole, so remote from man and his towns. An old shepherd came in, and we began to eat the one dish which was our dinner, a thick soup of potatoes, bacon and cabbage.

'When the little meal was over, I went and sat outside, my heart full of the melancholy of the desolate countryside, with the feeling of distress which travellers sometimes experience when the evening is gloomy and the place is desolate. On those occasions it seems as if all were nearly at an end – one's own existence and the world itself. One sees, with a flash, the awful misery of life, the loneliness of mankind, the emptiness, and the dark solitude of hearts which lull and deceive themselves with dreams to the very end.

'The old woman came out to me, and worried by the curiosity which ever exists in even the most resigned hearts, she asked: "Are you from France?"

' "Yes, I am having a holiday here."

' "You come from Paris, perhaps?"

' "No; from Nancy."

'It seemed to me that an extraordinary agitation shook her. How I saw, or rather felt it, I do not know.

'She repeated slowly: "You come from Nancy?"

'The man appeared in the doorway, impassive, as the deaf always are.

'She continued, "It doesn't matter. He can't hear."

'Then, after a few seconds: "You know a good many people in Nancy, then?"

' "Certainly, nearly everybody."

' "The Sainte-Allaize family?"

' "Yes, very well. They were friends of my father's."

' "What is your name?"

'I told her. She looked at me steadily. Then in the low voice of one who is calling back the unforgettable past, she went on: "Yes, of course, I remember quite well. And the Brisemares? What has become of them?"

' "They are all dead."

' "Dear, dear! And the Sirmonts? Do you know them?"

' "Yes. The last of them is a general."

'Then, shaking with distress, with some indefinable feeling, at once powerful and sacred, with some desire to lay bare her heart, to tell everything, to speak of those things which, up till then, she had kept securely within her, and of those people whose names so moved her, she said: "Yes: Henri de Sirmont. I know him well. He is my brother!"

'I looked up at her, thunderstruck. Then, all of a sudden, a bygone memory came back to me. There had been a great scandal in high circles in Lorraine. Suzanne de Sirmont, a rich and beautiful girl, had been carried off by a non-commissioned officer of a regiment of hussars which her father commanded.

'He was a good-looking boy, of peasant parentage, but handsome in his blue tunic, this soldier who had run away with his colonel's daughter. No doubt she had seen him, noted him, and loved him as she watched the squadrons go by. But how she had been able to speak to him, how they had been able to meet, to understand each other, how she had been bold enough to make him see that she loved him – that was never known.

'What followed was neither guessed nor anticipated. One evening, just when his term of service was finished, he disappeared with her. They were hunted but not found. No news of them was ever to be had, and she was looked upon as dead. And now I found her in this gloomy valley!

'Then I said, in my turn: "I remember quite well. You are Mademoiselle Suzanne."

'She nodded, and tears fell from her eyes. Then, looking towards the old man standing motionless on the threshold of his cottage, she said: "That is he!"

'I knew then that she was still loving him, and that she still saw the enticing light of bygone days in his eyes.

'I asked: "Have you at least been happy?"

'She answered in a voice that came straight from her heart: "Oh, yes! Very happy. He made me very happy. I have never had a single regret."

'I looked at her, sorrowful, surprised, wonder-struck by the power of love! This rich girl had followed this man, this peasant. Herself had become a peasant. She had fashioned for herself a life, like his, devoid of grace, of luxury, of any kind of daintiness, and she had trained herself to become accustomed to his simple habits. And she still loved him! With her peasant's bonnet and cloth petticoat she had become a peasant herself. Seated on a rush-bottomed chair at a plain wooden table, she ate out of an earthenware dish a stew made of cabbages and potatoes and bacon. She slept on a straw mattress at his side. She had never thought of anything but him. She had never regretted her jewels, her fine clothes, the softness of chairs, the scent of warm rooms with their tapestries or the delicious comfort of a feather-bed. She had never needed anything but him; as long as he was there, she desired nothing else.

'Quite young, she had given up life, society, and those who had brought her up and loved her. She had come, alone with him, to this wild valley. He had been everything to her, everything that one desires, everything that one dreams of, everything that one is always waiting for, always hoping for. From beginning to end he had filled her life with happiness. She could not have been happier.

'All night, as I listened to the hoarse breathing of the old soldier on his pallet beside her who had followed him so far, I thought of this strange and simple adventure, of this happiness, which was so complete yet made up of so little.

'At daybreak I left the house, after shaking the hands of the old couple.'

The storyteller finished. One of the women said: 'All the same that woman had too simple an ideal, with her too primitive needs and her little wants. She must have been a fool.'

Another said quietly: 'What does it matter? She was happy.'

Away on the horizon Corsica buried itself in the darkness, disappearing slowly in the sea, from which it had risen as if itself to tell the story of the two humble lovers whom its shores had sheltered.